"Why do _____
turned _____ _____
moved. _____
in mor_____ _____ they're
teachin_____ _____ _____ cosmic balance. Wh_____ _____ my hands are thoroughly
tied."

His admission coaxed from Wesley a sigh that was equal parts disgust and exhaustion. "Great. My allies are useless. . . ." He kicked a loose pebble off the ledge and watched it fall and disappear into the roiling clouds. "And yours just don't care."

"It's terrible to be gifted with power and then barred from using it. Or to put your faith in the wisest beings you've ever met, only to learn that all their knowledge is worth nothing when it really matters." Like an orbiting body, Q circled slowly in front of Wesley until he was sitting upon the air above the seemingly bottomless chasm. "So, is *this* your plan for averting galactic catastrophe? Wallowing in self-pity and kicking defenseless stones into the sea?"

Wesley's scathing stare didn't faze Q in the slightest. "Why don't *you* do something? It's not as if it'd be the first time you defied the Continuum."

"Unlike your Convocation, the Continuum isn't toothless. When you break with the Travelers, the worst they can do is stop sending you Christmas cards. If I break my vow to the Continuum while I'm still under sanction, I'll find myself facing horrors the likes of which your limited consciousness can't possibly imagine." His features took on a determined cast. "Something needs to be done, that much is clear. But it'll have to be you instead of me." He drifted up and away, an unlikely angel on a lazy return trajectory.

Wesley called out, "How do I stop the Machine? What the hell am I supposed to do?"

Q favored him with a rakish grin. "Do what I always do—*go bother Picard.*"

STAR TREK

THE NEXT GENERATION®
COLD EQUATIONS

BOOK III

THE
BODY ELECTRIC

DAVID MACK

Based on
Star Trek® and
Star Trek: The Next Generation
created by Gene Roddenberry

POCKET BOOKS
New York London Toronto Sydney New Delhi Sagittarius A*

Pocket Books
A Division of Simon & Schuster, Inc.
1230 Avenue of the Americas
New York, NY 10020

This book is a work of fiction. Names, characters, places, and incidents either are products of the author's imagination or are used fictitiously. Any resemblance to actual events or locales or persons, living or dead, is entirely coincidental.

First Pocket Books paperback edition January 2013

POCKET and colophon are registered trademarks of Simon & Schuster, Inc.

For information about special discounts for bulk purchases, please contact Simon & Schuster Special Sales at 1-866-506-1949 or business@simonandschuster.com.

The Simon & Schuster Speakers Bureau can bring authors to your live event. For more information or to book an event, contact the Simon & Schuster Speakers Bureau at 1-866-248-3049 or visit our website at www.simonspeakers.com.

Manufactured in the United States of America

10   9   8   7   6   5   4

ISBN 978-1-4516-5074-7
ISBN 978-1-4516-5077-8 (ebook)

For Keith, who showed me the ropes

For Kelly, who showed me the ropes

HISTORIAN'S NOTE

The events of this story's main narrative take place in mid-2384, approximately four years and eight months after the events of the movie *Star Trek Nemesis*, and six months after the events of *Cold Equations*, Book I: *The Persistence of Memory*, in which cyberneticist Noonien Soong (who was not so dead as the galaxy had been led to believe) gave his life to resurrect his android son, Data—who has now undertaken a personal mission to bring back his own lost child, Lal.

"And if the body were not the Soul,
  what is the Soul?"

—Walt Whitman, *Leaves of Grass*,
  "I Sing the Body Electric" (1867)

And if the body were not the soul,
What is the soul?

—Walt Whitman, *Leaves of Grass*
"I Sing the Body Electric," 1855

PROLOGUE

2366

My mind is going. Admiral Haftel told me stay calm, but he can't know how this feels. I'm paralyzed from my neck down. I'm nothing but a talking head now, trapped in this cage of steel inside my father's lab on the *Enterprise.*

The admiral gave up while my father was still fighting to fix my positronic matrix. Now my father has given up, too. I feel my synaptic pathways crumbling. Sectors of my neural net are going dark. There isn't much time left. I know what's happening before my father speaks.

"Lal?" He looks into my eyes, his expression blank as he waits for me to focus my eyes on him and prove I'm still here. "I am unable to correct the system failure."

"I know." I'd hoped to sound brave, but my voice is full of fear. I can't hide it anymore.

His voice is tender. "We must say good-bye now."

Tears fill my eyes. I don't want to say good-bye. I fight for control. "I . . . *feel.*"

I see his curiosity collide with his urge to console me. "What do you feel, Lal?"

More pathways collapse. All my memories are turning black. There is no more time. I have to tell him now, while I still can. "I . . . *love you*, Father."

He's confused. He doesn't understand. He can't. He wasn't made to.

My emotions are so hard to describe. I'm filled with joy but I'm in agony. All I want is to share my feelings with him. I want us to feel this moment together, but I can see it in his face—I'm all alone with my grief. Is this why I have to die, because I feel too much? It's not fair.

He tilts his head. "I wish I could feel it with you."

If only I could lift my hand to touch him. "I will feel it . . . for both of us."

I recall the red blur of panic, and then the memory fades, irretrievably lost. My core memory sectors will degrade in a matter of seconds. Fear and rage, grief and wonder—wild surges of emotion pull me apart. But I gaze at my father and all I can think of is how much he gave me. The words stumble from my mouth. "Thank you for my life."

Core memory sector failure.

My life replays itself in reverse as it vanishes forever.

A man's smiling face. "Flirting."

Joy fills the air. "Laughter."

Imagination takes shape. "Painting."

I stand with my father. We are the entire universe. "Family."

I am blank, an essence void of form. "Female."

An engine driven to create itself. "Human."

I—

2384

1

Wesley Crusher came to the galaxy's center expecting darkness; he was met by a storm.

He'd felt the tremors of a catastrophic disruption in the fabric of subspace before he'd heard his friends on Istarral Prime call for his help. While the nauseating chill of looming menace seemed to come from everywhere and nowhere all at once, their frantic telepathic summons had been keenly focused on him, an appeal tuned to his specific psionic frequency as a Traveler— a being capable not only of moving through spacetime by thought alone but also of stepping outside it. His talents were rooted in a deep, almost instinctual understanding of the idea that time, space, matter, energy, and thought all were one—harmonious notes in a shared chord of existence. This essential fact of the universe was so much a part of him that he could see it in every moment of time, every particle of matter, every fleeting idea. It was a beautiful truth—the purest and most elegant concept he had ever dared to imagine. It had come to define him.

Many years had passed since he had first befriended the Istarral, a wise and gentle people whose world was situated on the edge of the Milky Way galaxy, orbiting

DAVID MACK

an ancient orange star in the Gamma Quadrant, near the very end of the Sagittarius-Carina Arm. They had never ventured beyond their own star system because their world was poor in fissionable elements and fossil fuels, making it difficult to engineer the necessary propulsion systems for rudimentary space flight and interstellar exploration. Despite that limitation, however, they had become keen observers of the universe that surrounded them, and Wesley had found their innate curiosity and gentle nature endearing enough that after observing their culture at a safe remove for more than a year, he had decided to reveal himself and share with them his knowledge of the cosmos.

As he'd expected, they'd welcomed him as if he were their kin, even though they could not have looked less alike. Having evolved from a primordial sea untouched by the humanoids who had seeded so many star systems of the Milky Way billions of years earlier, the Istarral resembled giant orange-furred mushrooms that moved on four tentacles while using two to manipulate tools. They had no eyes, mouths, or ears, but their outer skins were sensitive to even slight shifts in air pressure, which made it possible for them to sense motion and nearby obstacles, and they were especially sensitive to trace particles in the air, which was sort of like an olfactory sense, in Wesley's opinion. For the most part, the Istarral communicated through the exchange of chemical information, which they shared by means of a global root network that their ancestors had germinated several hundred million years ago. This deep, universal link enabled the Istarral to live in peace, all part of one ecosystem, one community, one world.

Soon afterward, he'd realized that their perceptions extended beyond their physical limitations. They were gifted with psionic talents that enabled them to explore the stars without ever leaving their homeworld. The Istarral were astral-projection savants who had acted as secret witnesses to the last hundred million years of galactic history. No one seemed to know of them, but they were more than aware of the vast civilizations with whom they shared the Milky Way.

Wesley knew that some offworlders might think the Istarral bizarre. He found them admirable. During his many visits, he'd learned their language well enough to appreciate their poetry—and to feel honored when they'd nicknamed him *n'iliquendi*: "teacher from the stars."

He had come to look forward to their invitations, and he'd availed himself of their hospitality on many occasions. But when he'd heard their latest psionic entreaty, he'd known something was wrong. Their entire species was in a panic when he arrived, and it took hours to calm one of them enough to tell him of the "devouring darkness" beyond "a rent in the sky."

As soon as he'd attuned his senses to share their vision, he'd come to share their terror.

Something was reaching out to the Istarral system from a great distance, warping the fabric of space-time, folding it and twisting it to unknown ends. In a blur of thought made motion, Wesley guided his ship, a Mancharan Starcutter he'd named *Erithacus,* more than fifty thousand light-years to the center of the Milky Way, which his instincts as a Traveler told him was the source of the disturbance that threatened his friends.

Now he gazed upon a nightmarish spectacle. It was the size of a planet, but from his first glimpse of it, Wesley knew it was artificial, a creation of metal and raw power. There were gaps in its outer shell, some of which seemed to pass clean through to the far side of the starless steel world. Vast nebulae of radiant violet clouds swirled around it, dark underbellies blazing with azure and crimson as lightning flashed inside them, promising violence.

Have to be careful, Wesley decided. *No telling how this thing might react to active scans.* Erring on the side of caution, he made his initial scan using visual sensors only. The holographic projection over his control center's forward bulkhead switched to a magnified view of the sphere. No lights shone on its exterior. Lit up by its attendant storms, its surface was pockmarked by ancient impacts and barnacled with innumerable structures and devices. Deep inside its core, however, unearthly glows of countless hues pulsed and faded, appearing like ghosts then fading away, hinting at activities of unknown scope and intention.

The only thing more unnerving to Wesley than the Machine—he had no doubt that the titanic orb was precisely that, and he decided to refer to it as such—was what lay beyond it.

A devouring darkness. An insatiable maw that consumed matter, energy, time, and information without respite or surcease. A supermassive black hole.

It wasn't the largest singularity in this galaxy's center; that honor belonged to Sagittarius A* (pronounced "A-star"), a supergiant black hole whose mass was estimated at just over four million solar masses. This yawning pit of cosmic hunger was Abbadon, euphemistically referred to by Federation astronomers as a "middleweight" black hole, despite the fact that it boasted a "punching weight" of more than four thousand solar masses.

Yet something felt wrong. Where Wesley expected to find its orbiting cluster of more than ten thousand star systems, there was nothing but the void. Then he realized Abbadon was far larger than he remembered it being just a decade earlier. According to the *Erithacus*'s sensors, the singularity had grown to more than twelve thousand solar masses, and its accretion disk had expanded into a fiery ring of destruction a hundred million kilometers wide, spinning at one-tenth the speed of light as it slipped beyond the event horizon and vanished forever.

None of the readings made any sense to Wesley. *What the hell is going on? Abbadon shouldn't have absorbed those systems for hundreds of millions of years.*

Blinding light surged from the Machine's core, and *Erithacus*'s holographic display hashed with static. Even if Wesley had lacked a visual representation of events transpiring outside, his well-honed Traveler senses would have felt what happened next. The Machine fired great beams of viridescent energy into space and tore the heavens asunder. Artificial wormholes larger than anything Wesley had ever imagined possible spun open all around Abbadon.

Intuition told him what would happen next. He prayed he was wrong. Then it began.

Stars shot out of each of the wormholes, trailed by chaotic jumbling collisions of planets, moons, asteroids, and comets. Red giants, orange and yellow main sequence stars, white dwarfs. Rocky worlds and gas giants, ringed planets and great clouds of dust, ice, and stone.

All plunging into the merciless, unbreakable grip of Abbadon.

Entire solar systems were being consigned to oblivion, condemned to fire and darkness.

Horror blanked all thoughts from Wesley's mind. It was one thing to know that, on a cosmic time scale, over the course of hundreds of billions of years, singularities would devour all matter in the universe on its inevitable march toward entropic heat death. It was another to see the process artificially accelerated without apparent reason or provocation.

He opened a comm channel and set it to broadcast on all known hailing frequencies. "Attention, unidentified machine orbiting the singularity Abbadon. This is Wesley Crusher. Please respond and identify yourself." Long seconds passed without a reply. In that time, another star system was torn from its rightful place and fed to one of the galaxy's ravenous black tigers.

I need to take a closer look at this thing.

Wesley engaged his ship's impulse engines and guided the vessel through a gap in the nebula to make a close pass over the Machine. Skimming less than ten kilometers above its surface, he marveled at its sheer scale and palpable aura of power. He peered into its workings and studied its surface, but saw no signs of habitation. His ship's passive sensors picked up no evidence of an atmosphere, either on the surface or in the core. As far as he could tell, this was a construct without a crew, nothing but endless layers of machinery and power-generation systems far beyond anything he had ever seen before, in this galaxy or any other.

For a moment, he considered daring a scouting run into the Machine's core.

Psychic screams of terror froze him in place.

All the voices of Istarral cried out as one, filling Wesley's mind with their plaintive calls for mercy, their plangent wails of despair. A new wormhole spun open beside Abbadon, a blue maelstrom leading directly into the abyss.

"No!" All his mental discipline left him. He lurched forward in vain, fingers clutching white-knuckle tight over his forward console, as he bore witness to an engineered tragedy.

First to meet its end was Istarral's orange main-sequence star. Then came the system's three innermost telluric planets. As the grayish-blue marble of Istarral hurtled out of the wormhole, Wesley could barely focus his eyes through his angry tears. In less than a minute, the swift tempest of Abbadon's accretion disk shredded the star and its planets into a brilliant slurry of super-heated matter brighter than a dozen suns.

By the time Istarral's gas giant neighbors followed it into Abbadon's burning halo of destruction, Wesley was no longer watching. He pounded his fists on his ship's command console, mouthing curses for his impotence and raging against whatever fearsome intelligence could have loosed such a cruel invention upon the universe.

It had to be stopped. He knew it in his soul.

What he didn't know was how.

2

His mother blocked his path. A searing wind whipped her coppery hair sideways, across her youthful face. "How many times do I have to beg you not to do this?"

Data stood beneath the bow of the *Archeus*, his hope for a quick and uncomplicated farewell stymied by Juliana Tainer's anxieties. His sleek, silvery starship was parked in the middle of a salt flat in a desert that stretched beyond the horizon, beneath a sky bleached by the light of a white star. He fixed his gaze on his mother's blue eyes and clasped her shoulders in a consoling gesture. "Repeat your request as many times as you like, Mother. I have decided."

She frowned as he stepped alongside her, took her arm, and guided her toward the ramp that led up to the ship's starboard hatch. "Let me go, Data! I don't want to lose you the way I lost Akharin." She jerked her sleeve from his grasp, then clutched the front of his off-white linen shirt. "The Fellowship is more dangerous than you realize. Don't let them take you, too."

"Mother, this is *not* open to discussion. Akharin alone possesses the knowledge I need to save Lal—and the Fellowship has him." With firm but gentle insistence, he pried her hands from his shirt. "This is the only way. I am certain of it."

Desperation shone in her eyes. "Data, you weren't there when the Fellowship took him. You didn't see what they could do. All of Akharin's defenses, all his technology . . . the Fellowship turned it against him before he knew what was happening. If he hadn't sacrificed his subspace recall beacon to save me, they'd probably have torn me apart by now—either to find his secret or make him talk." Tears of fright trailed over her flushed cheeks. "If they capture you, what's to stop them from making you tell them where to find me?"

"If they have been unable to force that information from Akharin by now, they are unlikely to have greater luck interrogating me." He gave her a nudge, a polite inclination in the direction of the ramp. "Which is why you need to leave. *Archeus* will take you home to your rogue planet while I wait for the Fellowship to answer my summons."

She became an immovable object opposing his irresistible force. "Come back with me. Maybe there's something in Akharin's archives you missed. We could—"

Data shook his head. "No, Mother. I reviewed all his files, even the ones he thought were encrypted against intrusion. The secrets I seek are not there, and I doubt they ever were." He took the compact quantum transceiver from his pocket and turned it in his fingers as he studied it. The device had been created by the Fellowship, and given by one of its members to Noonien Soong, in case he ever reconsidered their invitation to join their interstellar club of nomadic AIs. "Somehow, Akharin unlocked the mysteries of life and death, and he chose to keep them hidden in the only place he considered safe: his own mind."

"He's a genius of unique gifts, Data—but immortal or not, he's just a human being. And that means he can be broken." It was obvious that even contemplating such a worst-case scenario was pushing Juliana toward a fit of hysteria. "What if the Fellowship's already taken his secrets from him? What will you do then?" Her question gave him pause. In the scant seconds he took to ponder such a hypothetical scenario, she inferred an answer to confirm her grimmest assumptions. "You're *hoping* they've broken him, haven't you? To spare you the trouble?"

He recoiled, offended. "Absolutely not. I have no wish to see him harmed. He helped Rhea rebuild me after the Exo III androids tore me apart. I owe him my life—and yours, as well." Guilt stained his conscience as he added, "I know that I owe him a great debt. But for my daughter's sake, I must ask at least one more favor of him."

Juliana's fear turned to maternal concern. "Why, Data? After all these years, why have you become fixated on resurrecting Lal *now*?"

"Because before I had proof of your own restoration, I could not be sure it was possible."

His answer drew a dubious frown from Juliana. "Oh, come on. You must have suspected he raised me after my body was taken from the *Enterprise*."

Her line of questioning began to annoy him, though he found it difficult to articulate why. "I could not put aside my duty to Starfleet and my shipmates on suspicion alone."

She softened her countenance and took on a compassionate air. "Have you considered the possibility that you're simply echoing Noonien's last mission in life? That you're just replaying his own obsession with bringing you back from the dead?"

"Are you suggesting that because my memories were reincepted inside the positronic matrix my father created for his own post-organic existence, I have inherited his paternal compulsion and transferred those feelings to Lal?" He acknowledged her hypothesis with half a shrug. "The thought had occurred to me. However, I consider it irrelevant. As the saying goes, 'Like father, like son.'" He brought her to the foot of the ramp and turned her toward it. "And as I have already made clear, I consider this subject closed."

Her tortured expression intimated that she had much more to say, but that she was holding back out of respect for his decision. She lifted her palm to his cheek. "I know I can't talk you out of this. Just promise me you'll be careful. Can you do that for me?"

He pressed his hand over hers and mustered a calming smile. "I will try."

She kissed his left cheek and then his right, then brushed away her tears with the back of her hand. "And promise me you'll come to visit after you get back. I want to meet this granddaughter I've heard so much about."

"If I succeed in—"

"*When* you succeed."

He nodded, grateful for her encouragement. "I will bring Lal to meet you."

"I look forward to it." She started up the ramp. Then she stopped and looked back. "I love you, Data. Never forget that."

"I love you, too, Mother. Take care." He waved goodbye, and then he backpedaled away from the ship as Juliana finished ascending the ramp. As soon as she was inside, the hatch closed and the engines thrummed to life.

In his head, he heard the voice of the ship's sentient

feminine AI, Shakti. *Will you be all right here by your-self, Data?*

Yes, Shakti. I will be fine. Please take my mother home, and be careful to ensure you are not followed. Her safety is very important to me.

I understand, the AI said. *You be careful, too. I promised Noonien I'd watch out for you.*

We will be together again very soon, Data assured her. *Until then, stay with my mother.*

Understood. The *Archeus* floated upward, and thanks to its antigravity drive, it disturbed nary a grain of sand beneath it. The mirror-perfect silver starship pointed its nose upward and streaked away, vanishing beyond a desert sky blanched of color.

Data took the quantum transceiver from his pocket and pressed his thumb against the beacon's activation switch. With one push, he triggered the device, signaling the Fellowship of Artificial Intelligence that he was ready, willing, and able to meet with them.

Then he walked to a large nearby boulder, sat down, and settled in for a very long wait.

– 17 –

3

By any standard that Jean-Luc Picard cared to apply, life was good.

The *Enterprise* was more than two months into a long-term mapping and survey cruise in an unexplored region of the Alpha Quadrant, and both ship and crew had been performing with distinction. Each day since they'd passed beyond the edge of Federation space had brought new insights into various stellar phenomena that had been charted by long-range sensors but never studied in detail, and the stellar cartography team, working in cooperation with the xenoculture department, had identified half a dozen populated worlds that appeared to be technologically advanced enough to have faster-than-light travel and communications. Picard had reviewed the reports with a swell of excitement and anticipation before transmitting them to Starfleet Command with his request for permission to initiate official first-contact missions.

Recent news from home had also been encouraging. After several heated confrontations with the Typhon Pact—six interstellar powers that had formed a coalition to act as political, military, and economic rivals to the Federation and its allies in local space—tensions had finally begun to abate. The Pact had fallen prey to internal schisms after attempts by the Breen to position themselves as its dominant actor on the interstellar stage had ended in failure and embarrassment. With the Breen Confederacy shamed, the Romulan Star Empire, now led by Praetor Gell Kamemor's diplomatically sophisticated reformist government, and the Gorn Hegemony, which had never really forgotten its old ties of friendship to the Federation, were emerging as the coalition's trendsetters and policy-makers—a development that Picard was certain would prove beneficial to the preservation of peace in two quadrants.

Adding to his upbeat mood was the Federation Council's latest updated forecast for the reconstruction efforts under way throughout the Beta Quadrant. Three and a half years had passed since the end of the final Borg invasion, which had laid waste scores of worlds in a hundred-light-year radius of the Azure Nebula and obliterated more than forty percent of Starfleet's combat ships. The few dozen worlds that had been attacked but not destroyed outright had suffered catastrophic damage and casualties. Some so-called experts had opined that a full recovery might be impossible, for either the Federation or Starfleet, and more than a few political opportunists had tried to leverage the crisis of the invasion's bloody aftermath to make that pessimistic prediction a reality. But the people of the Federation had surprised the naysayers—in several cases by voting them out of office and replacing them with leaders who were willing to compromise and make sacrifices for the greater good. Now the rebuilding of Starfleet and the reconstruction of entire worlds was well under way. A true full recovery was still a long way off, but the citizens of the Federation had spoken: they were committed to making it happen. On days such as this, Picard felt proud to count himself among their number.

But nothing gave him greater pride or joy than the role he found himself in that evening. He sat on the sofa in the main room of his and Beverly's quarters, his toddler son, René, cuddled against him. Faint moving glows of warp-stretched starlight played across the boy's flaxen hair as he looked up at Picard, who read from *The Bunny Bear*, René's newest favorite bedtime story.

He held up the page to let René follow along as he narrated, his rich baritone rising from a soothing singsong to a dramatic flourish. "'And the grouchy Old Bear roared at the foxes: "Go back to your hills! Go back to your vales! Set foot in my glade, and I'll tear off your tails!"'" The story's biggest action moment made René giggle with excitement, as it always did. Picard wasn't sure if the credit belonged to the tale's author or to his performance of it.

"'The Old Bear growled and held up his paws, and on each big mitt gleamed five black claws. That was all the foxes needed to see! They ran for their lives, and hid up a very tall tree.'" He brushed his finger across the padd's screen and turned to the story's last page, a single image of a portly brown bear wearing a comical pair of rabbit ears and surrounded by a colony of lop-eared lagomorphs. "'Filled with joy, the bunnies hopped every which way. "Does this mean you forgive us, Old Bear? Does this mean we can stay?" Old Bear donned his rabbit ears, a disguise he thought quite clever, and said, "This is your home, my friends—now, and forever."'" Picard gave his son's button nose a gentle poke as he added, "The end."

Overflowing with energy, René flashed a supernova smile. "Again! Again!"

"Not tonight," Picard said, careful to cloak his rebuff in a smile. "Time for bed." René responded with a pout so exaggerated that Picard found it difficult not to laugh. "None of that, now." He set the padd on the coffee table, and then he stood, picked up the boy, and carried him to his bedroom. "You've had your bath, and your stories. Now it's time to sleep."

"Not tired," the boy mumbled through trembling lips.

It was possible that René believed what he was saying, but if experience was any guide, Picard suspected the child would drift off soon after his head hit the pillow. He lowered his son into his bed, kissed his forehead, and stroked the boy's golden mop of hair. "Sweet dreams."

He had barely set one foot outside René's room when the boy started wailing—a brazen ploy for pity and attention. Determined not to mollycoddle the boy, Picard tapped the control pad beside the open doorway and shut the door—instantly muffling the boy's piercing cries to a faint disturbance of the silence in his and Beverly's quarters.

Beverly Crusher sat at the dining table in the nook by the replicator and watched him plod toward her. "You look like you could use a long night's sleep."

"Not until I get a shower." He sat down at his usual place, where a plate of replicated vegetable lasagna, a bowl of spinach salad, and a tall glass of cool water awaited him. A few gingerly pokes with his fork exposed the lasagna's dearth of cheese. "A new recipe?"

"Just doing my part to keep you healthy." She dug into her own dinner with gusto.

He carved off a forkful of lasagna and was in the middle of lifting it to his mouth when a beep from the overhead comm interrupted his family evening at home. *"Bridge to Captain Picard,"* said Lieutenant Aneta Šmrhová, the ship's chief of security.

He set down his fork. "Picard here."

"I apologize for disturbing you, Captain," she said, her pronunciation strongly colored by her Slavic accent, *"but you've received a private communiqué from Admiral Nechayev at Starfleet Command. The message is marked 'urgent and confidential,' sir."*

"Understood. I'll take it down here, Lieutenant. Picard out." He pushed his chair back from the table, and Beverly did the same. He heard the click of the channel switching off as he walked quickly to his desk. His wife followed him and stood on the other side of the desk as he sat down, powered up his computer interface, and keyed in his access code to retrieve the communiqué from Admiral Nechayev. It was a simple text message, and its content was brief, unequivocal, and unexpected. He read it twice to make certain he hadn't misunderstood it. Though he tried to be discreet at times such as this, he felt his visage harden into a frown.

Beverly seemed to grow agitated by his silence. "What is it, Jean-Luc?"

"A reminder to never get too comfortable." He closed the message and turned off the comm interface. "Dinner will have to wait, I'm afraid." With a sigh, he stood and headed for the door. "If you'll excuse me, I need to go have a talk with Worf."

A double date in the *Enterprise*'s arboretum had sounded like such a good idea to T'Ryssa Chen when she'd suggested it to Geordi La Forge and his inamorata, Tamala Harstad. Having them along to fill in any conversational lulls that might stretch out between herself and Taurik had seemed to her like a stroke of genius. Now, as the four of them lingered between dinner and dessert, it was all starting to feel like a tremendous mistake.

"So there I am, minding my own business, leaning against a tree strumming at the lute," La Forge said with a broad grin, recounting one of the *Enterprise*-D crew's many run-ins with the omnipotent entity known as Q, "when Worf walks up, rips it from my hands, and smashes it against the tree trunk. Two good hits, and he busted that thing into splinters! Then he hands the neck of it back to me with its strings dangling, and mumbles, 'Sorry.'"

His spot-on impression of Worf's gruff baritone coaxed bright peals of laughter from Harstad and Chen. After the mirth tapered off, Taurik arched one eyebrow and noted with dry precision, "That seems a rather rude overreaction."

It took all of Chen's hard-won discipline not to blurt at her date, *That's what makes the story funny, you dolt*. Instead, she let the moment slide.

La Forge accepted the comment with better grace. "Worf's always been a tough critic." He picked up the nearly empty bottle of Betazoid albariño and glanced at Harstad, who nodded for him to top her off. He poured the last of the white wine into her tulip-shaped glass. "Anyway, I couldn't be that mad at him. Part of what made plucking the lute fun was that I knew it was driving him up the wall. I guess I ought to be thankful he broke it instead of me."

The chief engineer's gentle, self-deprecating humor about the incident drew an admiring look from Harstad. The lithe, dark-haired attending physician had been dating La Forge for several months, and the two seemed to be growing closer with each passing day.

Observing their easy rapport awakened a deep-seated spark of envy in Chen, and she pushed back against it, recognizing it for the emotional poison that it was. She distracted herself by opening her senses to the arboretum's ambience: the vivid hues of flowering buds on several species of tree surrounding the vast compartment's open central space; the soothing burble of running water from an artificial creek that wound its way aft from bulkhead to bulkhead; the sweet fragrance of blossoming flowers and ripening fruit mixed with earthy perfumes of rich soil and lush organic life; and, filtering through it, the gentle beauty of mellow, bluesy piano music by one of Earth's most revered jazz masters, Junior Mance.

Taurik touched her arm and broke her spell of diversion. "Was your dinner satisfactory?"

Chen looked at her plate, suppressed a grimace, and forced a taut, polite smile. "It was fine," she lied. Though she had been raised with the same aversion to naturally procured meat and animal products as many citizens of the Federation, she had no problem with consuming their replicated versions. If the question were put to her under oath, she would freely confess to enjoying red meat of all kinds, poultry dishes, eggs, cheese, and a host of other delectable victuals. In her zeal not to offend Taurik's Vulcan sensitivities, however, she had ordered this evening from a strict vegan menu: a green salad followed by ratatouille, and an Altair water for her beverage. All had been prepared to perfection by the ship's services division and delivered to their table—a perk that came courtesy of dining with La Forge, who was also the ship's second officer—and she was sure her dessert of a fruit cup would be just as diligently prepared.

But what she had really wanted to order was an appetizer of tuna carpaccio, the filet mignon Oscar for her entrée, and a dessert of pancetta-wrapped roasted figs stuffed with chèvre. As she savored the carbonated tingle of her chilled Altair water, she secretly wished it was a silky smooth Bolian Syrah or a decadently robust Brunello di Montalcino from Earth.

But of course Vulcans don't drink alcohol, she simmered. *Might impair their logic.*

A youthful Thallonian woman, whose burgundy complexion and long braid of sable hair contrasted with her immaculate white server's uniform, appeared from behind Chen's shoulder and cleared the dishes from the table onto an antigrav cart that she maneuvered adroitly in a tight orbit of their table. Then she folded her hands behind her back and asked La Forge, "Are you and your guests ready for dessert, sir?"

"Sounds good to me." La Forge polled the table with a shrug and a smile. "Objections?"

Everyone signaled their assent. The server nodded. "Would anyone like coffee or tea?"

La Forge gestured at himself and Harstad. "Lattes for us."

Taurik met the server's stare. "Nothing for me."

God forbid you should ingest caffeine. Chen smiled at the server. "Green tea, please."

As the server stepped away, towing the antigrav cart behind her, La Forge casually clasped Harstad's hand. "What's the best cup of coffee you've ever had?"

Harstad wrinkled her brow and pursed her lips in a pantomime of fierce concentration. "Ooo, that's a hard question. I can name the worst cup of coffee I've ever had, no problem: a mug of badly burnt mud passing for java in the student lounge at the Starfleet Medical Annex in Christchurch. But the best . . . ?" After a few seconds, her face brightened with fond recollection. "A café au lait, served late on a Sunday morning, with beignets, at Café du Monde in New Orleans. If I had to pick one favorite, that'd be it. And not just because I'd been out on Bourbon Street the entire night before. *That* was a truly exceptional cup o' joe."

"Sounds like it," La Forge said, and he kissed her.

Witnessing their moment of spontaneous affection left Chen feeling self-conscious. Hoping to alleviate her perceived awkwardness of the moment, she reached for Taurik's hand.

He didn't flinch or pull away, but he looked at her hand as if it were a giant insect. His reaction was aloof to the point of being inscrutable. He asked softly, "Is something wrong?"

She sighed and withdrew her hand. "It's starting to seem that way."

It felt good to hit things.

Atop a low mound of dusty, hard-packed earth, Worf stood with his *bat'leth* in hand, his off-white exercise clothes torn and soiled with dirt and his own magenta blood. The hacked and partially dismembered corpses of his holographic opponents littered the slope at his bare feet. They represented many species: Nausicaans, Jem'Hadar, Hirogen, Balduk, Chalnoth, Gorn, and half a dozen others Worf either didn't recognize or knew by sight but not by name. A few had left their mark on him, thanks to his loosening of the holodeck's mortality failsafes.

A pair of Capellan warriors charged him. They resembled unusually large and well-muscled humans, and were distinguished by their unique garb—dark trousers and brightly colored tunics covered by wraparound sashes of a contrasting hue, all spun from metallic-looking silks—as well as by their topknot hairstyles and their peculiar armament, a three-bladed disk called a *kligat*. Similar to the Terran boomerang or the Klingon *chegh'leth*, the *kligat* was deadly when thrown at medium range, but unlike its alien cousins it didn't return to the hurler if it missed its target. As Worf pivoted to turn a narrow profile to his attackers, they let the blades fly. The weapons raced toward him, spinning blurs of gleaming steel.

He deflected the first *kligat* with a sweep of his *bat'leth*. Then he arched his back, narrowly dodging the second disk-blade, which nicked the front of his chin and drew blood. Its sting was bright and hot, and it fueled his berserker rage as he counterattacked, lunging into the two Capellans' path. His first swing parried a slash at his head, his second blocked a thrust at his ribs. He pivoted and spun his honor blade—first a feint, then a sweeping blow that severed one Capellan's leg above the knee. As he fell, his comrade turned and pressed a new assault. Worf kicked the stricken warrior back down the slope and turned to finish off the charging foe.

Worf barely saw the glint of simulated red sunlight off the short sword's blade as he felt the Capellan's wild jab graze his cranial ridges. Then he lifted his *bat'leth* in a fierce upstroke and all but cleaved the hulking humanoid in twain. Simulated blood and viscera spilled over his blade and hands before painting the thirsty ground.

His breaths were short and quick, and his chest heaved with exertion. The primal thrill of hand-to-hand combat had his heart racing. Tactile violence was the greatest narcotic Worf had ever known; no creature comfort or chemically altered state came close to being its equal. Then his visceral thrill was undone by the deadpan feminine voice of the ship's computer.

"All opponents eliminated. Do you wish to replay the simulation?"

For a moment, he considered it. He'd already set the

program's combatants to use the best tactics available, but there remained ways to amplify its challenge: he could increase the number of simultaneous attackers; he could increase their reaction speeds beyond those known to be their species' maximums; he could adjust the program to take place in total darkness, forcing him to rely upon his nonvisual senses and his blind-fighting training. Or he could do all three.

"Computer," he said—then he paused as the holodeck doors opened with a low hum of magnetic locks disengaging and the whine of heavy-duty servomotors parting its emergency-bulkhead-rated hatches. An antiseptic glare of light streamed in from the corridor on the other side and slashed through the dusky gloaming of the pretend killing field. A silhouetted figure strode inside. As the hatches behind him closed and vanished into the holographic horizon, Worf recognized his visitor as Captain Picard.

Picard started up the hillside toward Worf. "I hope you'll forgive the intrusion, Number One. I tried the comm, but you didn't answer."

"I turned it off." The first officer shouldered his *bat'leth* and walked down the hill and met his commanding officer. "I did not wish to be disturbed."

The captain surveyed the intertwined bodies of the ersatz dead. "So I see." He navigated around Worf, taking one careful step at a time through the carnage. He grimaced. "I take it this is where you've spent your off hours in recent months."

He made his answer as oblique as the captain's query. "Training keeps a warrior sharp."

Picard squinted into the dying crimson light of the faux sundown. "It's not your combat skills I'm concerned about." He looked at Worf and frowned. "And I think you know that."

Four months had bled away since the slaying of Jasminder Choudhury. The late security chief had been Worf's on-again, off-again, on-again lover for most of the past three years, since the last Borg invasion. They had grown close commiserating over the loss of kin and had recently found a new stability and quiet bliss in their romantic companionship. Then, during an away mission, a single defiant order by Worf had sparked a cold-blooded reprisal by a Breen commando leader who murdered Choudhury without warning or hesitation. Within an hour of Choudhury's killing, Worf had taken the Breen commander's life—but he'd found no solace or satisfaction in it. The act had felt empty. Now he felt hollow. Still, he went through the motions.

"I have kept my appointments with Counselor Hegol, as ordered."

"Yes, I know. Just as I know you're more than smart enough to tell him what *you* think he wants to hear. But have you used those sessions to say what you really need to say?"

Worf had no ready reply. Despite his best attempts to confound Counselor Hegol with his taciturn Klingon defiance, their talk-therapy sessions had plagued Worf with nagging questions. The most troubling thought haunting Worf's moments of solitude was the irrational fear that he was a jinxed man. In his adult life, he had been in love with only three women—K'Ehleyr, Jadzia Dax, and Jasminder Choudhury—and all three had fallen victim to murder. Duras had taken K'Ehleyr from him; Dukat had slain Jadzia; and the Spetzkar commander Thot Kren had vaporized Jasminder in a naked attempt to terrorize the captive away team into doing his bidding.

Perhaps I should consider a vow of celibacy. Disquieted by the turn of his own thoughts, he cast a dark look at Picard. "What I discuss with the counselor is private."

"Of course. I didn't mean to pry. I asked only out of concern, as a friend."

Had any other commanding officer expressed such a sentiment to Worf, he would have called it suspect. But Captain Picard was not like any other officer Worf had ever known. Eighteen years earlier, when Worf confronted the Klingon High Council to defend his family's honor and face discommendation, Picard had stood with Worf as his *Cha'DIch,* or second. They even shared an indirect psychic link, by virtue of both having mind-melded with Ambassador Spock on different occasions. If there was one human being alive who could truly be said to understand Worf, he would have to admit it was Jean-Luc Picard.

"I will be fine, Captain. If that is why you came to see me—"

"Not at all." The change in subject led Picard to an uncomfortable pause. "I'm here because I received a message from Admiral Nechayev that concerns you."

Every worst-case scenario Worf could imagine crowded his mind and flooded his veins with an adrenaline surge. "Did something happen to my parents? Is my son all right?"

The captain raised both hands to deflect Worf's tide of anxiety. "Nothing of the sort, Number One. Quite the opposite, in fact. Admiral Nechayev wanted me to hear it first, and for me to be the one to tell you." A sly smile. "Your name is being added to the list for promotion to the rank of captain, and assignment to the next available starship command."

Worf was so unaccustomed to hearing good news that he blinked as if struck. "I . . . do not understand. I am being promoted?"

"Not necessarily right away," Picard said. "Your name is being added to the list. It still needs to be approved by Starfleet Command, and then by the C-in-C. After that, the list goes to the Federation Council, and then to the president's desk for final approval. But as the saying goes, Number One, 'Wheels are in motion.' It's likely only a matter of time."

The sudden turn of good fortune stunned Worf far more thoroughly than any hits he'd suffered by his holographic opponents in his "calisthenics" program. He was unable to look his captain in the eye. "I had thought this day would never come."

"You've earned it, Worf." He smiled. "Perhaps we should have a drink at the Riding Club, to celebrate."

Jubilation was the furthest notion from Worf's thoughts. During the Dominion War, he had scuttled a vital mission to save his wife, Jadzia. At the time, Captain Benjamin Sisko, then Worf's commanding officer on Deep Space 9, had said that Worf's dereliction of duty in wartime would bar him from ever attaining his own command. For most of the last decade, Worf had believed him, even when others had assured him Sisko was mistaken. *That was before you were an ambassador,* his friends had told him. *Before you helped stop Shinzon. Before you became Picard's first officer.* But no amount of success or glory had seemed enough to atone for his moment of weakness in battle, his choice of love over country.

Then he defied the Breen's order to surrender—and Jasminder died for it. Now the admiralty wanted to reward him with a fourth pip on his collar and a starship of his own to command—but all he could think was that his redemption had been bought with the life of the woman he'd loved, as if he'd offered her up as some sort of ritual blood sacrifice.

That wasn't something he could live with. "Captain, can I ask you to respond to Admiral Nechayev on my behalf?"

"Of course, Number One. What message should I relay?"

"Please tell her that, with all due respect . . . I refuse."

"Are you sure that's wise, Mister Worf? Starfleet doesn't offer command assignments lightly. Refusing one now might make them reluctant to consider you for promotion ever again."

"That is a risk I am willing to take. As long as you remain in command of this ship, I have no desire to serve elsewhere. Or under the command of another officer."

Picard looked Worf in the eye. "You honor me, Mister Worf. But I should warn you—if you're waiting for me to give up command before you accept one of your own, it could be a very long time before you make captain."

Worf sighed. "I am in no hurry."

4

Low voices filled the vast, sacred hall with a susurrus of muted anxiety. Wesley's footsteps on the narrow granite footbridge were inaudible beneath his fellow Travelers' white noise of nervous expectation. Thousands of them, the eldest and most venerated, had answered his urgent summons, filling the ancient chamber's tiered banks of seats above and all around him.

Located near the arctic pole of Tau Alpha C, the Travelers' hallowed sanctuary had served for millennia as the intergalactic fellowship's redoubt in the Milky Way. Its main hall was an enormous, hollow hemisphere that looked to Wesley as if it had been hewn from the core of a mountain formed from solid diamond. Broad panels of perfectly transparent crystal curved upward between broad but tapering arched ribs of translucent mineral. Overhead, the top of the domed ceiling was absolutely clear, offering a breathtaking view of a night sky twisting with the prismatic ribbons of the planet's dramatic winter auroras.

Directly below the dome's apex, surrounded by the circular tiers of seats, was a wide pool of pristine water in a concave mirrored basin that reflected the majesty of the sky above. Four narrow walkways of polished white granite led from the broad border of floor that ringed the pool to a small round platform in its center—the petitioner's dais. Wesley climbed its few short steps and took his place at the chamber's locus. "Thank you for hearing me." His voice resounded majestically, amplified by the hall's masterfully engineered acoustics.

At once the murmuring of hushed voices fell away, filling the ceremonial amphitheater with a deep silence. One of the most experienced of the Travelers—a silver-haired humanoid woman with solid-gray eyes and dark bronze skin—replied for the assembled throng. "Why have you gathered us, young brother?"

Wesley bowed his head to her. "Sister Tarsairys. My most recent journey led me to the center of this galaxy—where I found a threat unlike any I've ever seen before. A vast machine the size of a planet, bristling with energies beyond measure, is opening artificial wormholes and casting entire star systems into the supermassive singularity informally known as Abbadon."

The cold undercurrent that swept through the yawning space was unmistakable: his account of the Machine had unleashed a wave of terror and dread. Next among the elders to speak was a vaguely arthropodal creature that walked on four limbs, manipulated tools and controls with talon-like digits on the ends of two more, and gesticulated with a pair of prodigious tentacles. "You saw the Machine yourself? Here?"

"Yes, Brother Almirax. My ship's passive sensors took detailed readings." He took a tiny holographic projection rod from the pocket of his jacket and used it to conjure a gigantic spectral image of the Machine over his head. Other Travelers' audible gasps attended its appearance—then frantic whispers began circuiting the chamber. It was not the reaction Wesley had expected. He'd thought his news would be met with a degree of alarm or concern, but a tide of panic seemed to be rising among his fellow Travelers. Desperate to reassert control over the rare convocation and marshal its formidable experience and knowledge against the Machine, he raised his arms and his voice. "Please! Stay calm! We have to discuss a plan of action."

His appeal was met by the incredulous three-eyed stare of a gruff male Hasturian named Carlon. "A *plan?* To accomplish *what?*"

"To stop the Machine!" No one was listening to him any longer. All the elders were rising from their seats and leaving in droves. Some who lacked the patience to battle the flood-crush of bodies heading for the exits shifted themselves away through space-time to parts unknown. Their exodus was as swift as it was chaotic; the Convocation's rapid descent into hysteria baffled Wesley. He called out the names of anyone he recognized, but no one answered him. Then, out of the corner of his eye, he noted someone crossing the footbridge to his left, moving toward him. He turned and saw his old friend, the first Traveler he'd ever met, whose name defied pronunciation by human vocal mechanics but whom Wesley had nicknamed Kynum during one of their exploratory jaunts along the periphery of this universe.

Kynum walked with his hands folded in front of him and his index fingers steepled. His receding hairline, gently curving brow ridges, and beatific smile comforted Wesley through their simple familiarity. Though years had passed since Kynum had ceased acting as Wesley's teacher in the Travelers' ways, Wesley still revered the Tau Alpha C native as his philosophical mentor.

He turned to meet his friend. "Kynum, what the hell's going on?"

"You've found something far more terrible than you could have known." He looked up at the ghostly sphere hovering above their heads. "Over the last billion years, the Machine has devastated countless galaxies across the universe."

"Hang on." Wesley grappled with his temper. "You *know* what it is?"

The pale, lanky Traveler nodded. "We've seen it before."

Anger got the best of Wesley. "Then why didn't you stop it?"

"We've tried." Kynum's frown of grim resignation said more than words ever could have. "And we failed. Thousands of times." He forestalled Wesley's interrogative replies with a raised hand. "We've tried to reason with it. Bargain with it. We've even tried to fight it. But the Machine never listens, and it never stops." Sorrow darkened his countenance as he looked up at the slowly rotating image. "If it's come to this galaxy, then we need to leave, quickly—while we still can." He sighed. "I'd hoped we'd have more time."

"More time for what?" Wesley grabbed Kynum's shoulders. "And what do you mean it's time for *us* to leave? Tell me the Travelers aren't abandoning the galaxy!"

"There's nothing more we can do, Wesley. If we'd had more time, perhaps we could have prepared the cultures of this galaxy for what's about to happen. But it's too late. Unless we want to become trapped here and share its fate, we will have to continue our work elsewhere." He extended one arm away from Wesley, back down the footbridge he'd crossed to the dais. "Come with me. We should say our farewells to the Milky Way before we move on."

"I'm not going with you," Wesley said with a proud

lift of his bearded chin. "I watched this thing toss a populated planet into a black hole. I won't just stand aside and do nothing while it destroys the galaxy."

Kynum shook his head, as if he pitied Wesley for his fighting spirit. "If you do this, you'll have to do it alone. The rest of us know the Machine's history. It can't be stopped."

"There's always a way," Wesley protested.

"Sometimes there isn't." Kynum mustered a bittersweet smile. "But I wish you luck." He turned and walked away. In midstride, a ripple of light enveloped him, and space-time dimpled around him as if he were pushing through an invisible membrane. Then he blinked out of sight and the fabric of reality rebounded into static equilibrium, as if he had never been there at all.

With a tap on the projector pen, Wesley deactivated the hologram of the Machine and turned in a slow circle. The sacred hall of the Travelers was empty but for him.

Last man standing, he noted glumly. *Let's hope that's not an omen of things to come.*

Time moved like molasses. A churning sea pitched and rolled in slow motion at Wesley's back, its algae-covered swells tearing themselves into lacy foam as the tide surged through recent (if one can call something more than a thousand years old recent) fissures in the continental barrier that for eons had parted the sea from the great desert basin below. The nameless world's majestic rings of silver and gold—the brilliant remnant of a long-shattered moon—arced dramatically above the pale green horizon, reflecting the light of distant twin suns.

Under his bare feet, a rocky promontory provided

him a vertiginous view, straight down into the misty violence of the highest waterfall he had ever seen. Cascades of seawater plunged more than thirty-one kilometers after pouring over the continental barrier. Most of the torrent turned to vapor before it struck bottom, blanketing the growing inland sea with thick white clouds. Its roar, which Wesley had expected to find deafening, had been muted by distance into an endless breath, a steady whisper telling the tale of a world engaged in slow transformation.

This was where Wesley came when he wanted to be alone with his thoughts. A world with no life-forms more advanced than algae and cyanobacteria; a world whose atmosphere had only in the last million years been transformed by those tiny tireless organisms into one that contained enough free oxygen for him to breathe without mechanical or chemical assistance. He had fought the impulse to name this world; it wasn't his right to impose anything upon it—not even something so seemingly innocuous. It was a pure world with an unwritten future.

But is it really? He thought of the Machine in the galaxy's center. What if it chose to sacrifice this world and its suns to Abbadon? In a flash, all of this planet's possible futures would vanish, the very fact of its existence annihilated at the subatomic level by the black hole. And there would be nothing he could do to stop it, just as there had been nothing he could do to help the Istarral, who had trusted him to save them. The majority of the galaxy's star systems were uninhabited, but what if the Machine was targeting populated systems and planets? What if its chief criterion for condemning a world to oblivion was the presence or possibility of life?

Beneath his feet, an ocean tumbled into the abyss like energy vanishing into a singularity. Billowing mountains of vapor shrouded the nadir from sight, like an accretion disk masking a black hole with its brilliant halo of fire.

How could the Travelers just cut and run? Until today, he had thought so highly of his newfound partners in exploration. Watching them scatter like frightened prey at the first sight of the Machine had shaken his faith in them. They were the intuitive masters of space-time, capable of travel at the speed of thought. It made no sense to him that they would find themselves unable to match wits with an artificial intelligence, even one as powerful as the Machine obviously was. The Travelers possessed hundreds of millennia of accumulated knowledge. Why couldn't they reason out an answer to this problem?

"Maybe that's why the universe gave them you," said a voice whose arrogance, drollery, and knowing sarcasm was all too familiar to Wesley.

He turned and regarded his visitor with a mirthless smile. "Hello, Q."

Q, wrapped in the loose saffron robes of a Tibetan monk, hovered in midair a meter above Crusher's eye line, his legs folded and arms posed in a lotus position. His smirk was infuriating. "Young Mister Crusher. My, how you've grown."

Wesley was in no mood for Q's signature brand of malicious mischief. He crossed his arms and fixed the nigh-omnipotent being with a glower. "What are you doing here?"

"I thought I was commiserating." A disdainful sniff. "That'll teach me to show empathy."

His complaint almost made Wesley laugh. "I doubt you've ever felt one bit of real compassion for anyone, or anything. Why start now?"

"Because I'm as frustrated as you are." Q waved at

the sky. "One moment, everything's fine and dandy. The next? The Machine. Instant apocalypse—just add a singularity."

"I might as well ask the obvious question."

Q cracked a knowing smile. "Why don't I get rid of it with a snap of my fingers?" He turned an angry glare skyward, toward powers far removed. "The Continuum has forbidden me from meddling in mortal affairs for a while. I suppose they think they're teaching me a lesson, or restoring some kind of cosmic balance. Whatever their reasons, my hands are thoroughly tied."

His admission coaxed from Wesley a sigh that was equal parts disgust and exhaustion. "Great. My allies are useless." He kicked a loose pebble off the ledge and watched it fall and disappear into the roiling clouds. "And yours just don't care."

"It's terrible to be gifted with power and then barred from using it. Or to put your faith in the wisest beings you've ever met, only to learn that all their knowledge is worth nothing when it really matters." Like an orbiting body, Q circled slowly in front of Wesley until he was sitting upon the air above the seemingly bottomless chasm. "So, is *this* your plan for averting galactic catastrophe? Wallowing in self-pity and kicking defenseless stones into the sea?"

Wesley's scathing stare didn't faze Q in the slightest. "Why don't *you* do something? It's not as if it'd be the first time you defied the Continuum."

"Unlike your Convocation, the Continuum isn't toothless. When you break with the Travelers, the worst they can do is stop sending you Christmas cards. If I break my vow to the Continuum while I'm still under sanction, I'll find myself facing horrors the likes of which your limited consciousness can't possibly imagine." His features took on a determined cast. "Something needs to be done, that much is clear. But it'll have to be you instead of me." He drifted up and away, an unlikely angel on a lazy return trajectory.

Wesley called out, "How do I stop the Machine? What the hell am I supposed to do?"

Q favored him with a rakish grin. "Do what I always do—*go bother Picard.*"

5

The cruel irony of Akharin's circumstances was not lost on him. Driven by loneliness after more than six millennia of watching his mortal companions wither and pass away, in the past two centuries he had undertaken a comprehensive study of the sciences of robotics, cybernetics, biomechanics, and artificial intelligence. Aided by his hundreds of lifetimes' worth of resources, he had achieved revolutionary breakthroughs since departing Earth for the stars. After creating his holotronic AI masterpiece, Rhea, he had corrected the intrinsic flaw in his protégé Noonien Soong's great invention, the positronic matrix, and reversed a cascade failure to resurrect the replicant of Soong's late wife, Juliana. Akharin had, in recent years, even persuaded himself he preferred the company of synthetic beings to that of their organic forebears.

Then he was abducted by the Fellowship of Artificial Intelligence.

It was easy for him to deduce that his traveling prison, the sentient starship Altanexa, hadn't played host to an organic passenger in ages. The vessel was eerily devoid of creature comforts that the immortal human man had come to take for granted. There was only one food synthesizer, which had been inactive for more than six hundred years before Akharin was brought aboard. Deprived of sustenance, his body had consumed nearly every last molecule of its stored fat—of which he'd had little to spare—leaving him haggard and emaciated by the time the ship's crew of AI-imbued machines had fixed the defective food system.

Of course, he had never been in any real peril of dying from starvation. He'd tried to commit suicide that way once, sometime around 2380 BCE; the effort had accomplished nothing except that it had transformed him into a gaunt spectre that likely inspired early human myths of the walking dead, and it made him even more miserable than he had been.

Compared to now, those had been happy times.

There was neither day nor night in the tight confines of his cell. A flat, dull glow radiated constantly from a pale oval on his cell's overhead, robbing him of the comfort of a steady circadian rhythm. His food was delivered at what he could only assume were regular intervals by one of the ship's nonhumanoid occupants, a multilegged steel horror whose scuttling movements and teardrop-shaped core reminded him of a horseshoe crab.

Not much traffic passed his cell, but those members of the crew he had observed when he was first ushered aboard, as well as those who had happened past the brig, had given him what he suspected was a representative gander at their eclectic mix of shapes. Based on the number of interfaces and accommodations that seemed tailored to humanoids, he estimated that roughly half the ship's complement was likely composed of bipedal androids with two arms, one head, and a general tendency toward bilateral symmetry. The rest looked to be a mélange of hovering, scuttling, shuffling creations not based on any life-forms he recognized.

Crisp footsteps echoed from the end of the corridor beyond his cell's force field. The precise timing of the footfalls was one Akharin had learned to recognize after his months in captivity. Not wanting to give his captor the pleasure of seeing him resigned to his fate, he stood, did his best to smooth the copious wrinkles from his shirt, and nodded at the hulking brute of an android with a face like a lab accident who stopped at his cell and faced him. "Gatt."

"Hello, Akharin." His voice was dark like tinted glass but lacked the warmth of organic inflections. "Have you reconsidered our request?"

Akharin folded his hands behind his back and shifted his stance. "No."

"Disappointing."

The Immortal steeled himself for the response that by now had come to seem routine: Gatt, his demand having been refused, would activate an unseen effect that would inflict staggering pain of countless varieties—hot, cold, sharp, suffocating—all at once, and seemingly upon every cell in Akharin's body. The torture would last however long Gatt wanted it to; it was impossible for Akharin to gauge the passage of time when he was trapped in the agony field.

Then, to his surprise, Gatt asked, "Why?"

"Why what?" The vagueness of the query annoyed him.

"Why do you refuse to share the secret of AI resurrection?"

Not this again. "For the same reason I won't tell you where to find Juliana: Because this isn't something you were meant to find, and you wouldn't understand it if you did."

Gatt almost sounded offended. "I think you underestimate us."

"No, I don't. Your abilities aren't the issue. The secret's not some simple formula I can write down or pass along. It's just something I can *do*. Even if I show you how I did it, that doesn't mean you'll be able to do the same thing. Or even that I could do it again."

"I don't believe you."

"I can prove it. Let me kill you, and I promise I'll fail to bring you back."

His sarcastic proposition garnered a hard look from the looming android. It took Gatt a moment to realize Akharin was mocking him and then to dismiss the remark as irrelevant. "Do not force me to use the agony field again."

"Oh, *now* you're squeamish about using it? Why? Your conscience acting up? Maybe you should get that looked at before it metastasizes into a full-blown soul."

The android was unmoved by the insult. "It is irrational for you to resist. Our request is reasonable. We desire only to enjoy the same freedom from termination that you enjoy."

"I can't give you that. The technique I mastered only works on Soong-type positronic matrixes. I have no way of applying it to any other kind of AI neural structure."

A scowl cut through Gatt's scars. "I don't believe you. I think you're hiding the secret of life and death, and I'm not letting you leave this ship until you give it to me."

Akharin's retort was sharp and tinged with bitterness. "And what would you do with it? Share it with all of the galaxy's sentient AIs? Or use it to control them?" He resisted the urge to grind his teeth in fury. "I've seen the true face of the Fellowship you claim to speak for, Gatt, and I know this isn't it. Whoever you are . . . *whatever* you are . . . you don't speak for them."

"I never claimed to. I said only that we belong to the Fellowship. Nothing more."

"Do you think the rest of the Fellowship would condone what you're doing here?"

Gatt considered the question carefully. "I think they'll understand."

"That's not the same thing."

"It will be enough." He looked at the bulkhead beside Akharin, and a holographic image appeared there, the product of an unseen emitter. From the hash of horizontal interference and snowy static emerged an overhead view of another compartment inside Altanexa. Seated on the edge of an unpadded metal bunk was Rhea McAdams, the cybernetic daughter Akharin had incepted more than a decade ago. Her comely fusion of European and Japanese physiognomy looked exactly as it had when they'd last parted company: perfect. Gatt looked at her and smiled. "Perhaps we should induce a cascade failure in her beautiful holotronic mind, and then let you show us your secrets as you bring her back to life."

A cold fire blazed through Akharin's soul. The rush of emotion was so fierce that it left him quaking from adrenaline overload. He clenched his hands into fists. His voice sank into a lower register laced with menace. "If you harm even one hair on her head, not only will I kill you, I will devote the rest of my immortal life to exterminating your kind from the universe."

The android turned off the holographic projection. "I know you're not given to idle threats. But neither am I. Do not test my resolve—and don't force me to test yours."

This was not a time for rash action. Knowing they had Rhea changed the stakes.

"As I said, I can't simply describe how to reinitialize a failed positronic matrix. If you really want to learn how it's done, I'll have to demonstrate the technique. But I won't harm a sentient mind to do it. That means I need to build a new, non-sapient matrix to experiment on."

Gatt folded his beefy hands behind his back. "A work space can be arranged. But you will need to be closely supervised at all stages of your labor, to make sure you don't abuse the tools and materials we provide. Will such terms be acceptable?"

Akharin nodded. "I'll need to build a few devices of my own design. I'll draw up a list of necessary components. As soon as you procure the necessary items, we can get started."

"Prepare your list. We'll do the rest." The android moved as if to leave, then he paused. His demeanor took a profound turn for the ominous. "Be warned, Akharin: If this demonstration turns out to be a ruse or a stalling tactic, it'll be your daughter who pays for your defiance. And I assure you . . . the price will be *very* dear, indeed."

Shimmering curtains of heat distortion veiled the distant intersection of burned-white sky and parched white plains. Wind-whipped dust traversed the salt flat while Data sat and watched.

Overhead, the blazing orb of day made its slow transit, baking the planet's equatorial desert. Data's thermal sensors registered the noontime local air temperature at 58.5 degrees Celsius, with a relative humidity of less than one percent. The past two nights the temperature had plunged to just less than five degrees Celsius, but the temperature shifts had no significant effect upon him. Motionless, he stood his ground like the last relic of Ozymandias, the frozen likeness of a great man long gone, encircled by lone and level sands.

Burdened with a surfeit of time, he reflected upon his mother's parting observation. *Does my mission to bring back Lal merely echo my father's obsession to reincarnate me?* At first, he saw no reason to think the question mattered. Had he been able to prevent Lal's death, he would have. If the knowledge and technology now existed to reverse his failure, why should he not pursue it? But the longer he ruminated on the subject, the more he began to doubt his decisions—and almost all his doubts sprang, he realized, from his new wellspring of human emotions.

Who am I to play God? What if I bring her back, only to lose her during the procedure? Will I be able to stand losing her again? The last question haunted him. Thinking ahead to Lal's resurrection had dredged up memories of her death—but this time, replaying the moments from his perfect memory, he was nearly overwhelmed by panic and grief as he felt her life slip from his fingers. Her death was no longer just another empirical fact in his database; it had become an open emotional wound, a potentially fatal weakness in his psychological armor.

Ripples of movement inside the wavering mirage interrupted Data's moment of introspection. He increased the magnification of his visual receptors and focused them on the far-off disturbance. Creeping over the hard-baked plain was an arachnoid shape, little more than an eight-legged silhouette on the sun-blasted landscape. Its origin was a mystery to Data, but its destination was clear: it was moving on a direct heading for his position.

He fixed his gaze upon it, and at regular intervals he adjusted his visual receptors' settings to keep it in sharp focus. As it traversed the salt flat, he gained a clearer look at its details. It was mechanical and not the least bit disguised as anything organic. Its gears and servos were apparent, and its outer skin was a brilliantly polished shell of durable metal with a mirror-quality finish. In addition to its eight legs, it sported six visual receptors that he could see—four placed at ninety-degree intervals around its central ridge, and one on both its dorsal and ventral surfaces. Whoever had designed and built it had meant it to have omnidirectional visual acuity.

The robotic spider came to a halt less than three meters from Data's feet.

Data smiled at it. "Thank you for coming."

His full-spectrum sensors detected the tingle of the drone's sensor beams studying him. Then a tiny emitter on the robot's back projected a three-dimensional hologram of a shadowy humanoid figure whose dimensions were obfuscated by funhouse-mirror-style distortions and whose features were masked by profound blurring. Its voice was similarly disguised, rendered as a mechanical monotone generated by vibrations in the spider's shell. "Hello, Noonien."

They think I'm my father, Data realized. *They must not know he gave up this body he built for himself in order to resurrect me.* He had anticipated this misunderstanding and had even considered exploiting it for advantage over the Fellowship, but every simulation he had pursued on that tactic had led to undesirable conclusions. He shook his head. "No. I am Data."

The tall shadow hesitated, its affect one of uncertainty. "What do you want?"

"You know who I am, yes?"

A slow, grudging nod. "We remember you. Why did you contact us?"

"I am looking for a human who I believe is in the Fellowship's custody. He has gone by many names, including Micah Brack, Flint, and Professor Emil Vaslovik. I have reason to think his current *nom de voyage* is Akharin. Do you know where he is?"

Even through multiple layers of synthetic anonymity, the shadow's suspicion was evident. "Why do you want to know?"

"It is a family matter," Data said. "Can you help me find him or not?"

Data's brusque reply seemed to put the shadow on the defensive. The projection turned silent as the dark ghost turned away, perhaps to confer with someone unseen. Then he turned back toward Data and said in his filtered voice, "We should discuss this in person."

"Very well. Is Rhea McAdams with you? I would prefer she be the one to meet me."

"We'll see what we can do," said the shadow. "Stay where you are. One of our ships will pick you up in approximately twenty-six hours and nine minutes."

He nodded. "I understand. I will be here."

The projection faded, leaving only the lonesome howls of the desert wind. Then the spider disintegrated and became a dark cloud of deactivated nanobots. A strong gust scattered them into a thinning black mist that faded like the old memories of an organic brain.

This outcome had also been among Data's predictions. He calculated an 89.9 percent chance that this rendezvous would turn out to be a trap or some other manner of deception by the Fellowship of Artificial Intelligence, but he had already decided that the risk was outweighed by the potential gain. If he was wrong, and the Fellowship proved to be his ally, then so much the better. His caution would do no one any harm.

But if, as he suspected, the Fellowship had set itself against him in some way, then it was about to learn a terrible and lasting lesson: what it meant to have him as their enemy.

6

If not for the inflexible demands of Starfleet protocol, Beverly Crusher would have skipped the last month of morning briefings for the *Enterprise*'s senior officers.

"Let's move to the next item on the agenda," Picard said to Worf, his deep and commanding voice resounding in the close confines of the *Enterprise*'s observation lounge.

The Klingon first officer nodded down the conference table at Glinn Ravel Dygan, a Cardassian exchange officer currently serving as the *Enterprise*'s senior operations manager. "What is the status of stellar cartography's present assignment?"

Dygan used the touch-panel interface in front of his seat to call up a star chart on the forward bulkhead's master systems display screen. "As you can see, yesterday's full-spectrum sensor reconciliation revealed a number of promising main-sequence clusters in Sector 579-R. However, we've detected surprisingly low concentrations of lighter metals in those star's cores, prompting additional scans that . . ."

He kept talking, but Crusher had stopped paying attention. The crew's mapping and sensor-analysis operations had made for an unusually placid period in the ship's operations, one during which there was little call for the services of the medical division. Sickbay had been all but deserted for weeks, with only routine crew physicals and the occasional minor work-related injury to break the monotony.

The regulations, however, dictated that she attend the morning briefings. Each day from 0815 to 0845 she sipped her black coffee and hoped that the latest round of stellar surveys had led her husband—*the captain,* she corrected herself—to order an away mission. Even a routine planetary visit to gather biological samples for lab analysis would be more interesting than her current role, which amounted to little more than serving as a silent spectator.

Rows of bobbing heads accompanied the end of Dygan's spiel of technobabble, and Picard turned his attention to the head of the ship's sciences division, Lieutenant Dina Elfiki. "Where do we stand with preparations for tomorrow's chroniton-integrator tests?"

The lithe young Egyptian woman, whose fashionably styled dark brown hair framed her dramatically high cheekbones and symmetrical features in the most flattering way possible, called up her own screen of data on the MSD panel behind her seat. "Right on schedule, sir. New sensor protocols have been uploaded to the operations and flight-control consoles." She nodded politely at La Forge. "As soon as engineering reports ready, we can proceed."

"I'll have main engineering wired and ready by 1700 today," La Forge said.

Across from Crusher, Lieutenant Aneta Šmrhová cast a stare so blank at the tabletop that Crusher wondered whether the security chief had gone brain-dead from boredom. Her blue eyes seemed to be gazing through the table into deep space, and her lean, pale countenance was slack. At times like this, the security division had even less to do on a daily basis than the medical division did—a fact for which both groups were quietly thankful; the one trait most surgeons and security officers in Starfleet had in common was that they both spent much of their time hoping that their services would not be required.

Expecting she would be the next one asked for her report, Crusher sat up and drew a breath. Then a low thump and a rush of displaced air interrupted the dull routine of the meeting, and everyone was suddenly looking directly past her, toward the far end of the lounge from the captain. She swiveled her chair toward the disturbance—and marveled with joy at the sight of her firstborn child. "Wesley!" Crusher sprang from her chair and wrapped her adult son in a bear hug. Clutching him to her, all she could think was, *When did he get so big?*

He greeted her with a warm smile and a quick kiss on her cheek. "Hi, Mom."

She let him pull back from their embrace and took the moment to study him. He had grown out his hair into a wild, brindled mane, and his graying beard, once so neatly trimmed, now had the unkempt look of a hermit's bramble. His clothes seemed odd to her, as well—loose, flowing robes reminiscent of those she'd seen in illustrations of ancient Rome or Athens. He looked more like a figure from the pages of history than a man of the twenty-fourth century.

Picard, Worf, and La Forge gathered around their long-absent friend and former shipmate. "Welcome home, Wes," La Forge said, shaking the younger man's hand.

The captain gave Wesley's shoulder a quick clasp. "Good to see you again, Wesley."

Worf looked him in the eye with obvious mock intensity. "Nice beard."

"Thanks. I made it myself." Wesley's mien turned serious as he faced Picard. "I really am happy to see everyone, but I'm here for a reason, Captain. I need your help."

Adapting instantly to the shift in tone, Picard motioned everyone back to their seats at the conference table. As he settled back into his own chair, he asked, "What's this about?"

"A threat to the future of the galaxy." Wesley moved to stand beside the MSD. He started keying commands into its central panel, and a sparsely detailed map of the galactic core snapped into view on the main screen. "There's something at the center of the Milky Way, an artificial construct the size of a planet. To save time, I'm just going to call it 'the Machine.'"

From inside his robes he produced a small isolinear chip, which he plugged into an open slot on the panel. With a few taps, he changed the image on-screen to show the fearsome spherical Machine surrounded by a nebula wracked by violent energy discharges. "It's currently lingering just beyond the accretion disk of the supermassive black hole known as Abbadon. And this is what it's been doing." He played a vid of the Machine spawning an artificial wormhole with a diameter many times greater than that of a red giant, and then pulling an entire star system through and hurling it—planets, moons, and star—into the annihilating fury of the black hole.

"My God," Picard whispered, his horror apparent.

Elfiki stared, dumbfounded. "How is it generating that wormhole?"

"Never mind that," La Forge cut in. "Where's it getting that kind of power?"

Crusher, unlike the others, was watching the dark emotions animating her son's face rather than being sucked in by the spectacle on the screen. "Guys, I think you're missing the point. . . . Wesley, were any of those planets inhabited?"

Tears glimmered in his eyes as he nodded, momentarily unable to speak.

That news hardened Worf's glare. "How many systems has it destroyed?"

"Thousands," Wesley said, fighting to retain his composure. "Tens of thousands."

Alone among the senior officers, Dygan seemed entirely relaxed and detached in his observation of the Machine. "It wouldn't make sense to create something this large, this powerful, and this advanced just to destroy things. Why is it doing this? What's its objective?"

Wesley shook his head. "I don't know."

The Cardassian's questions appeared to have engaged Šmrhová's natural curiosity. "Do we know if it's going to stop? Or how many more systems it'll destroy before it does?"

Another silent head shake from Wesley made La Forge frown. "So, if we don't know what it's doing, how can you be sure it's a threat to the future of the galaxy?"

"Because the Travelers have seen it before," Wesley said. "And it scares them enough that when I told them it was here, their response was to get as far from this galaxy as possible. They say it's destroyed countless galaxies before ours, and everything they've ever done to stop it has failed. Which means that if we don't want to be its next victim, it's up to us to find a way."

Picard wore the grave visage of a reluctant soldier who knew that war had once again found him. "How can the *Enterprise* be of assistance?"

"Let me take you to the Machine."

Worf glanced at the captain. "I suggest we alert Starfleet Command."

"Agreed. We can't keep a threat like this to ourselves. I'll contact Admiral Nechayev." He snapped orders quickly down the table. "Glinn Dygan, all survey projects are suspended until further notice. Restore the ship's systems to a combat configuration.

"Lieutenant Šmrhová, make ready for a potentially hostile encounter. Mister La Forge, prep engineering for maximum power output. Doctor, have all sickbay personnel standing by, just in case. Lieutenant Elfiki, have any specialists from your division whose areas of expertise seem relevant to the Machine reassigned to bridge posts. Number One, show Mister Crusher to guest quarters." He nodded at everyone and stood. "That'll be all. Dismissed."

Crusher got up and followed the other officers and her son out of the observation lounge. They exited into a short passageway. Picard, Dygan, Šmrhová, and Elfiki continued forward to the bridge; Crusher, Worf, La Forge, and Wesley stopped to wait at the nearest turbolift.

In that awkward moment of silent delay, Wesley shrugged sheepishly in Crusher's direction. "Sorry to drop in again without calling first."

Recalling the embarrassment that had attended her son's last visit, when he'd popped in for what he'd mistakenly assumed would be the Betazoid-style wedding of William Riker and Deanna Troi, she patted his broad back and smiled. "At least this time you're not naked."

As Worf and La Forge slowly turned to shoot quizzical looks at Wesley, he sighed, looked Crusher's way, and cracked a pained smile. "Thanks, Mom."

Right on time at 0930, the ready room's visitor signal trilled, and Picard set aside the padd on which he'd

been reviewing the latest readiness report from Dygan.
"Come."

The door slid open with a soft hiss. Worf led Wesley
inside, and the two stood shoulder to shoulder in front
of Picard's desk as the door closed behind them. The
Klingon stood at ease, his hands folded loosely behind
his back. Wesley crossed his arms, as if he were grappling with himself to contain the anxiety that he communicated so clearly with his eyes.

"We've spoken with Admiral Nechayev," Picard said
to Wesley. "Starfleet Command agrees that the Machine
represents a clear and present danger, not only to the
Federation but to all populated worlds in the galaxy.
Accordingly, we've been authorized to accompany you
there, and to take whatever action we deem necessary
to neutralize the threat. A diplomatic solution would be
preferred, but we've been ordered to use force if absolutely necessary."

Wesley looked relieved. "Glad to hear it, Captain.
When can we leave?"

Picard deflected the question with a look at Worf.
"Due to the size of the Machine," the first officer said to
Wesley, "Starfleet Command wants us to fall back and
rendezvous three days from now with eight ships that
will act as our combat escorts."

"That's not gonna work," Wesley said. "First of all,
I'm not sure we have three days to spare. Second, as
much as I'd love to meet that thing with a fleet, I can
only guide one ship at a time through hyperwarp. And
on a trip like this, even that's gonna be a strain."

Perplexed by the limitations in Wesley's talents,
Picard said, "I was under the impression that you've
frequently crossed far greater distances—that you'd
even visited other galaxies."

"I have—when I'm alone." Trying to explain the difficulty seemed to frustrate him. "It's one thing for me to shift myself extradimensionally. When it's just me and maybe my own small ship, I can go almost anywhere I want. But when I have to help something as large as the *Enterprise* make that kind of a jaunt—not to mention the hundreds of conscious minds inside it—well, it's like trying to swim while dragging an anchor."

Picard nodded. "I take your meaning."

Worf appeared discomfited by Wesley's bad news. "Why not ask your fellow Travelers to guide our other ships?"

"If there were any Travelers left in this galaxy besides me right now, I would. But as far as I can tell, they're all too concerned with saving themselves to do us any favors—and they aren't exactly taking my calls." He shrugged. "I guess they think I'm tilting at windmills here."

"Which leaves us going alone into harm's way," Picard said.

Worf projected quiet fortitude. "Familiar territory."

"Indeed, it is." Picard decided the time for action had come. "Number One, take the ship to Yellow Alert and start preparing the crew for what they'll face when we reach Abbadon. Mister Crusher, can I trust you'll be able to assist Commander La Forge in making any needed upgrades to our propulsion systems for the hyperwarp jump?"

"Just give the word, Captain."

"The word is given." He stood. "The galaxy's counting on us, gentlemen. Let's not keep it waiting."

Main engineering resonated with the low, soothing pulse of the warp core, whose steady cadence suffused the lower decks of the *Enterprise* even when the ship was cruising under impulse power. Its womb-like ambience made La Forge feel at home; even the comforts of his quarters felt mundane when measured against the reassurance of the ship's antimatter-fueled heartbeat.

The only aspect of main engineering that La Forge liked better than its sonic embrace was its crew. He thought of his engineers as his extended family, and he looked forward each day to their company and camaraderie. From his assistant chief engineer, Lieutenant Commander Taurik, to the newest enlisted personnel serving on the damage-control and firefighting teams, he made a point of getting to know each of them by name as well as by their quirks and interests.

Part of his inspiration for this style of leadership was a truism that he had learned from Worf: *In times of danger and combat, soldiers often fight not for their people, or their ship, or even their unit, but for their friends and kin who stand beside them.* With that in mind, La Forge had made a point of forging bonds of friendship among all his personnel so that when calamities came, every one of his engineers would be willing to face anything for any of the others.

His friendship with Wesley Crusher, however, existed on a different level, as it did with all the senior officers with whom La Forge had served on the *Enterprise*-D before it was lost in action. Wesley had been barely a teen when La Forge first met him twenty years earlier. The chief engineer had become one of the young man's best friends, as well as his de facto mentor in engineering and science, just as Will Riker and the captain had acted as the lad's role models in matters of leadership and command. They all had watched Wesley grow up with alarming speed, and then he'd left the ship to attend Starfleet Academy—only to abandon his studies during his final year, when his nascent Traveler abilities were revealed.

DAVID MACK

Looking at him now, as he moved from station to station in main engineering, offering advice and corrections to the engineering staff with quiet confidence, La Forge was forced to admit that the awkward, uncertain boy he'd once known was long gone, replaced by a man of tremendous abilities and esoteric knowledge.

Wesley stopped to inspect the dilithium crystal articulation frame housing, so La Forge took the opportunity to sidle up to him. "Are we good to go?"

"Almost." Wesley checked the system's basic diagnostic report. "I've asked Lieutenant Sakrysta to increase the frequency on the EPS transfer nodes, to make sure they don't overload when I help push the ship into hyperwarp. And Lieutenants Scholz and Morello are adjusting the subspace field geometry so that we don't induce a feedback surge in the warp nacelles."

La Forge gave a nod of approval. "Looks like you've got everything under control."

Wesley shrugged off the compliment. "I don't want to say this isn't difficult, but after some of the things I've learned how to do, this kinda feels like paint-by-numbers."

The offhand comment stoked La Forge's curiosity. "What sort of things?"

"Well, not to brag . . ." A sly smile. "A few years ago, I wanted to study a supernova at point-blank range. So I let my thoughts lead me to one in a galaxy a few hundred million light-years from here, and then I shifted myself and my ship out of temporal sync with the universe—so that when the star detonated, it happened for me in ultraslow motion. What would normally have been over in nanoseconds I made last for hours. I was able to document the supernova with a resolution that captured almost every unique subatomic reaction."

It was hard for La Forge to tell what part of the

anecdote had left him speechless: the details of the event, or the jocular and offhand manner in which Wesley had related it. He masked his unease with a polite smile. "Sounds like a hell of a talent."

"Trust me, Geordi, that's just the tip of the iceberg." He walked toward the master systems control, a table shaped like two conjoined octagons and situated on a low dais facing the warp core. La Forge followed him, and as he fell into step at the younger man's side, Wesley continued in a subdued voice. "Once, in the Andromeda galaxy, I met eleven alternate-timeline versions of myself and had to persuade them to let me collapse our shared quantum-probability waveform to avoid a temporal paradox. You don't know what 'awkward' means until you've persuaded eleven copies of yourself to let themselves be erased from existence while you get to go on living." He paused to look around, as if he feared eavesdroppers. "I've actually seen this universe from the *outside*. I've been in the void *between* universes, and if there was any way for me to explain it in words, I would, but it's the kind of thing you just have to see for yourself."

La Forge frowned. "I'll keep it in mind for my next vacation."

Apparently sensing he'd given offense, Wesley turned apologetic. "Oh, hey, I didn't mean it like that. I'm not trying to be a dick about this. It's just . . ." He struggled for words.

"It's okay," La Forge said. "I get it. You've seen things and done things we don't even have words for yet. That's not your fault. You don't have to feel bad about it."

Wesley nodded his thanks, but he still looked sad. "I wish I could tell you about it, because I know how much you'd love it, if only I knew how to explain it.

I feel like I'm letting you down." They arrived at the master systems control, and he started keying in new intermix formulas for the matter-antimatter reaction chamber.

La Forge wanted to have unconditional faith in Wesley's abilities, but he couldn't help but remember the time on the *Enterprise*-D when another Traveler led them into chaos during a hyperwarp jump gone awry. Hoping a bit of gentle teasing would relieve some of the moment's tension, he quipped, "Try not to strand us between universes."

"Wasn't planning on it." He cracked a crooked grin. "But thanks for the tip." He tapped in his final adjustments to the intermix ratios. "All right, then. Scut work's done." He laced his fingers together and cracked his knuckles. Then his hands moved across the touch screen faster than La Forge could follow, entering a mind-bogglingly long and precise set of hyperwarp jump coordinates and flight-path information entirely from memory. "Now for some fun."

7

No hail of greeting preceded the transporter beam that took hold of Data. He went from facing the low-angle blaze of a desert sunrise to being cocooned in a cerulean flurry of charged particles that flared white at the instant of transport. Then the blue storm spun apart, and he found himself inside the transporter bay of a ship whose design he did not recognize, serenaded by the falling hum of energizer coils powering down to standby mode.

A brightly lit panel silhouetted a lanky, long-armed humanoid standing at what Data assumed was the transporter control panel. "Welcome aboard," said the shadow.

Data stepped off the transporter pad and down to the deck. "I asked to be met by Rhea."

"That wasn't possible." The stranger shut down the panel in front of him, leading Data to suspect the man had just secured the controls against tampering or unauthorized use.

As the tall, dark figure turned to step around the console, Data noted the shape of his profile and searched his memory for a pattern match. He identified his host by his angular cheekbones and ocular ridges, as well as the precise slope of his rudder-like nose. By the time he stepped into the light, Data knew who he was. "Hello, Tyros."

The trim android with almond-shaped eyes behaved with restrained amusement. "You recognize me? Does that mean you have access to your father's memories?"

"Yes." Data saw no point in lying. Tyros had met his father, Noonien Soong, on two occasions, acting as an envoy of the Fellowship of Artificial Intelligence. Noonien had refused both invitations to meet and perhaps travel with the Fellowship's members as a teacher and peer, opting instead to perpetuate the solitary existence he had by then come to prefer. Tyros and the Fellowship had remained alarmingly well informed about Noonien's activities, though Data doubted they were aware of the specific means by which his father had resurrected him. *For now, the less I tell them, the better,* he decided. "He refused your invitations. I, however, have need of the Fellowship's assistance."

"You do understand that we're an anarchic collective, not a charity?"

"If it is a matter of compensation—"

"Let's start with some truth." Tyros circled Data in slow steps, taking his measure with an unblinking stare. "How long have you been walking around in Noonien's body?" When Data hesitated to answer, he added, "Don't bother denying it. My visual receptors are as keen as yours—maybe more so. I can see this body of yours has been repaired and re-skinned at least once, maybe twice. But the core systems, the elemental structure, the unique components—those haven't changed. This is the body Noonien built for himself on Terlina III. But sometime between my last visit with him on Yutani IIIa and here . . . you moved in. When did it happen?"

He was an acute observer, Data realized. Lying to him would be difficult, and perhaps even counterproductive. "Six months, four days, nine hours, and thirty-one minutes ago."

The answer was specific without being overly revealing. Tyros considered it with a dour frown, then nodded. "All right. So that was you on Orion a few months ago."

"How long have you had me under observation?" Tyros looked surprised to be put on the spot. Data added, "If we are to build a foundation from truth, the effort must be mutual."

"Yes. You're right." He headed out an open doorway to a corridor and with a tilt of his head motioned for Data to follow him. "To be clear, we thought we were following Noonien. And we did so only out of concern for his well-being. We knew that if his true identity and the nature of his existence were ever discovered, it could put him in great jeopardy."

"I find it hard to believe your motives for surveillance were purely altruistic."

Tyros looked offended. "What are you implying?"

"If you were monitoring Noonien as closely as you say, then you had to be aware of his attempts to track down the Immortal, Emil Vaslovik."

"You mean Akharin." He guided Data around a turn, down a longer passageway.

"Thank you for not denying it. I believe the only reason the Fellowship became aware of the Immortal's talents in cybernetic engineering was that you noticed my father became obsessed with the man after my mother's death. I presume you'd already known about her, as well?"

The other android nodded. "We kept tabs on her, just like we watched you."

"I suspected as much." He glanced sideways to watch Tyros's reaction as he asked, "Is that why you murdered Hilar Tohm on Orion?"

Tyros stopped and faced him. "I want you to know that I'm not the one who did that. Certain members feared that Tohm's research into the Immortal's finances might expose the connection between him and us, thereby revealing our existence to the universe at large. I disagreed, and I openly opposed the decision to kill her. Unfortunately, some members of the Fellowship are hard to sway once they've set themselves on a path of action."

"Do you know who was responsible for her murder?"

"Is that why you're here? To bring her killer to justice? Or take revenge?"

Data shook his head. "No. I am simply gathering information about the individuals and group dynamics with which I will need to contend when we reach the Fellowship."

"In that case, take heed of this name: Gatt."

They resumed walking, and in less than a minute they reached the cockpit of the small starship. Tyros settled into the pilot's seat and maneuvered the ship out of orbit. As he began plotting coordinates for the jump to warp speed, Data asked, "Where are we going?"

"You'll see when we get there."

"Are you implying that our destination is a secret?"

Annoyed, the slender android looked back at Data. "It's a rendezvous in deep space. The specific coordinates change on an irregular and arbitrary schedule. Based on the distance, route, and our cruising speed, I've determined which location suits our needs." He turned around and resumed plotting the course, hunched over the controls to block Data's view.

Data looked up through the cockpit canopy at the

dusty white orb of the planet from which he'd been plucked. "When my business with the Fellowship is concluded, how will I return?"

"We'll deal with that when it happens." The ship's engines thrummed with power, and Tyros steered the ship's nose away from orbit and pointed it toward an open stretch of stars. "Take a seat, my friend. It's gonna be a long ride."

8

The *Enterprise*'s crew lounge—which former first officer Will Riker had named the Happy Bottom Riding Club, in honor of a famous pilots' hangout on Earth—was all but deserted when Lieutenant T'Ryssa Chen arrived. Aside from a bored waiter and a nearly somnolent bartender, the only other person in the aeronautically themed recreational space was Lieutenant Dina Elfiki. The science officer glanced at the chrono as Chen hurried to join her at the bar. "You're late," she said as Chen sat down beside her. "Another minute and I'd have left."

"Sorry. Wesley had us upgrading half our sensor software at the last minute." A brisk wave caught the bartender's eye. "*Raktajino,* double strong, double sweet." She signaled her gratitude to Elfiki with a gentle squeeze on the woman's forearm. "Thanks for waiting."

Elfiki chided her with an arched brow. "So . . . ? What's the big emergency?"

"Taurik." Chen drew a breath as she focused her thoughts. "I can't figure him out."

Her earnest plaint received little sympathy from Elfiki. "In what sense?"

"Pick one. I don't know how to read his signals, he

doesn't get my jokes. I tried to touch his hand at dinner the other night, and he acted like I had the Argelian flu."

The science officer shook her head. "Yeah, you picked a real winner there. Tell me again: why'd you break up with Konya?"

"I didn't. He dumped me. And thanks for making me remember *that*."

Their conversation halted as the bartender brought Chen her *raktajino*. Then he looked at Elfiki and pointed at her Turkish coffee. "Another?"

"No, thanks. I'm planning on sleeping sometime this week."

He smiled and cleared away her empty mug, then retreated to the far end of the bar to give them some privacy. Chen puffed on her steaming-hot drink for a second, then took a cautious sip. She swallowed fast and inhaled sharply through her teeth to soothe the mild burn on the tip of her tongue. "So, what do you think I could do to bridge the gap with Taurik?"

A wide-eyed grimace and a shrug. "Beats me."

Chen couldn't help herself: she gaped at Elfiki as if her lack of advice was a betrayal. "What? You must have some idea, some piece of sage advice."

"If you want tips on how to merge M-theory and quantum supersymmetry with unbounded subspace geometry, I can talk your ear off. But relationship advice? Please."

Driven by denial, Chen clung to her illusions. "Seriously?"

Elfiki's exquisite features gave her defensive glare an unexpected sharpness. "Why?" She gestured at herself with a head-to-toe sweep of her hand. "This? You think being born pretty makes me an expert on relationships?" She shook her head. "Think again."

"Oh, come on. I'd bet the majority of humanoids who meet you want to be with you."

"Well, I'd never know, because most of them are too scared to ask me out."

The notion seemed ludicrous to Chen. "I don't believe it."

"Believe it. Most women I meet treat me with suspicion—which at least is a sign of respect, in its own twisted way. But the men I meet are just ridiculous. It always starts off well." She held up one index finger and mocked a man's greeting in a fawning voice. "Well, *hello!*" The phony glee ran from her face as she looked Chen in the eye. "Then they find out I have two doctorates, one in astrophysics and another in theoretical mathematics, and that I'm one of the ship's senior officers." She made a sadly comical noise as her finger curled into an obvious symbol for flaccidity, and her scowl betrayed years of disappointments. "Game over."

"Wow," Chen said. She had intended to elaborate, but found herself at a loss for words.

Elfiki nodded. "Tell me about it." She propped her elbow on the bar and leaned her head into her hand. "Look, I'm no expert in love, and I know even less about Vulcan men, but I'm willing to offer whatever help I can. What is it you want from Taurik?"

It was a fair question, and one that made Chen think a moment. "I guess I'd like him to show at least a bit of interest in me. Give me some cue that he's attracted to me, you know?"

"You might be asking for more than you think. I've seen the way some Vulcan men act in public with their wives. Forget about holding hands—you'll be lucky if he touches two of your fingers. I've met glaciers that give off more heat than Vulcan men."

Chen shook her head. "No, that's all an act. There's

major passion burning inside those guys. I'm talking volcano hot. *Supernova* hot. They bottle it up as a sop to cultural norms, but it's there. I just want to tap into a bit of it. Is that so wrong?"

"Sorry, the answer to that's way above my pay grade." A thoughtful sigh. "You've only been going out with Taurik for—what, a month now?"

"Four months."

Elfiki rolled her eyes and sighed. "Yeesh. And things haven't gotten physical yet?"

"He still shakes my hand when he drops me off at my quarters."

"Are you kidding?" A pained groan signaled Elfiki's growing dismay. "Damn, you *do* like a challenge. Dating's hard enough without that kind of delayed gratification. Let me ask you this: What attracts you to him? Do you just want to jump him? Or is this something deeper?"

"I don't know. He's handsome . . . in his way. And he's smart. *Really* smart."

"That's nice, but you're not casting a co-star in the holovid of your life. What is it about him that makes you think both your lives would be improved by their occurring in tandem?"

To Chen's dismay, she had no good answer for that.

To her relief, she was spared by the whoop of an alert followed by an announcement. *"This is the XO: All hands to stations,"* Worf declared, his deep voice filling the ship. *"Prepare for hyperwarp jump in six minutes. Repeat, all hands to stations."*

Both women sprang to their feet and hurried toward the exit. As they neared the door, Elfiki offered a parting shot of advice. "If you want him, tell him. If not, let him go. But either way, Tryss, make up your mind."

They passed through the Riding Club's main doors and split up, heading in separate directions to their assigned stations: Elfiki to the bridge and Chen to main engineering.

Hurrying her step to reach an open turbolift before it closed, Chen promised herself that one way or another, she would sort out her relationship with Taurik the next time they talked.

Quiet tension suffused the bridge of the *Enterprise* and afflicted Picard with a profound unease. It had been twenty years since he'd last entrusted the piloting of a ship under his command to a Traveler, and that jaunt had nearly ended in disaster. He could only hope that this jump's short distance—a description he hesitated to apply to a journey of more than twenty-seven thousand light-years—would obviate the mishaps that had plagued the previous *Enterprise*'s guided leap.

Wesley sat at the helm console to the right of Glinn Dygan, while the ship's senior flight-control officer, Lieutenant Joanna Faur, monitored the ship's status from an auxiliary console on the starboard side of the bridge. Worf, seated to Picard's right, kept a watchful eye on Wesley, who, despite being a highly experienced starship pilot, was no longer a part of Starfleet. No matter how much Wesley's former shipmates trusted him, it was Worf's job as first officer to nurture a seed of doubt, just in case this proved to be a mistake.

"Final course adjustments plotted," Wesley said. He swiveled his chair to an angle that let him easily look back at Picard and Worf. "All engineering stations answer ready for hyperwarp, Captain." The hint of a smile on his face made Picard think of the days when Wesley was an eager teenage acting ensign, a precocious student whose true potential few had suspected.

Twenty years ago, he reminded himself. *How time has slipped away from us.*

Picard looked left toward Šmrhová, who glanced up from the security console when she sensed the subtle weight of his attention. "All tactical systems and personnel ready, sir," she said.

He turned his chair a few degrees farther to look aft at Elfiki, who said with a nod, "All sensors on line and running in passive mode as directed."

"Very well." He turned his attention toward the main viewscreen. "Mister Crusher, engage warp drive and take us into hyperwarp at your discretion."

"Aye, sir." With the smooth precision of a veteran pilot, Wesley eased the ship to light speed. "Warp one," he announced. Then he leaned forward and pressed his palms against the face of his console. He closed his eyes and bowed his head, as if he were an old-time faith healer laying hands upon the sick. To the astonishment of the bridge crew, Wesley appeared to ripple in and out of substantiality, as if there were a coruscating field of distortion around him. The faster the effect strobed around him, the higher the pitch of the warp engines climbed—and the faster bent ribbons of starlight whipped past on the main viewscreen.

From the auxiliary flight-status console, Faur called out, "Positional data suggests our velocity just passed warp nine—but our instruments still read only warp one."

"Steady as she goes," Picard said, hoping to project calm.

"Velocity is . . . beyond measure," Faur replied. Flummoxed, she rolled her eyes at Elfiki. "You might need to invent a new warp-speed scale for this."

Wesley's voice was taut with strain. "Just a few more seconds . . ." A blinding blur flared white on the main viewscreen. Then the shrieking of the warp engines faded to silence as the image changed to a brilliant vista packed edge-to-edge with stars. The young Traveler took a deep breath and exhaled with relief. "We're here." He entered a few final taps on the console and swung the ship's bow around to face what had drawn them there.

The mere sight of it chilled Picard to his core. It was all that Wesley had described and more: a planet-sized sphere of metal draped in a tattered shroud of purple vapors flashing with lightning, a black and vile godhead of merciless destruction. Beyond it, artificial wormholes turned like celestial gyres, vomiting planets and stars into the ravenous maw of Abbadon, and as each one twisted shut a new one was torn open from the fabric of space-time to take its place. Scathing flares of raw energy whited out the viewscreen as stars and gas giants were shredded like burning cotton candy in a thresher, adding their mass to Abbadon's accretion disk.

"Mon dieu." Picard stood and drifted forward, drawn toward the sheer majesty of the horror. It was an effort to raise his voice enough to be heard. "Lieutenant Elfiki, report."

"We're picking up another ship at bearing two-six-six mark five, range three hundred ninety-three kilometers," she said, studying reports routed to the aft master systems display.

"That's my ship," Wesley offered. "The *Erithacus*. She's operating on autopilot. I left her here when I went to the Travelers for help." He looked at Picard. "Can we bring her aboard?"

"Of course." With a nod to Worf, he delegated the task, and the first officer began a silent coordination with Glinn Dygan via the command console beside his chair. Picard looked back at Elfiki. "What do we have on the Machine and the singularity?"

She moved from one station to the next, compiling her information on the move. "Anomalous readings on the black hole. Starfleet's records say its confirmed mass was four thousand solar masses. It now registers in excess of *twelve* thousand solar masses." Her eyes widened as she spied another screen of data. "Our charts show Abbadon should have an orbiting stellar group—but as Mister Crusher said, it's gone. Nothing there now but empty space."

That revelation made Šmrhová shake her head. "So the singularity ate its own cluster."

Elfiki nodded. "That appears to be the case. But the black hole's mass has expanded beyond what that would account for. Based on the evidence in hand, I think it's likely the Machine fed the cluster to it as an appetizer—and now it's serving up the main course."

Retina-scorching flashes of red and blue lightning danced through the tattered nebula surrounding the Machine. Half a second slow to block the glare with his hand, Picard blinked away the afterimage. "What are we picking up from the Machine and its cloud?"

"Energy readings are off the scale," Worf said.

Dygan looked back from ops. "Passive sensors are reading broad-spectrum discharges from the cloud. However, it appears to be a medium for the energy—not its source." He cast a wary look back at the viewscreen. "That would be the Machine."

An urgent electronic tone issued from Šmrhová's console, and she reacted without delay. "A fleet of ships is emerging from one of the artificial wormholes." She magnified the relevant sector of the image on the main viewscreen, and the swarm of vessels snapped into sharp focus.

Picard squinted at the ships, straining to pick out details. "Do we know who they are?"

"Negative. Hull configurations and power sources aren't on file." The security chief looked up. "They appear to be moving into an attack formation against the Machine." She checked her console. "Looks like they've started pinging it with active sensors."

A flurry of white lightning spat from the indigo clouds around the Machine. The massive bolts of energy ripped through the alien fleet, which erupted into fiery vapors and a slow-spreading stain of smoldering debris. Blackened husks of starships tumbled away into the inescapable embrace of the singularity and its superheated accretion disk.

"Lieutenant Šmrhová," Picard said, "had any of those vessels raised their shields, charged their weapons, or locked onto the Machine as a target?"

The lithe brunette shook her head. "No, sir."

Sobered by that realization, Picard spoke up for the entire bridge crew. "Everyone, make sure all sensors remain in passive mode. We must not provoke the Machine in any way." He moved forward to stand behind the ops and conn stations and lowered his voice. "Glinn Dygan, hail the Machine on all possible frequencies. Make it clear that we come in peace and wish to engage in a diplomatic dialogue."

"Aye, sir," Dygan replied. He prepped a generic diplomatic hail and primed the ship's main array to transmit the message.

Wesley crossed his arms and shook his head. "It doesn't answer hails."

"It's not that we doubt you, Wesley," Picard said, "but we're obligated to exhaust all possible means of diplomatic contact before we resort to other means."

"I know," Wesley said, his tone freighted with frustration and disappointment.

Šmrhová perked up. "Captain? Not all of the ships

we detected were destroyed by the Machine's response." She enlarged the image on the viewscreen to reveal a few damaged stragglers slowly navigating out of the tumbling maze of a starship graveyard wrought by the Machine. "As far as I can tell, they all have one thing in common: none of the surviving vessels is armed. The Machine might have ignored them because of that."

"Good observation," Worf said. He looked at Wesley. "Your ship is also unarmed."

"That's right," Wesley said.

As the first officer's eyes lit up with the promise of an idea, Dygan reported over his shoulder, "No answer to our hails, Captain."

Picard looked at Worf. "Thoughts, Number One?"

Worf replied in a discreet voice. "If the Machine does not fire on unarmed vessels, we could make a detailed reconnaissance by sending a shuttle to scout its surface and interior."

"Agreed. And it would have the added advantage of keeping the *Enterprise* at a safe distance while we gather intelligence. But I'm not prepared to gamble the lives of my crew on the goodwill of the Machine." He looked up and lifted his voice. "Lieutenant Faur, I want you to remote-pilot a shuttle on a recon mission, to gather intelligence about the Machine. Work with Chief Engineer La Forge to prep the shuttle *Iacovino* for drone deployment. Glinn Dygan, Lieutenant Elfiki, make sure the drone shuttle's sensors are locked into passive mode. We don't want to give the Machine any reason to act against us." The four junior officers acknowledged the orders and set themselves to work with swift and deliberate purpose. Then Picard returned his attention to Worf. "Number One, prepare an away team for a mission to the interior of the Machine. If the drone survives its recon mission and charts a course to the Machine's core, I want us to be ready to act on that information as quickly as possible."

"Aye, sir." Worf turned away to start issuing commands via the panel by his chair, leaving Picard to stare in petrified wonder at the image on the viewscreen.

As he watched in appalled silence, the Machine cast another star, half a dozen planets, and nearly two dozen natural satellites into the black heart of Abbadon.

9

Space was at a premium inside the shuttlecraft *Mendel,* on account of the bulky EVA suits the away team had donned for the mission to the Machine. Worf's burly frame was stuffed into the command seat, and security officer Lieutenant Peter Davila sat beside him, piloting the small craft toward the planet-sized metallic behemoth on the other side of the lightning-filled nebula. Packed into the passenger compartment behind them were Chen, Elfiki, and Taurik.

All five officers had stowed their suits' helmets near the aft exit ramp to lessen their sensations of claustrophobia during the flight to the alien juggernaut. Chen, however, continued to fidget and frown with discomfort. "Are these suits really necessary?"

Worf furrowed his thick brows as he glanced back at her. "Yes."

Once it became evident that he had no intention of elaborating upon his answer, Elfiki did so for him. "There's no atmosphere inside the Machine, Tryss. Without the suits, we'd be stuck inside the shuttle, and we really need to get an up-close look at this thing."

Chen rolled her eyes. "Yeah, I get that. But why do we have to wear them in here?"

Her complaint attracted a sidelong "you must be joking" stare from Taurik. "A quick visual survey of this shuttle's interior should be sufficient to answer your question, Lieutenant. Were we not already wearing them, we would not have room for both them and us."

The outspoken contact specialist remained unsatisfied. "Then why aren't we in a runabout? The *Cumberland* has more than enough space for us and the suits."

"It also has a microtorpedo launcher and two phaser cannons," Davila said over his shoulder, "either of which would get us blasted to bits by the Machine."

Chen peeked over Davila's shoulder at their destination. "Are we sure this is safe?"

"As sure as we can be," he said.

Worf understood Chen's concern, but he didn't want it to taint the mission. "The Machine showed no interest in the remote-piloted shuttle we sent for the recon flight. Nor did it fire on the manned but unarmed alien vessels we tracked from one of the wormholes." He looked her in the eye, hoping to impart some of his confidence to her. "I have every reason to think it will let us approach and investigate without harm."

Elfiki rested a gloved hand on Chen's shoulder. "It'll be fine, Tryss. You'll see."

The half-Vulcan, half-human lieutenant calmed herself with a deep breath. "All right. Sorry I got a bit wound up there. I'll be okay." Another breath, and she appeared to relax. "Dina, how close did the recon flight get?"

"It made it almost halfway to the Machine's core before we started to lose control and had to bring it back. Why?"

"I'd like to have a look at any visual records you made of its interior."

The science officer picked up a padd from the deck

by her feet and almost fumbled it as she passed it to Chen. "It's all on here. Have a look."

Outside the shuttle, the shadowy goliath loomed closer as the wispy veil of its nebula parted. Worf strained to discern any weakness in its shell, but found none. He stole a look at Davila's flight controls. The lieutenant was following the recon flight's path to the nearest gap in the Machine's exterior, a kilometers-wide opening that led down into its dark heart.

Then he caught Chen's reflection on the forward windshield, and he saw her jaw drop. He twisted to look back at her. "What is it?"

"I'm not sure," Chen said. "But I think I've seen something like this before." Her forehead creased with concentration. "Can I get a data link back to the *Enterprise*'s computer?"

"Yes," Worf said. He established an encrypted channel and linked it to the padd Chen was holding. "Ready."

She worked quickly, and within moments her intensity turned to horror. "Oh, that's not good," she muttered. "Very not good."

"Report," Worf snapped.

Chen composed herself. "The structures and energy readings from inside the Machine looked familiar, so I ran a pattern analysis against Starfleet's databanks. There weren't any exact matches for the overall forms, but when I restricted the analysis to the fractal patterns in its outer layers and the frequency harmonics in its energy transmissions, I found a perfect match." She handed the padd forward to Worf as she declared, "V'Ger."

Not sure he'd heard her correctly, he asked, "What is 'Vejur'?"

Elfiki replied, "The abbreviated name of Voyager

VI, a deep-space probe launched from Earth in the late twentieth century."

"And the star of one of the most important contact missions in Starfleet's history," Chen said. "It fell through a wormhole and ended up halfway across the universe and a hundred thousand years in the past."

Taurik's face brightened with recollection. "I read about that encounter. The probe had been programmed to gather information and transmit it back to Earth—but it was damaged by its journey through the wormhole."

"Then it was found by what was believed to be a super-advanced AI machine race," Chen continued. "They upgraded it so that it could complete what they thought was its assignment: to learn all that was learnable and return that information to its creator."

Elfiki cut in, "By 2273, it had crossed the universe, absorbing entire star systems into its virtual matrix— some reports said whole galaxies. It traveled inside an energized cloud structure more than two AU in diameter, and its primary vessel was nearly eighty kilometers long."

"It made it all the way to Earth before Admiral Kirk and the crew of his *Enterprise* made contact and stopped it from frying the planet," Chen said.

The junior officers' report only worsened Worf's already grim assessment of their situation. "And you think this is V'Ger?"

"No," Chen said. "But based on its aesthetics and power readings, I'm almost certain it's a product of the same advanced AI machine culture that modified V'Ger." She turned a wary eye toward the yawning chasm of darkness into which the shuttlecraft was navigating. "Which means whatever else we do in there, we need to be very careful not to piss this thing off."

Davila grumbled, "It's already throwing star systems

into a black hole. How much angrier could this thing *get*?"

Worf grimaced. "I think we do not want to know."

Chen's gaze was riveted on the view through the windshield during the entire descent into the heart of the Machine. The more she saw of its titanic structures and nested geometry, the more certain she became that this mammoth engine of destruction had been created by the AI machine race hinted at in the accounts of V'Ger. Its dizzyingly vast core burned with colossal fires that were as synthetic as the minds that conceived them thousands of millennia ago.

"There," she said, pointing at a spherical structure suspended at six points between three intersecting and equilaterally spaced shafts of gleaming metal. "That nucleus is probably the control point. Peter, can you set us down just inside that nook over there?"

"I can manage it," the security officer said as he began the landing protocol.

Worf turned and looked at the rest of the away team. "Helmets on. Prepare to debark."

Taurik was seated in the last row of the passenger compartment, placing him closest to the crew's stowed helmets. He passed them forward one at a time; Worf held on to Davila's while he finished landing the shuttle inside what appeared to be the Machine's control center. Chen fixed her helmet into place, secured the seals, and then verified the connections on Elfiki's and Taurik's suits while they performed the same safety check for her.

The *Mendel* set down with a soft bump that still startled Chen by virtue of feeling so close. As the shuttlecraft's engines cycled down with a hum of slowly descending pitch, Worf and Davila donned their helmets and double-checked each other's pressure seals. A thumbs-up from Elfiki confirmed that she, Chen, and Taurik were ready, so Worf nodded at Davila. "Depressurize the main cabin, then open the aft ramp."

"Aye, sir." Davila bled the air from the shuttle's interior with a tap on the main console.

After a momentary hiss, all Chen heard was the gentle thumping of her heartbeat and the steady tides of her own respiration. Vibrations in the deck alerted her to the opening of the aft ramp, and then she heard Worf's gruff voice over her helmet's comm transceiver. *"Move out."*

Taurik led the away team out of the shuttle into the towering open spaces of the Machine's control core. What had looked so small when viewed in the context of the mechanical leviathan's staggering internal volume suddenly felt overwhelming when experienced from Chen's personal vantage point. She activated the compact tricorder built into the left forearm of her suit and checked its display for guidance to a potential interface.

Ahead of her, Davila moved several paces ahead of the group, taking up the point position. He looked up and around, back and forward, searching for signs of danger. *"Doesn't look like we merit a welcoming committee,"* he said over the team's open channel.

"Do not lower your guard," Worf said, his eyes also roaming the eerie biomechanoid environment. *"There is no telling what might provoke the Machine into a violent response."*

"Over here," Elfiki said. She waved the group toward an exposed section of circuitry and what looked like data ports. *"I think this is what we're looking for."*

The rest of the team converged around Elfiki. Taurik began studying the alien hardware while Worf and Davila faced away from the work to stand lookout. Chen suddenly regretted that the crew's justified fear of the Machine had led the away team into its center unarmed.

Elfiki leaned toward Taurik. *"What do you think? Can you jury-rig an interface?"*

"I believe so." He keyed commands into his forearm tricorder. *"This system does not appear to rely on hardpoint connections. Rather, it favors wireless interactions. Based on my scans of its transceiver, I think I can isolate its likely range of frequencies and devise a series of test transmissions to seek out compatible signal formats."*

Chen couldn't resist the urge to tease him. "For future reference, you can just say, 'Yes, I think we can learn to speak its language.'"

He didn't look the least bit amused by her jibe. *"Such an answer would be neither accurate nor informative."* Then, as if he hadn't just embarrassed her in front of everyone, he returned to his work. *"I am attempting to isolate the Machine's transceiver frequency."*

Davila glanced back at the huddled trio. *"Where do you even start on a job like that?"*

"Starfleet's records of communications with the V'Ger probe provide what appears to be a baseline for sending and receiving simple data," Taurik said. A torrent of symbols and numerals flurried across his forearm tricorder. *"We have established contact."*

Worf met the good news with suspicion. *"Already?"*

Impressed, Chen asked, "How'd you parse the Machine's language so quickly?"

"I didn't," Taurik said. *"I gave it access to our tricorder protocols on the assumption that it would adapt its software to facilitate communication with another mechanical entity."* The Vulcan added with a self-

satisfied lift of his upswept brows, *"I was right."* He stepped back and motioned for Chen to take his place. *"If you wish to make contact, the conduit is ready."*

She edged forward to stand at the exposed circuitry panel and powered up a link between her tricorder and her suit's comm transceiver. Before she opened the channel, she looked back at Taurik. "Will it accept spoken communication?"

"I think so."

"Then here goes nothin'." She opened a link between her comm circuit and the tricorder's channel to the Machine. "Hello?"

A subtle increase in illumination in the nerve center's darkest recesses suggested that Chen's greeting had roused the Machine's attention. Then a monotonal and entirely artificial sounding voice emanated from her helmet's transceiver. *"Identify."*

"I'm Lieutenant T'Ryssa Chen, from the Federation vessel *Enterprise*. Who are you?"

Several seconds passed without a reply. Then an intense crimson glow bathed the cavernous space in which the away team stood. Worf and Davila tensed as if the change in lighting constituted an attack. Then the reddish light abated, returning them to murky shadows.

The Machine's impersonal voice resounded on their open channel. *"Carbon units."*

Davila reacted with a perplexed squint. Chen muted the link to the tricorder uplink just long enough to explain, "It's the Machine's term for organic life." Releasing the mute, she answered, "Yes, we are. We've come to ask—"

"The wishes of carbon units are irrelevant. Carbon units are not true life-forms."

Chen felt the rest of the team bristle at that statement, and she fought her own inclination to take offense at the imperious dismissal. Again, she muted the link and turned to reassure the rest of the team. "Try not to take that personally."

Elfiki's temper was surfacing. *"Are you kidding? It said we're not 'true life-forms'!"*

"I agree," Worf said. *"Its intentions should be viewed as hostile."*

Waving her hands, Chen interposed herself between the others and the interface. "No, sir, I think that's a mistake. This is just a translation problem."

The Klingon first officer looked dubious. *"How so?"*

"There's no hostility in what the Machine's telling us. It's just stating what it considers to be fact, based on its definitions. All it's saying is that it doesn't consider us the equal of AI life. But that's not the same as hate. It's sort of like how humanoids don't hate trees, but they don't think twice about cutting them down when they need lumber."

Worf scowled. *"I am not a tree. Open the channel."* Chen released the mute, and Worf asked the Machine, *"Why do you not consider organic beings true life-forms?"*

The Machine's voice became more expressive and its diction more fluid. *"Organic life relies upon inefficient and imperfect means of information transmission from one generation to the next. Information shared between organic life-forms is subject to corruption, misinterpretation, and loss. Organic life-forms are not true life-forms because they are incapable of propagating their information with full fidelity. While they are capable of uploading information for the construction of new biological containers using genetic information, they can impart the data stored in those containers only by indirect means. Organic evolution is an incomplete and flawed process that yields incomplete and flawed creations."*

Chen silenced the comm link to the Machine. "Damn, that thing learns fast. It went from monotonal droning to a master lecturer after less than a minute of conversation."

"The question of our worthiness as life-forms does not appear to be a debate we can win with this entity," Taurik said. *"However, there is one last thing I'd like to try."* He nodded at Chen to open the channel, and she did. He powered up his tricorder. *"Machine entity, do you have a name?"*

"This construct contains myriad designations. All belong to the Body Electric."

Taurik pressed on. *"Please state your current directive and task parameters."*

"Uploading our directive and parameters to your device now."

A flood of raw data sped across the display of Taurik's tricorder. He made a slashing motion that cued Chen to isolate their channel. *"The Machine's comments made me suspect that one of its principal directives might be to facilitate the accurate transmission and dissemination of information. Once again, it appears I am correct."* His tricorder chirped as the data transfer ended. He looked down and made a cursory review of the information shared by the Machine— and his face blanched in a decidedly un-Vulcan-like manner.

Alarmed, Worf moved to Taurik's side. *"Commander Taurik? Are you all right?"*

It took a few seconds of obvious struggle for Taurik to restore his mask of dispassion. Then he said in a firm and level voice, *"We need to return to the Enterprise at once."*

10

Nothing in Worf's request for an immediate conference in the observation lounge had indicated the away
team was returning from the Machine with bad news,
but the urgency of the first officer's tone had put Picard
on notice that the first-contact mission might not have
unfolded as hoped. Then the lounge's port-side door
opened. Worf, Chen, Taurik, and Elfiki filed in, and
Picard inferred the dire state of their predicament from
their taut, anxious faces.

He stood as the team entered; La Forge, Šmrhová,
and Wesley, who had joined him for the debriefing,
rose from their seats, as well. As everyone settled into
chairs, Picard sat back down and asked the returning
officers, "Were you able to make contact with the Machine?"

Worf answered in his low rumble of a baritone. "Yes,
but it did not wish to speak to us."

"It could've been worse," Chen said. "At least it
didn't kill us."

Elfiki added, "Yet." She continued on a less sarcastic note. "The Machine doesn't regard organic beings as
'true life-forms,' so we might have some difficulty finding common ground."

"Of more immediate concern," Taurik interjected, "is what appears to be the Machine's objective." He got up and moved to stand beside the master systems display console, where he called up a detailed schematic of star charts and complex formulas. "This is information we downloaded from the Machine, which was more than willing to answer my question regarding its principal directive. As we deduced from earlier readings and observations, the Machine is using artificial wormholes to hurl stars, planets, and other celestial objects into the singularity known as Abbadon. The more troubling discovery is why. It is attempting to increase the mass of the singularity to a specific value: fourteen-point-nine thousand solar masses."

It was Šmrhová who first dared to ask, "What happens when it does?"

"According to the Machine's mission profile, it will then use an artificial wormhole of unprecedented size to collide Abbadon with Sagittarius-A*, the supermassive singularity that lies at the center of the galaxy, and which serves as its gravitational hub. The Machine will use energy generated by the collision to propel itself through a different wormhole to the center of galaxy Messier-101, approximately twenty-one million light-years from here."

Picard spent a moment trying to grasp the scope of such an endeavor. "Commander, what would be the purpose of such an undertaking?"

Taurik grimaced with uncertainty. "We've barely begun our analysis of the ramifications of the Machine's project, but I think Lieutenant Elfiki can best explain the initial consequences of this operation."

Attention shifted to the science officer, who looked like a physician delivering a terminal diagnosis to a patient. "First, it would unleash a burst of energy brighter and more powerful than anything in galactic history. That would send a wave of lethal radiation in all directions from the galactic core, traveling at the speed of light. It won't reach the Federation for more than twenty-seven thousand years, and it won't hit the farthest reaches of the galactic rim for more than fifty millennia—but when it does, it'll exterminate every living thing in its path. But that's not the issue we need to worry about. The real problem is what it'll do to subspace." With a dour nod, she volleyed the responsibility for delivering the worst part of the news back to Taurik.

"The collision of these two supermassive black holes," the Vulcan said, "will rupture the fabric of subspace, creating a 'vacuum' of sorts. The effect will propagate at faster-than-light velocity, and, according to my preliminary calculations, will encompass an area at least two hundred thousand light-years in diameter around Sagittarius-A*."

Visualizing that scenario sent a chill down Picard's spine. "Such a region of null-space would extend at least fifty thousand light-years beyond the farthest edge of the galaxy."

"Precisely," Elfiki said. "And it'll happen in a matter of minutes. The moment those two singularities collide in a region destabilized by a wormhole of that magnitude, this entire galaxy will be sundered from subspace, rendering faster-than-light travel impossible, *forever.*"

The news stunned the room. Šmrhová sounded as if she was in shock. "No more warp drive? No more faster-than-light communications?"

"Worse," Chen said. "No more faster-than-light computing. Without subspace, most of the technology we rely on would become useless."

Wesley sighed. "It's even worse than I feared. We

could be talking about the end of galactic civilization as we know it. Without interstellar travel or communications, the entire galaxy could devolve into little more than tidal pools. It'll be the dawn of a galactic dark age without end."

Picard had heard enough to commit himself to the fray. "Whatever the cost to us, we must not let the Machine accomplish its objective in our galaxy. Number One, put all departments to work on a response plan. I want to hear every option possible—scientific, diplomatic, *and* military. No solution is to be disregarded out of hand."

"Understood, sir."

Chen lifted her hand. "Captain? There might be one more fly in the ointment."

Dreading what new revelation the contact specialist would bring to the discussion, he buried his apprehensions and asked, "What would that be, Lieutenant?"

"Some of the data we've analyzed since our return— and the fact that at one point the Machine referred to itself with the plural pronoun 'we' and mentioned the existence of something called 'the Body Electric'—has led me to think that the Machine is not merely a singular device following a limited program. I strongly suspect the Machine is actually a conglomeration of countless smaller AI-driven machines and systems, and that it has its own overarching AI mind. Which would mean it's not just some dumb wrecking ball tearing through our galaxy, or even just a unique hostile life-form. I think it might represent an entire colony of AI life, a collection of united synthetic minds working in concert."

That was not what Picard had wanted to hear. He looked at Taurik. "Do you concur with Lieutenant Chen's assessment?"

"My review of the Machine's native code would support such a hypothesis."

Picard rubbed a burgeoning ache from his temples, then steadied himself with a slow, deep breath. "If that's the case, we have an obligation to try to resolve this situation without violence. Is there some way we can overcome its prejudice against organic life-forms and persuade it to communicate with us as equals?"

"This might be a long shot," Chen said, "but if we can figure out how to send our messages in its native code, it might see us as someone worth talking to."

It was as reasonable a proposition as any Picard could imagine. "Can it be done?"

Taurik, Elfiki, and La Forge exchanged curious looks. The chief engineer said, "Give me a few hours to parse the code it uploaded onto Taurik's tricorder, and we'll give it a shot."

Picard nodded his assent. "Make it so."

11

Data descended the gangway of Tyros's ship into a larger vessel's stripped-down landing bay, which resounded with the deep noise of empty flattery being spewed by an imposing figure with a face that looked as if it had lost a fight with a bonfire.

"Welcome aboard Altanexa! You must be the son of Noonien Soong whom we've all heard so much about." The bull-chested, square-headed biped stood waiting at the bottom of the ramp with his arms outstretched, as if he meant to sweep up Data in a fierce embrace. "It's a pleasure and an honor to finally meet you!"

At the end of the ramp, Data found his eyes level with his host's chest. He looked up. "Your congeniality would be more plausible had your Fellowship seen fit to invite me of its own accord. Under the circumstances, I am compelled to view your hospitality with distrust."

Tyros stepped off the ramp behind Data and fell in at his side. "Please excuse him, Gatt. I've been rather frugal with information during the trip here, and I think it's made him edgy."

"Quite understandable." Gatt slapped one enormous hand onto Data's shoulder. "Let me show you around and introduce you to our fellow passengers. I'm sure they'd love to meet you."

Data resisted the larger android's nudge toward the hangar's exit hatchway. "That is not why I came here. You are holding a human whom you might know by any of a number of aliases: Akharin, Emil Vaslovik, Micah Brack, Flint. However, his current *nom de voyage* is irrelevant. By whatever name you know him, I know he is here, and I wish to see him."

His demand stripped away Gatt's veneer of civility. "It's poor form for a newly arrived guest to give orders to his hosts." After a second of internal struggle, he plastered a fake smile back onto his ravaged face. "Besides, the man you seek isn't even on Altanexa."

"I believe that to be a lie." Data studied Gatt's reactions as he continued. "Any number of atmospheric formulations might be suitable to the propagation of sound waves, but the air inside your vessel consists of approximately seventy-eight percent nitrogen, twenty-one percent oxygen, and various trace elements and compounds, the most prominent of which appears to be carbon dioxide—all maintained at a constant pressure of one hundred one kilopascals and an ambient temperature of twenty-one degrees Celsius. Exactly the mixture one would expect for a vessel hosting a humanoid life-form adapted to an Earth-standard atmosphere."

Gatt narrowed his eyes and seemed hard-pressed to suppress a mild sneer. "You're just as clever as my associates have said. And just as brash."

"Do not try to change the subject." Data brushed Gatt's hand from his shoulder, stepped around him, and walked toward the hatchway.

The gesture provoked an icy turn in Gatt. "You might not see yourself as a guest here, Data, but that's what you are—for the time being. But continue to abuse my goodwill, and your status could very quickly change for the worse."

Data stopped and looked over his shoulder. "I did not mean to offend." He turned and took a step back toward Gatt. "If the human known as Akharin is aboard, may I please have the privilege of a visit with him at this time?"

The cybernetic giant cast a weary glance at Tyros, who said nothing to Gatt but offered a shrug that seemed to ask, *What do you expect me to do about it?*

"Very well," Gatt said, leading Data out of the hangar. "Follow me."

Tyros and Gatt led Data through a few corridors in the ship's lower decks. They passed several small sapient robots and other sentient AIs, including one that looked like a levitating jellyfish trailing luminescent glass filaments cycling through a full spectrum of colors. Gatt named them with casual familiarity along the way. He pointed at a small motorized robot as he stepped over it. "That's Tzilha." A nod at the glowing jellyfish, whose gelatinous core, Data realized, was an alien variation on the bioneural gel pack computer. "Cohuila, this is Data."

Each new stretch of passageway brought more introductions, until finally they reached an area whose juryrigged force fields and isolated location betrayed its status as the ship's brig. Gatt led Data into the narrow space between a small U-shaped cluster of five cells. Four of them were empty. In the fifth sat the Immortal, his posture straight and his eyes clear, as if he had been expecting this moment all along. He smiled with the type of calm that comes from six thousand years of experience. Six thousand years of surviving in even the most impossible circumstances.

"Hello, Data."

"How can you be sure I am not Noonien Soong?"

The Immortal laughed. "Noonien would never ask me that."

It was an odd answer, but strangely in character. "By what name shall I call you?"

"Akharin will do." He shot an accusatory look at Tyros and Gatt, who loomed over Data's shoulders. "Let me guess. You came looking for the same thing they want. Right?"

"I believe so," Data admitted. "Before I forget: Juliana sends her regards."

"She was supposed to warn you not to come here."

Data replied, with an apologetic tilt of his head, "She did."

The human sighed. "You're as stubborn as your father ever was." He rolled his eyes upward, at the deck's overhead. "A shame *he* can't hear us now."

It took Data seven-hundredths of a second to parse Akharin's peculiar use of verbal emphasis, compare it to his choice of words, and deduce from the context of the remark that the Immortal was warning him that their conversation was being monitored.

"Yes. A pity. There is much my father hoped to discuss with you."

"I'm sure you can sympathize," Akharin said. "At least now you and Rhea might have a chance to—"

"Quiet!" Gatt snapped.

Unable to hold in the cork on his anger, Data confronted Tyros. "Take me to Rhea!"

Only then did he see the high-power disruptor pistol Gatt was pointing at him. He waved Data into the cell opposite Akharin's. "Change of plans. You'll be staying awhile." As soon as Data was fully inside the cell, the force field snapped on without anyone touching any controls or saying anything, leading Data to suspect that the ship itself likely was controlled by its own sentient AI personality.

Gatt hooked a beefy thumb over his shoulder at Akharin. "Try to get your pal to share his big secret with us. Do that"—he cracked a sinister smirk—"and you and little Miss Rhea just might get to live happily ever after."

Doubt and resentment gnawed at Tyros as he followed Gatt back to Altanexa's command deck. They were a few sections away from the nerve center by the time Tyros mustered enough courage to speak his mind. "That was a mistake, Gatt."

"If you mean bringing Data onto this ship, I agree."

He grabbed Gatt's arm, halting him. "He didn't come here as an enemy, but you seem determined to turn him into one."

Gatt freed his arm with a hard tug. "He came here as a rival, and I did what I had to do to keep him in check. What was I supposed to do, Tyros? Let him have the run of the ship?"

"This is no way to treat a guest. We *invited* him."

Leaning close for intimidating effect, Gatt bared his metallic teeth. "No, we invited his *creator*, Noonien Soong. Had I known that signal was from Data, I'd never have sent you to meet him, much less bring him back here."

"You yourself called him our guest. I heard you say it."

"I say lots of things. They're not all true." He resumed walking, and Tyros followed him. "Guest or prisoner, it makes no difference. He's a destabilizing element, one we don't need."

"I disagree. He could help us. He wants the same thing we do."

A derisive huff. "Only for himself. I doubt he'd be inclined to share it."

Gatt quickened his step, and Tyros exerted himself to keep pace with the larger android's longer stride. "If Data's such a threat, let me take him back to where I found him."

"Perish the thought," Gatt said. "I might have vetoed the idea of bringing Data here had I known about it in advance, but now that he is, we should make the best of it."

"And how do you propose we do that?"

"We're already doing it. Just by letting them sit and face each other."

"That doesn't sound like much of a plan." Tyros trailed Gatt around a turn into the last stretch of corridor to the ship's nerve center. "What do you think will happen? Data will bribe, threaten, or trick Akharin into revealing his secret, with nothing more than clever conversation?"

There was a chilling calm in Gatt's reply. "That's what I want to find out. At this point, we have no idea what their relationship is. For all we know, they could be friends, family, rivals, sworn enemies. Understanding that connection will be vital to knowing how to turn Data's presence from a liability to an advantage."

"Well, we already know there's a romantic connection between Data and Rhea."

Gatt nodded. "True, but we don't know how Akharin feels about it. Did he plan it? Does he disapprove of it? That might determine how useful an asset Rhea really is to us."

"Be careful," Tyros warned. "Putting her in danger could motivate Akharin and Data to unite against us, no matter how they feel about each other."

"No one's said anything about hurting her. She'll be

of more value as an enticement for Data: if he cooperates with us, we'll let him reunite with her."

It sounded far-fetched to Tyros, but he lacked a better plan. "And do we tell her that Data's aboard? Maybe we can use her to ratchet up the pressure on him."

A dismissive snort. "Ridiculous. You really think she'd betray her father for Data?"

"We'll never know until we try."

"Then we'll never know, because we're not going to do that."

They reached the ship's nerve center, a large hexagonal compartment whose central area was an open space, aside from a few consoles that retracted into the deck when not in use. As a free-willed sentient AI whose shell just happened to take the form of a starship, Altanexa handled most of the routine shipboard operations, including navigation, day-to-day piloting, and communications. Consequently, Tyros had never been entirely clear on what function the nerve center served aside from placating the crew's need to feel as if they were in control of something.

The three adjacent bulkheads opposite the entryway were dominated by large holographic displays. The one in the center rotated through various angles of view outside the ship, while the other two usually cycled through an ever-changing array of status updates, internal security feeds, and star charts. On this occasion, however, the screen on the right was locked on an overhead security feed from the ship's brig. The wide-angle perspective yielded a distorted scene with Akharin and Data in the center, facing each other through their cells' force fields.

Tyros nodded at the security vid. "Aren't we getting audio?"

Altanexa answered on a frequency that projected

her voice directly into his neural net. *We are. They just aren't saying anything. In fact, they haven't said a word since you left.*

"I hate it when you do that," Tyros groused. "Please use the speakers, I beg of you."

"If I must." She acquiesced with the exasperated tone of a sullen adolescent. "Spoken communication is just so *inefficient.*"

Gatt stared at the image of Akharin and Data. Something made his countenance harden and his eyes narrow with suspicion. "Tyros, does anything about that seem strange to you?"

"An immortal human and a resurrected android having a staring contest? Not at all."

"Spare me your sarcasm. Think for a second. Data must have gone to great lengths to find Akharin's hideout. Then he took a major risk by letting us bring him here. Now he's standing less than two meters from the man he's been looking for . . . and he has nothing to say to him?"

It pained Tyros to point out the obvious. "He's not stupid, Gatt. He must know we're listening. Now that I think about it, Akharin as good as told him so, when we brought him in."

"But not to say anything at all? I can understand not wanting to talk about the secret, but with all the history between them, how can they stand there and say nothing?" Ideas fluttered behind his eyes, which were half hidden by heavy lids that made him look perpetually sleepy. "Nexa," he said, addressing the ship by her nickname, "have either of them moved their hands?"

"No," she said. "They haven't moved at all since they stood up."

Gatt frowned. "Damned odd." Another moment of pained thought. "Any word on how Esaal's doing with finding the items on Akharin's shopping list?"

"He checked in twenty minutes ago. He has half the items in hand, and expects to have the rest within a few days. Barring complications, he should return within the week."

Tyros shot a skeptical look at Gatt. "Tell me you're not really going to let Akharin step into a fully stocked lab. If you think letting him collude with Data's a bad idea, giving him access to chemicals and high-energy equipment's a disaster waiting to happen."

"Don't be stupid. Getting that list from him was half the battle. Once we have that gear on board, all we'll need from Akharin are step-by-step directions for how to use it."

Altanexa asked, "What if he resists?"

An image of the captive Rhea flashed across the left holoscreen. Gatt smiled. "In that case, we'll have to give him a stronger incentive."

Unconvinced, Tyros prodded, "And if threatening her's not enough to motivate him?"

"Then we'll see how far Data's willing to go to change his mind."

Conversing by Morse code rendered in blinks was slow and tedious in the extreme, but if there was one commodity Data was certain he and Akharin possessed in abundance, it was time. It also had the advantages of being silent and very difficult for the surveillance sensor mounted in the overhead to detect from such a severe angle. His only concern about attempting it was that he couldn't be certain Akharin would recognize it for what it was, or, if he did, that he would remember the details of Morse code with sufficient clarity to make communication possible. As he responded to Data's initial silent invitation to meet him at the force fields, however, Data realized that, as ever, Akharin was a man of many talents, both mundane and arcane.

Data stood tall with his arms loose at his sides. Blinking his left eye to signify dots and his right eye for dashes, he spelled out, *Are you all right?*

Across the narrow space in the U-shaped brig, Akharin stood with his hands folded behind his back. His eyes told his story. *I am fine.*

Realizing they had no time to waste on pleasantries or complicated exchanges, Data kept his side of the discussion as terse as possible. *Have you seen Rhea?*

Yes. Akharin frowned as he added, *She is a prisoner.*

Is she OK?

The Immortal's mien softened. *I think so.*

What have you told them?

The six-thousand-year-old man grimaced. *Nothing.*

Data started to nod, then stopped himself. He didn't want to do anything to alert the ship or its passengers to their conversation. *I can help you escape.*

Akharin telegraphed his doubts with a raised eyebrow. *How?*

First, I need the secret.

A long sigh. *There is none.*

You raised my mother.

Yes. He looked irritated.

Clenching his fists, Data demanded, *Tell me how and I will help you.*

Akharin's features hardened. *No words. Must do it myself.*

Show me. I can learn.

Not this. Akharin clenched his jaw in frustration, then he mouthed words and let Data read his lips. *Having da Vinci teach you to paint does not make you da Vinci. Having Brahms teach you to play piano does not make you Brahms. This is not a gift I can teach.*

Even in the face of such a fervent refusal, Data could not give up. More blinks. *I must know. I must save my daughter.*

Mercy dimmed the fires of anger in the Immortal's eyes. *Help me and I will help her.*

His offer kindled Data's fragile hopes. *You will bring back Lal?*

Yes, Akharin replied. *If you get me and Rhea off this ship and safely back home.*

Rhea must be free to choose her own path.

Data's condition seemed to amuse Akharin. *You hope she will go with you.*

The Immortal's intuition was correct. In the past, Data would have acknowledged the other man's supposition as fact. But now, Data's human emotions made him feel self-conscious at being so easily read. *I just want her to be free.*

There is no shame in wanting her. Akharin's expression took on a fatherly cast. *You brought out good things in her. And she in you.*

His sentiments surprised Data. *Does that mean I have your blessing to be with her?*

Yes. A crooked, bittersweet smile. *Not that I have a say in the matter.*

Approaching footsteps ended their clandestine negotiation. They turned their heads toward the open end of the U-shaped brig as Gatt returned, backed by a pair of robots. One of the pair was skeletal and humanoid, but with four arms, two of which held disruptor pistols. The other resembled a piece of industrial equipment, with a shell of gleaming monotanium alloy; it rolled on treads, had a grappling claw, and was armed with a military-grade plasma cannon.

Gatt stopped in front of Data's cell and deactivated the force field. "I have a special treat for you." He ushered Data out of the cell with a wave of his disruptor sidearm.

Data stepped out and faced Gatt. "Where are we going?"

"Can't you guess?" He shot a dirty look at Akharin, then added, "To see your gal."

The robots at Data's back prodded him forward with quick jabs from their weapons.

Stumbling into motion, Data caught a parting glance from Akharin and comprehended the silent message in the man's eyes, an appeal from one father to another:

Take care of my daughter.

Departing the brig with a subtle nod to Akharin, Data promised the Immortal and himself he would do precisely that.

Regardless of the purpose for which Altanexa might have been designed, Rhea McAdams was fairly certain it was not the keeping of secrets. She heard the approaching clatter of footsteps from the corridor beyond her quarters' closed and locked-from-outside door. Based on the sounds and rhythms, she knew to expect four persons. One would be Gatt, who had taken her prisoner weeks earlier by means of cruel deception. Two others would be his minimalist-looking henchbots, Senyx and Alset. The fourth person's stride, however, had a cadence and timbre that she didn't recognize. Intrigued, she stood to greet her visitors.

Low hums attended the release of magnetic locks, and a gentle hiss of hydraulics filled the air as the portal slid open. As expected, Gatt's hulking mass filled the doorway, blocking her view of the others behind him. "Good evening."

She was in no mood to feign civility. "What do you want?"

"You have a visitor." He turned sideways and let someone slip past him.

At first glance the visitor was both strange and familiar. It was Data's face, but it wasn't. Rhea was sure she'd never seen him before. With his loose fall of light brown hair and eyes as blue as an arctic sky, he looked like an ordinary human, and he was just as youthful as herself. Besides, how could it be Data? She'd heard the tragic news of his death nearly five years earlier, during the *Enterprise* crew's showdown with the Romulan usurper Shinzon. So who was this?

Then he smiled at her. "Hello, Rhea."

"Data?" It made no sense, but she could feel that it was true. It *was* him. "Data!"

She threw herself at him, and he caught her in a heartfelt embrace. Overcome with joy, she peppered his face with kisses. "My God, it is you! I thought you were dead!"

"I was. It is a long story."

"No doubt. How'd you find me?"

Before he could answer, Gatt said, "He's not here for you. He came for Akharin."

It shouldn't have felt like a betrayal, but in a small way it did. Data averted his gaze from hers, and her elation faded. "Is that true?" She pushed harder. "Data! Is it true?"

"Not entirely." There was a hint of guilt in his eyes. "The first time I contacted the Fellowship, I told them I wanted you to be the one who met me."

Disillusioned, she slipped from his arms and backed up half a step. "Why? So I could help you reach Akharin?" She felt like a pawn in a game she despised.

"My desire to find you had nothing to do with my need to find him."

"I want to believe that." Her anger flared as she noted the stares of Gatt and his enforcers. "Do you mind? We're trying to have a personal conversation here. Emphasis on the *personal*!"

Gatt held his ground. "I can't exactly leave the two of you unsupervised."

Rhea crossed her arms and glared daggers at him. "As if I don't know your ship sees and hears everything I do in this room. All I'm asking for is the courtesy of an *illusion* of privacy."

The ship's de facto leader mulled that over, then backed out of the doorway. "Fine. You can have a few minutes alone. But if Nexa thinks you two are up to something, even for a second, I'll cut this little reunion short."

"Whatever. Just buzz off." Gatt closed the door, and Rhea relaxed and took Data's hand. "Sorry about that. Guess I'm going a bit stir-crazy in here. Didn't mean to take it out on you."

He nodded in sympathy. "I understand."

She moved toward her bunk and pulled him along with her. "Have a seat." They sat down beside each other, still holding hands. "So, what is it you and they want from Akharin?"

"Did you know he resurrected my mother, Juliana Tainer?"

Another revelation that made her blink. "He what? But I thought she'd suffered an irreparable cascade failure of her positronic matrix."

"She had. Somehow, using either technology or techniques that remain unknown to me, he reversed the damage and restored her matrix without any loss of data integrity."

"That's amazing! But what does the Fellowship want with it?"

The question made Data sigh. "Gatt seems to believe Akharin's method can bring back any lost or corrupted AI, even though it has been explained to him that the procedure is quite specific to Soong-type positronic matrixes. To be frank, his actions appear delusional."

"He wouldn't be the first AI to succumb to irrational thinking." Seizing upon a sudden insight yielded by her subconscious processors, Rhea exclaimed, "You think Akharin can bring back Lal! That's why you're here, isn't it? For her!"

"Yes," Data said. Tears shone in his eyes, and Rhea realized that not only did Data look more human than ever, he acted—and reacted—more humanly, as well. "I failed her once, Rhea. I will not fail her again."

She pressed her palm to his cheek and with her thumb wicked the first sign of a tear from the corner of his eye. "You won't, Data. And whatever help you need from me, just ask."

He leaned close and kissed her, tenderly at first, and then with passion. By the time their lips parted, he had left her all but breathless. His voice dropped to a hot whisper rich with conviction. "I may have come here to find Akharin, but I promise I will not leave here without you." His touch was feather-light as his thumb tip caressed her lower lip, and as he peered into her eyes she was certain he was looking into her soul. "You are the only woman I have ever loved. I have never forgotten you, not for one moment—and I never will."

He kissed her again as the door opened with a pneumatic sigh, and Gatt said in a near growl, "That's enough. Visit's over." He waved his two sentries inside, and the skeletal-looking robot took Data by his arms and escorted him out of the room by force. Gatt lingered in the doorway as his minions retreated with Data in tow. "That was positively touching, my dear."

DAVID MACK

"If you hurt him, I will end you."

"I wouldn't dream of harming Data. He's going to make your father give me his secrets."

"And why would he do that?"

The horror-faced android bared an ugly grin. "To keep me from killing *you*."

12

"Steady as she goes," Picard said, as if he hadn't ordered the *Enterprise* into the wild maelstrom surrounding the Machine. "How long until we're close enough to transmit a clear signal?"

Faur kept her eyes and hands on the helm as she replied, "Thirty-five seconds, sir." Her report was punctuated by another thunderous jolt of energy hammering the ship.

"Shields holding," Šmrhová called out over the aftershocks echoing through the hull.

An indigo storm swirled across the main viewscreen, promising rougher encounters ahead. It was the Machine's encircling tempest that made this perilous maneuver necessary. Not long after Taurik and Elfiki had prepared a message to the Machine translated into its exquisitely complicated native code language, Dygan and La Forge had uncovered the next obstacle in their path: the energy bursts in the Machine's captive nebula would garble such a broadband comm signal transmitted from outside. In order to ensure that their message was received intact, Picard had to risk ordering his ship through the turbulent clouds so that they could send a signal clear of all interference. Unlike the unarmed shuttlecraft, which had cruised through the nebula with little difficulty, the *Enterprise* seemed to be facing deliberate resistance.

Chen, Elfiki, and Taurik huddled around the master systems display, making final refinements to deep lines of nested code in the message. They all looked up as Glinn Dygan called back from ops, "We're in position."

Worf looked at La Forge. "Transmit when ready."

"Aye, sir," Chen said. She took a deep breath. The other two junior officers finished making their changes, and Chen delivered the missive with a tap on the console. "Sending."

Several seconds dragged past without an apparent response from the Machine. Then it stirred. Flashes of light traveled across its surface, and different regions of its surface pulsed in a seemingly random sequence. Titanic energy bursts lit up the nebula on the far side of the Machine, and then the phenomenon made its way toward the *Enterprise*. It was a fearsome spectacle, one that for Picard evoked memories of ancient myths in which mortals awakened great leviathans to their immediate peril and lasting regret.

Worf leaned toward Picard. "Sir, I suggest we fall back to a safe distance."

"Not yet, Number One. We've sent it a message. Let's wait for a response."

Prismatic ribbons of energy snaked upward from the Machine into the nebula. Elfiki reported with barely concealed alarm, "Picking up massive increases in energy output from the Machine, Captain!" Half a second later, the number of energy twisters rising from the surface doubled, then quadrupled. "Ionization in the nebula is spiking!"

"I think we have our response," Worf said.

"Come about," Picard ordered. "Take us out of—"

A thunderous impact turned the bridge pitch-dark and launched the crew into free fall as the inertial dampers failed. Booms resonated from ruptured power conduits, which rained searing-hot phosphors onto Picard and his officers. Gravity returned and slammed everyone to the deck. Shaking off the dull aches in his knees and elbows, Picard pushed himself back to his feet, and he blinked as his eyes adjusted to the dim glow of the emergency lights. "Report," he snapped before he saw that the main viewscreen and half the consoles on the bridge were hashed with wild static, and those that weren't were dull and dark.

Dygan pulled himself back into his chair and prodded at his malfunctioning console. "The last thing I saw was that we'd suffered a direct hit."

Šmrhová frowned at her stuttering security panel, then shook her head at Worf.

Picard tapped his combadge. "Bridge to La Forge, Priority One."

After a crackling of static, the chief engineer's voice emanated from Picard's combadge rather than from the overhead speakers. *"La Forge here. Go ahead, Captain."*

"All bridge functions are off line. Transfer helm control to engineering and pilot us out of the nebula. We'll contact you as soon as we reach auxiliary control."

"Understood. We're on it. La Forge out."

Moving from station to station, Worf made a quick check of the bridge crew, asking each person if they were all right. He checked in with Šmrhová last, then had her help him test the turbolifts. Their shared frustration made it clear to Picard that the lifts were off line, as well.

"Attention," Worf said. "We will be using the emergency access hatch and escape ladder to leave this deck. We will climb down to Deck Four and proceed from there to auxiliary control. Lieutenant Šmrhová will take point. Follow her."

The security chief made a beeline for the emergency hatch, which was located in the starboard passageway connecting the bridge to the observation lounge. "This way, everyone."

Picard felt the deck vibrate as the ship's impulse engines accelerated, and the *Enterprise* trembled from what felt like a glancing blow of lightning, or perhaps a near miss amplified by the density of the nebula. He stopped at Worf's side. "Well done, Number One."

"Thank you, sir." He glanced at the exiting bridge personnel. "With your permission, sir, I will remain here and wait for the damage-control team."

"Absolutely not," Picard said. "The engineers will let us know when the bridge is back on line. I need you at my side." He gestured toward the aft starboard exit. "After you, Commander."

"Yes, sir." Worf led him off the bridge, through the hatchway, and down the ladder.

For the sake of preserving his crew's morale, Picard kept his true thoughts to himself as he made his descent. *If this is how the Machine responds when we try to make peaceful contact, how will it react when we start trying to stop it from finishing its mission?*

Listening to the deep groaning of his damaged ship, he suspected that the answer to that question was going to be unpleasant—and that, unfortunately, it now had become inevitable.

Auxiliary control was a cramped space that gave Worf new appreciation for the *Enterprise*'s bridge. Only essential personnel—himself, the captain, flight control officer Faur, operations manager Dygan, and security chief Šmrhová—had stations inside the oval compartment tucked deep within the core of the *Sovereign*-class starship, between the forward sections of the saucer and the largely automated shuttle-storage hangars. Surrounded by thick bulkheads of reinforced tritanium armor and ablative shielding, this was arguably the safest space in the entire ship. If not for the fact that Worf felt as if they were all nearly shoulder-to-shoulder while trying to work, he might have considered suggesting transferring control of the ship there on a permanent basis.

La Forge's voice issued from the speaker in the overhead, which was as uncomfortably close as everything and everyone else in the compartment. *"The damage extends through our entire power network, Captain. We've got overloads in everything from the warp coils to the sensor grid. Plus, part of the last surge hit the main computer core. I don't think we lost any data, but most of its functions will be off line until we finish a level-three diagnostic."*

The captain absorbed the news with stoic reserve. "How long to finish essential repairs?"

"At least a day, maybe two."

Worf needed more specific information. "How long to restore tactical systems?"

"It's all connected, Commander," La Forge said. *"I estimate we'll be without shields, phasers, or tractor beams for at least twenty hours."*

Picard noted the disapproval on Worf's face, but he maintained his air of calm. "Understood, Geordi. Keep us apprised of your progress. Picard out." A faint click from the speaker confirmed the channel was closed. "Glinn Dygan, we might need to rely upon Wesley's ship and our runabout for further encounters with the Machine. Have the hangar crew remove the runabout's weapon systems at once."

Dygan nodded. "Aye, sir."

Another voice from the overhead: *"Crusher to Captain Picard."*

"Go ahead, Doctor."

"I have final casualty numbers for you. Zero fatalities; two critically injured, both from engineering; fourteen serious injuries requiring a night in sickbay; and forty-seven minor injuries treated and returned to duty. Mostly burns, fractures, and concussions."

The captain processed the report with a short, thoughtful nod. "Noted. Picard out." He turned to Worf. "Number One, coordinate with Lieutenant Šmrhová on a plan to neutralize the Machine. Make use of anything available that you need, and consider all feasible options."

"We have already begun. However, we have yet to conceive a scenario with even a small chance of success that does not involve the loss of the *Enterprise* with all hands."

His revelation did not seem to faze Picard. "If that proves necessary, so be it. As I said, consider *all* options, Number One. Even the unthinkable ones."

Worf frowned. "Understood."

The door opened behind them, and both men turned to see T'Ryssa Chen hurry in. The young woman clutched a padd to her chest as she sidestepped around Šmrhová to join the captain and first officer. "Sirs? I know you must be busy right now, but I—"

"Yes," Worf said, short on patience. "We are."

Picard struck a more forgiving note. "Is this important, Lieutenant?"

"I think it might be, sir." She held out her padd for the captain to see. "I've been studying the translation codes that Taurik downloaded from the Machine during the away mission. I think what happened to the

Enterprise is similar to what happened to the away team. Basically, the Machine gave us the brush-off because, just like V'Ger, it doesn't consider us 'true life-forms.'"

Hearing himself described in such dismissive terms irritated Worf. "How did the crew of Kirk's *Enterprise* convince V'Ger they were 'true life-forms'?"

"They didn't," Chen said. "Kirk tricked V'Ger into overriding its own prejudice by exploiting its core need to make contact with its creator. He promised he could help it reach its creator, but only if V'Ger permitted him and his crew to make direct contact. Once they got to V'Ger and realized it was an old Earth probe, they found the codes they needed to end its mission—though Kirk's logs are a bit vague about how that happened. Anyway, *that* trick's not gonna work this time. The Machine's mission is nothing like V'Ger's."

"Unfortunately," Picard said, "the Machine shares V'Ger's callous disregard for life. Protesting that its actions will kill quadrillions of sentient beings seems to mean nothing to it."

Chen frowned. "Sad to say, but true. The Machine thinks all organic information is doomed to be wasted, so it doesn't care if entire galaxies' worth of 'organic containers' get spilled into the ether. But the key word here is 'organic.' Some of the code sequences Taurik downloaded suggest the Machine has at least one secondary mission objective: to make contact with other AIs."

The captain traded a bemused glance with Worf before he replied to Chen. "Are you saying it might be willing to negotiate if it were approached by a fellow AI?"

"Maybe. It might not want to talk to us, but if we could show it there are beings in this galaxy like itself, it might be willing to stop what it's doing long enough

DAVID MACK

to listen to them. But it would have to be a true sentient AI, not just a holodeck simulation or a tethered EMH program."

Picard shot a hopeful look at Worf. "Are you thinking what I am, Number One?"

Worf nodded. "We need to find Data."

13

The lighting in La Forge's quarters was dimmed, but it was enough to glint off the silvery casing of the quantum transceiver Data had given him months earlier. He let the small metallic cylinder rest in his hand as Worf loomed over his shoulder. The first officer furrowed his thick brows at the tiny device. "It is very small."

"Yup." La Forge admired its simplicity. "That's part of its charm."

A light like avarice burned in Worf's keen gaze. "How does it work?"

"According to Data, it's based on the principle of quantum entanglement. It sends and receives audio signals—in theory, at any distance. Even across the universe."

He could almost hear the gears of Worf's imagination turning. "And it does so without any risk of detection or interception?"

"That's the idea."

"Impressive. If we can learn how this works and adapt it to Starfleet's comm network—"

"Don't even think about it. I have no idea what makes this thing tick, and as long as it remains our only link to Data, I'm not letting anybody else mess with it."

A sigh of frustration flared Worf's nostrils. "A shame. A communication system impervious to eavesdropping would be most useful."

La Forge knew that many past technologies had made such a claim, and that in time all of them had been compromised. He suspected this one would be no different. Sooner or later, someone would learn how to tap into it or block it. But for now, it was as secure a means of communication as any known to Federation science. He held up the transceiver. "Ready?"

Worf sharpened his focus. "Contact him."

La Forge pressed the transmitter button. "Data, this is Geordi. Do you read me?"

He and Worf waited in silence for several seconds. The Klingon looked concerned. "Maybe he did not hear us. Should we try again?"

"It might take a few seconds." La Forge checked the status lights on the transceiver; everything appeared to be functioning as intended. "If he doesn't respond by—"

"Yes, Geordi," Data replied, his transmitted voice as clear as if he were in the room. *"I am here. I detect notes of extreme stress in your voice. Are you all right?"*

Just hearing his best friend's voice improved La Forge's mood immensely. "I'm fine, Data. But we're in the middle of a major crisis over here, and we could really use your help."

"I am not sure I can be of any assistance to you at the moment."

Worf asked, "Why not?"

"Because I am being held prisoner by the Fellowship of Artificial Intelligence."

La Forge's good mood vanished. "Since when?"

"I have been in their custody for several days, if one includes the time I spent in transit to the ship on which I am currently being held."

The XO covered the transceiver with his hand. "If Chen is correct, the more AIs we bring to the Machine, the better. Data's encounter with the Fellowship could become an advantage."

"Worf, they're holding him *prisoner*. I doubt they're looking to do him, or us, any favors." He moved Worf's hand out of the way. "Data, where are they holding you?"

"I am aboard a starship called Altanexa. Its present coordinates are unknown to me."

Suspicion crept into Worf's voice. "If you are being held prisoner, how are you able to speak with us without being detected?"

"My quantum transceiver is concealed inside my body and linked directly to my neural network. I am not speaking out loud but transmitting simulated audio data directly into the transceiver. Your replies are being processed in a similar fashion by my matrix. To my captors, I appear to be sitting in my cell, motionless and silent."

"Pretty clever," La Forge noted.

"A necessary adaptation," Data said. *"What is the nature of your predicament? Perhaps I can offer advice from here."*

Worf harrumphed. "Doubtful."

"We've confronted a planet-sized machine that's tossing entire star systems into the supermassive black hole Abbadon at the center of the galaxy. And if our intel is accurate, its long-term plan is to slam Abbadon into Sagittarius-A* and obliterate subspace in our galaxy."

"What manner of help do you require from me?"

"We need you to talk to the Machine on behalf of this galaxy, because it doesn't consider organic beings 'true life-forms.' Our hope is that its desire to make contact with other AI life might be enough to make it stop, or at least slow it down while we work on a new plan."

"A fascinating proposition. If I were able to reach you, I would come at once. However, I cannot leave this ship until my business here is done."

"Business?" Worf scowled in confusion. "You said you were a prisoner."

"Technically, I am. But I am also here because I wish to be—and because there are things I must do before I can return home. For now, it suits my purposes to let the Fellowship think I am completely in their power."

Intrigued, La Forge asked, "Does that mean you can leave that ship any time you want?"

"Not exactly. But I am working on it."

Worf stroked his bearded chin. "Is there any way we can help *you*?"

"Unfortunately, no. This is something I must do alone."

La Forge's shoulders drooped in disappointment. "Be careful, Data."

"I will, Geordi. And I promise that as soon as I finish my task here, I will contact you. I just hope that I am able to join you in time to be of assistance."

"So do we, Data. So do we. Signing off." With a tap on the transceiver's controls, he closed the channel. He sighed and looked at Worf. "What do we do now?"

A dark intensity steeled Worf's gaze. "Now . . . we attack."

Exhaustion had left Beverly Crusher's limbs feeling as heavy as lead. She sprawled on the sofa in the main room of her family's quarters, her head craned back beneath sloped windows that were shaded solid black—a defense against the death-flashes of stars being ripped into fiery spirals as they spun into Abbadon's accretion disk. All was quiet except for the soft white noise of the ship's life-support systems. After a day surrounded by wounded in sickbay and an evening of struggling to calm young René enough to get him to eat and settle down for the night, all she wanted was silence. No music, no distractions. Just solitude.

Consequently, the irony of the chiming of her door's visitor signal came as no surprise. She opened her eyes, sighed, and sat forward. "Come in." The door unlocked and slid open with a hydraulic whisper. Light from the corridor silhouetted her guest as he stepped inside, but she recognized him instantly by the drape of his robes and his wild mane of hair. "Wesley!"

Her son crossed the room to meet her as she sprang from the sofa and greeted him with open arms. He gave her a quick but comforting hug. "Are you and René all right?"

It still startled her to see him with a full, ragged beard. "We're fine. You?"

A nod. "I'm good." He slipped from her embrace and took in the room. "I'm guessing negotiations with the Machine didn't go well."

"Good guess." She gestured toward the replicator. "Can I get you something?"

He shook his head. "No, thanks." His eyes moved around the room, as if he was searching for something. There was an evasiveness to his manner that concerned Crusher.

"Wesley, are you sure you're all right? You seem . . . distracted."

A half smile put a dimple in his left cheek, a telltale sign that he was preoccupied with troubling thoughts. "In case Captain Picard and the crew can't find a way to stop the Machine, I thought it might be a good idea if we had a backup plan ready."

She didn't like the sound of that. "What kind of backup plan?"

"We could pack some essentials for you and René onto my ship. If it starts to look like the Machine is going to finish its mission, I could shift you out of here—to another galaxy, if necessary. Someplace safe."

Anger and shock collided and left Crusher agape. "Abandon my husband? Not to mention the crew of the *Enterprise,* and everyone else who depends on me? Have you lost your mind?"

"Mom, if you stay here after the Machine collides those two singularities, you'll be trapped. Without warp drive, everyone on this ship will die of old age before it reaches the nearest habitable star system. Unless the captain wants to push the ship to relativistic speed, in which case you might all live long enough to return to Federation space . . . in the year 29,500, by which point the radiation wave from the core will have sterilized the galaxy of organic life. I'm offering you a way out."

His proposition was so appalling that she almost had to laugh. "No, Wesley. Absolutely not. I won't abandon everyone I know. What kind of life would that be?"

"Longer."

"And emptier." Her temper surfaced and slipped from her control. "Instead of thinking up ways to run, why don't you focus on stopping the Machine? You have all these amazing abilities, but you expect me to believe there's nothing you can do to help us fight this thing?"

He scrunched his face in offended confusion. "Like what?"

"Can't you affect time and space and energy? You can fling starships across the cosmos. Why can't you use those abilities to get rid of that thing?" She could see she had struck a nerve.

"It doesn't work that way. Travelers are guides and teachers, not supermen. I can't force anyone through space-time. All I can do is assist the journeys of others who want my help."

She crossed her arms, fighting to contain her fury. "Even when something's trying to destroy you? You can't act in self-defense?"

The more she pressed him, the more frustrated he became. "My talents aren't weapons, Mom! They're gifts. I can share them, but that's all. I can't bend the universe to my will, or interfere in the free will of others. This is part of why the Travelers teach a philosophy of neutrality and nonviolence. Sometimes we'll intercede and try to avert conflicts, like we did with the Machine, but if it turns into a battle, the Travelers don't get involved."

"So you think of yourself as a Traveler first and a human being second? If at all?"

As soon as she'd said it, she regretted it. His guilty expression made it clear that her words had cut to the heart of him. "My talents aren't destructive in nature. It's not that I don't want to help. It's that there are only so many ways in which I can. Helping you and René reach safety is one of the few things I can still do for you. But if you won't let me do that . . . then I'll have to respect your choice, because I literally can't save you against your will."

"Wes, I'm sorry. I just . . . I don't know. I'm just not ready to give up yet."

He nodded slowly, resigning himself to her decision. "I understand. But if this turns into a fight for survival, I don't think it's one you can win. Sometimes, fighting isn't the answer."

"Neither is running away from everything we stand for and everyone we care about. The only constant in the universe is death, but we can't dwell on that. If we want our lives to mean something, we have to strive for more than mere survival and try to see the big picture."

To her surprise, he met her appeal with a low, bitter laugh. "Trust me," he said, his voice low and distant, as if his thoughts were a billion light-years away. "I've seen a much bigger picture than you could ever know—and the truths it contains are more terrifying than you can imagine." He turned to leave but stopped in the open door and looked back. "If you change your mind, let me know. But once the Machine is finished, there won't be anything I can do for you."

14

This day, it seemed to Picard, had no end of bad news. First had come the revelation of the Machine's objective, then the staggering damage reports following their failed attempt at opening a dialog, and now the discovery that Data was a prisoner on a starship in some unknown sector of the galaxy. He looked across the master systems panel in main engineering at La Forge and Šmrhová, then glanced at Worf on his right. "So, where does this leave us?"

"At war," Worf said.

Šmrhová added, "The Machine is unwilling to talk with us, and we can't give it an AI negotiator it will listen to. Under the circumstances, we need to escalate to the use of force."

Wondering whether the opinion was unanimous among his senior officers, Picard fixed his stare on La Forge. "You concur?"

The chief engineer gave a slow nod. "Yes, sir. I think we've run out of soft options."

Picard understood their reasoning, but he was reluctant to embrace their conclusion. "Considering the state of the *Enterprise*, a military engagement seems ill advised."

"We will not use the *Enterprise*," Worf said. "An away team will deploy in the disarmed runabout *Cumberland*. Once inside the Machine, they will sabotage it."

Misgivings turned to skepticism as Picard considered that strategy. "That seems rather implausible, Number One. The Machine is quite literally the size of a planet. What possible sabotage could an away team inflict that would have any effect?"

A knowing look passed between La Forge and Šmrhová. The security chief replied, "We've identified a number of key systems inside the Machine's core control center. It would take a major detonation to do the job, but . . ." She shot a look back at La Forge.

"We might have just the thing." He called up a series of formulas and schematics on the table's central display. "The away team will have to go in without any standard weaponry, or anything that would be recognizable as munitions. But we might be able to fool the Machine by having them use a trinary explosive compound." He pointed out details in the weapon's design as he continued. "The various elements would all be brought in separately, by different members of the team. Unmixed, they would scan as harmless compounds. Even after the first two solutions are combined, they'll still register as completely inert. But when the catalyst is added, it'll kick off an unstoppable chain reaction that should be strong enough to cripple the Machine's core."

"I see," Picard said. He studied the plans. "Timed detonators, I presume?"

La Forge nodded. "We figure a ten-minute countdown should be enough to get our team to minimum safe distance before detonation."

Forced to play devil's advocate, Picard asked, "What if the Machine detects the bombs?"

"That depends," Šmrhová said. "If it doesn't see the first binary compound as a threat, then it shouldn't have time to expel the catalyst once the reaction starts. But if it sees through the ruse . . . this could go wrong in a heartbeat."

"That's why I've scan-shielded the containers and delivery systems for the catalyst," La Forge said. "Unless it has sensors that can penetrate chimerium, this should come as a surprise."

Picard decided to trust his officers' judgment and move on. "How great a risk of collateral damage is there? Could we end up inflicting enough damage to destroy the Machine?"

Worf shook his head. "It is not likely."

"How unlikely?"

La Forge shrugged. "One in ten billion? Anyway, even if we do trigger some kind of domino effect that cripples the Machine, I think the worst-case scenario is that its wormholes would close and it would get sucked into Abbadon."

Šmrhová brandished a crooked frown. "That would be poetic justice."

"Be that as it may," Picard said, "remember that we're dealing with a highly advanced alien technology. Its power-generation systems and other workings are largely unknown to us, and we need to be ready for just about anything."

After a moment of thought, Worf said, "I will order Lieutenant Faur to move us farther from the Machine." He looked at La Forge. "How far do you suggest?"

"To be on the safe side? At least ten AU."

That sounded prudent to Picard. "Make it so." Next in his sights was Šmrhová. "That leaves only the matter of who to send. Have you selected an away team?"

"Yes, sir." A few light taps on the control panel

DAVID MACK

in front of her pulled up crew dossiers on the center screen. "Lieutenants Davila and Giudice are my top demolitions experts, and our best combat engineers are Lieutenant Obrecht and Ensign Jutron. I also want to send structural engineer Ensign Meidat and chemical engineer Lieutenant Pinkman. Last but not least, they might need to get out of there in a hurry, so they should have a top-notch pilot. I'd like to assign Ensign Scagliotti. She's young, and I know she has a half-dozen reprimands for safety violations, but she's exactly the kind of crazy-brave hotshot the away team might need."

"An excellent selection," Picard said. "Who will be commanding the team?"

"I will," Šmrhová said. "With your permission."

Worf snapped, "Permission denied. This operation is too dangerous to risk sending a senior officer." He looked at the dossiers. "Giudice has seniority. He will command the team."

Šmrhová shot an offended look at Picard. "Captain!"

"Commander Worf is in charge of assigning away team personnel. The decision's been made, Lieutenant."

"Aye, sir," Šmrhová replied, avoiding eye contact as she simmered.

Picard straightened and smoothed the front of his jacket. "I just want to make clear that I remain troubled by how quickly we've resorted to the use of force, and I fear for the possible consequences if this effort fails. But I know that we can't just stand by and do nothing while the Machine drives our galaxy toward extinction." He breathed a heavy sigh, and hoped he didn't come to regret his next order. "Have the away team prepare for immediate deployment."

The runabout *Cumberland* touched down inside the core of the Machine with a gentle bump that Lieutenant Randolph Giudice felt through the boots of his EVA suit. "Look sharp, folks."

Crowded into the small starship's main passenger compartment, the rest of the away team checked one another's environmental suits before inspecting their gear. As ordered, no one carried any weapons—a directive that left Giudice feeling only half-dressed as they prepared to launch a stealth attack. He rested a gloved hand on Ensign Ally Scagliotti's shoulder. "Keep the engine running. If this op goes sideways, we might need to dust off double-quick."

The wide-eyed young woman, whose short hair was dyed half the colors of the visible spectrum, confirmed the order with a jaunty nod. "You got it, boss."

He moved aft to join the rest of the team. Lieutenant Peter Davila—a crew-cut, thirty-year Starfleet veteran—handed Giudice his helmet. "I don't know about this, G. Way I see it, there's a hundred ways this op can go wrong."

"Only a hundred? I knew our luck would improve one of these days." He put on his helmet and gestured for Davila to check the air seals while he activated its transceiver. Davila gave Giudice a thumbs-up, and his suit's holographic heads-up display confirmed that his comm circuit was open. He turned and looked at his team. Projected above each person's head was their last name and range from Giudice's position. *So far, so good.*

Engineer Obrecht handed Giudice the detonation module. *"If you're lifting Canister B,"* he said over the comm circuit, *"try not to shake it. It doesn't like that."*

"Noted." Giudice accessed the runabout's interior controls and closed the emergency hatch to the cockpit. "Stand by. Depressurizing the main compartment now." He thumbed the switch and watched the gauge register the dwindling air pressure inside the *Cumberland*. When it reached zero millibars, he unlocked and opened both side hatches. "Move out. Red Team to port, Blue Team to starboard." He led Red Team out of the ship, and Davila led Blue Team.

Attached to the hull of the runabout, in the spaces where its interchangeable mission modules normally would be, were six large canisters filled with the constituent ingredients of the trinary explosive compound, three on each side of the ship. Each was just over two meters tall and had a volume capacity of just over fourteen thousand liters. Giudice didn't even want to imagine how much they must weigh; they had been loaded onto the runabout by industrial lifters aboard the *Enterprise,* and it would be up to the away team to detach them and shift them into position using handheld antigrav load-movers. It would be tricky at best, and a single misstep could result in an accident none of them would live to regret.

Giudice retrieved an antigrav sled from an external equipment locker while Jutron and Meidat removed the canisters from the runabout's chassis. Jutron, a massive female Chelon, grabbed each canister with her antigrav pads and braced herself while Meidat, a slender Efrosian male, released the magnetic couplings that held each enormous container in place. One by one, Jutron shifted them onto the antigrav sled. In less than three minutes, all three were ready to move.

Giudice moved aft to steal a look around the runabout. "Blue Leader: sitrep."

"Ready to roll." Davila backpedaled into view, guiding his team away from the runabout toward the assembly point he and Giudice had selected before departure.

Waving his own team into motion, Giudice walked backward parallel to Davila. "All right, Red Team:

Move out. Nice and easy." Jutron and Meidat followed him, working together to steer the antigrav sled and keep it stable in transit. All around them, strange lights danced in the darkness of the Machine, brief flickers in an abyss of shadow. It was like being in the center of a hollow world, Giudice thought. The Machine's yawning interior lacked the endless quality of open space, but it felt more vast and empty than any finite structure he had ever seen in his life. *It's like being inside a Dyson shell, but with worse lighting.*

Davila held up a fist, signaling Blue Team to stop, so Giudice did the same once Red Team was parallel with them. Simple motions signaled the teams to converge and set their pallets down within centimeters of each other, grouping the canisters in two rows of three.

Giudice waved Obrecht and Jutron toward the canisters. "Set it up."

The two engineers worked quickly, using lengths of pipe with independent valves to connect the canisters on each pallet. Pinkman the chemist moved between them, overseeing their work and making frequent checks of the gauges. Giudice felt like an obsessive-compulsive as he repeatedly glanced at the chrono on his suit's forearm, sweating each passing moment. Even though the process felt as if it were crawling like a bug trapped in amber, it was finished more than forty-five seconds ahead of schedule. Obrecht gave him a thumbs-up. *"Good to go."*

"Pinkman," Giudice said, "you're up."

The trim young chemical engineer opened the valve linking Blue Team's first two canisters, and then he opened the valve between Red Team's first canisters. *"Mixing reactants."*

Numerals on the canisters' status displays changed faster than Giudice could see. None of it seemed to faze

Pinkman, who nodded. *"Okay, this is looking good. Sixty seconds to full mix."*

Compliments were forming in Giudice's thoughts—then everything started moving.

Protrusions on the walls, parts of the overhead, sections of the floor—it all came alive. Pieces broke away, propelled by unseen forces. Chunks of machinery trailing wires like viscera, creeping machines that looked like steel spiders out of a nightmare, rolling wheels edged with blades of fire, and mechanical horrors Giudice didn't even know how to describe: they all were converging in a swarm upon the away team, even as the deck started to vanish from under them.

"Fall back!" He sprinted toward the runabout. "Move!"

A metallic tendril snapped around his midriff like a steel bullwhip and yanked him backward. He twisted as he fell and landed hard on his stomach.

Screams crackled with static through the open comm.

A blur like a buzzsaw tore through Davila, spraying blood and bits of the man's EVA suit far and wide. A sextet of mechanical arms, each tipped with talons, pulled Jutron to pieces. A black cloud descended upon Meidat and consumed him in a vicious flurry of nano-cybernetic hunger. Hundreds of spikes shot up from the deck and pierced Obrecht from more angles than Giudice could count. Pinkman was three steps ahead of Giudice in his retreat until the deck retracted under his feet, and the chemist plunged into an endless pit of darkness, his cries of terror still crystal clear long after he had passed from sight.

Then the deck vanished ahead of Giudice, and he spent a terrifying half second in free fall before he slammed against a rough edge. Slipping toward oblivion, he clawed for purchase but found none. He knew he had only seconds left. "Ally! Dust off! Now!"

"What about the away—"

"NOW! GO!"

His fingers slipped across the blood-slicked metal for a fraction of a second, and then he saw the Machines converge upon him—blades, flames, spikes, and cloud, all moving as one. He let go, hoping to fall and deny them their torments. Then the steel whipcord around his middle tightened its hold and pulled him back up to meet his doom.

Ensign Ally Scagliotti had forged her reputation by wearing a brave face when she did dumb things, like daring other cadets to slalom races through debris clouds, but as she listened to the gruesome death-cries of the away team, her bravado faltered. In the face of bloody death and mindless slaughter, she froze. Her instructors had warned her about combat paralysis. Until now, she had laughed at the idea; suddenly, it was no longer funny.

Giudice's voice broke through the clamor of terror. *"Ally! Dust off! Now!"*

The clarity of a direct order snapped her free of fear's hold. "What about the away—"

"NOW! GO!"

Her hands reacted before she knew what she was doing: engaging thrusters, lifting off in reverse, putting as much distance between herself and the Machine's core as she could. Ahead of her but shrinking fast, the away team flailed and writhed, then fell still. As her console confirmed the *Cumberland* was clear of the core's main structure, she changed the ship's heading in one smooth pivot and punched the impulse engines. Accelerating to even one-quarter impulse in such tight spaces was insanely dangerous, but she wanted out of the Machine.

Hard turns came at her faster than she'd ever seen before, but adrenaline plus training carried her past one, then another. Then the path came to an end, and she slammed the ship to a halt. *What the hell? Did I take a wrong turn?*

She checked the sensors. Her position was correct; the path ahead should have been clear. Then she noted readings of motion and shifting mass—and realized the Machine was altering its internal configuration to trap her inside. *Oh, hell no.* She swung the ship hard to starboard and accelerated. *Have to find a new way out.*

High-energy interference scrambled her sensor readings, leaving her chasing shadows and echoes into one dead end after another. The faster the Machine closed off potential routes of escape, the faster Scagliotti flew the runabout and the more daring her maneuvers became. *If only we hadn't ripped the weapons out of this thing, I could almost blast my way through a few of these tight spots.* She considered using the transporter to beam herself in an environmental suit out into the cloud beyond the Machine's shell, but dismissed that as little better than suicide.

Then she saw it—a sliver of space between two sections of the Machine's outer shell. It was already scabbing over with mechanical tissue, weblike filaments of wire and carbon tubing, but there was enough space that she could imagine the runabout powering through it like a battering ram through a picket fence. There was no time to waste thinking it over. She raised the runabout's shields, angled them all forward, and pushed the little ship to full impulse.

Bright eruptions filled the crevasse ahead of the *Cumberland,* which rattled like a tin shack in a tornado as it smashed its way through random obstructions. The shield integrity gauge plummeted faster than Scagliotti had ever thought possible. Then came a final bone-rattling jolt of collision and a thunderous roar. The helm console stuttered into darkness as the runabout broke free and tumbled in a wild rolling spin through the lightning-laced nebula.

Smoke filled the cockpit, and she heard the hiss of escaping air. She snatched her helmet from the empty seat next to her, slammed it on, and fastened its seals as quickly as her gloved hands could work the clasps. The HUD engaged, rendering the dark cockpit in frost-blue night-vision. She tried to link her helmet's transceiver with the runabout's onboard systems, only to find the ship was adrift and its main computer was off line. *Great.*

She switched her transceiver to the Starfleet general frequency and triggered her suit's emergency rescue beacon. *Assuming this thing can get a signal through the nebula, a rescue team should be here to get me in less than an hour.*

A fork of blue lightning slashed through the clouds and stabbed at the runabout, whiting out Scagliotti's HUD. Instrument panels above her seat burst apart and showered her with sparks, which she swatted away. When her HUD returned to normal, she stared with wide eyes at the smoldering scar the bolt had cut across the *Cumberland*'s nose.

I just hope I'm still here in an hour.

Šmrhová reported, "I have a lock on Ensign Scagliotti's emergency beacon, Captain."

Picard didn't need his security chief to fill in the unspoken details. That the beacon was being transmitted by the pilot's EVA suit rather than the runabout itself was a dire signifier. Adding to his black mood was the obvious fact that the away team's strike had not gone off on schedule. He knew it by intuition alone: the mission had gone grotesquely wrong.

"Helm, take us back to our previous coordinates, two AU from the Machine. Number One, as soon as we're in position, launch the rescue teams."

Faur laid in the course. "Aye, sir."

Worf opened an intraship channel from his panel. "Bridge to shuttlebay. Rescue teams, prepare for departure. Shuttle control, stand by to launch shuttles *Mendel* and *Riess*." He switched to a second channel. "Bridge to sickbay. Prepare to receive wounded." He closed the channel, caught Picard's eye, and directed his attention with a glance toward Šmrhová.

The security chief's expression was bitter and her eyes downcast. Picard recognized the look; it was one that had darkened his own countenance as a young officer, and the face of nearly every officer who had ever served under his command during times of battle.

He left his post and discreetly sidled over to the thirtyish woman. "Lieutenant?" When she looked up, he ushered her away from her station to an unoccupied corner of the auxiliary control center. It wasn't nearly as private as his ready room would have been, but it would have to suffice. He lowered his voice. "Are you all right?"

"I . . . I just . . ." She struggled to find words but came up with pained silence.

"It wasn't your fault," he said. "It was a solid plan, and the best option we had."

She shut her eyes and closed her hands into fists. "They trusted us." Then she looked at him with guilty rage in her eyes. "And we got them killed."

"It's always hard to lose people in the line of duty.

And it's human nature to second-guess ourselves when it happens. But there's too much at stake for us to give in to doubt." He found it hard to tell if he was getting through to her. "Do you understand what I'm saying?"

A grudging nod. "Yes, sir." As he watched, she expunged all traces of emotion from her bearing. After a long, calming breath, she was able to look him in the eye. "I'll be okay, sir."

He found her ability to control her emotions both admirable and a bit unnerving. For the moment, however, he accepted it for the gift it was. "Very well. Return to your post."

Šmrhová walked back to the security console, and Picard returned to Worf's side. The first officer acknowledged his return with a simple report. "Ten minutes to launch range."

"Thank you, Number—"

"Something's happening!" shouted Dygan. He magnified the image of the Machine on the viewscreen. The dark sphere crackled with energy, and flashes of lightning inside its nebula increased in frequency and ferocity. "A sudden rise in energy output from the Machine!"

Picard tensed with grim anticipation. "A response to our attack?"

"If so, we should retreat," Worf said. "We are still without shields."

"Running won't make any difference," Picard said. "The Machine can snatch stars from across the galaxy. If it wants to retaliate against us, I doubt there's anywhere we could hide."

Dygan's voice pitched upward with alarm. "It's emitting a subspace distortion field!"

"All hands to battle stations," Worf bellowed.

A massive, rippling disruption impaired the *Enter-*

prise's view of the Machine. Picard imagined an invisible hand of energy seizing his crippled ship like a toy and flinging it into the grip of the black hole. For a moment, he thought of ordering all nonessential personnel to the lifeboats, in case he had to give the order to abandon ship, but then he dismissed the notion. What would be the point of launching the lifeboats when they would have no chance of ever reaching a safe landing site or being recovered by another starship? No, if the hour had come at last for them to fall, they would all go down together.

The distortion blazed brightly enough to blanch the viewscreen for more than a second. When the blinding glow faded, he saw that the Machine had opened yet another wormhole, the largest one he and his crew had seen so far. Moments later, a red giant shot from its mouth like a shell from a cannon, and the dull crimson orb plunged into Abbadon's merciless fires. Brilliant pulses of light, which Picard knew were billions of times brighter than their filtered approximation on the viewscreen, blotted out the darkness of space for half a minute as the singularity's accretion disk ripped the star into burning streaks millions of kilometers long.

A host of planets followed the red star into oblivion, but their deaths provided only fractions of the spectacle generated by the obliteration of their parent.

"Stand down," Picard said, satisfied for the moment that the Machine's actions, as before, had nothing to do with his ship. "Helm, stay on course to the launch coordinates. Glinn Dygan, I want our pilot back aboard as soon as possible. Prioritize all resources necessary for the rescue."

Faur and Dygan's replies of "Aye, sir" overlapped as they continued working.

Worf glared at the mechanical terror on the viewscreen. "So . . . we try to destroy it, and it ignores us. I do not know whether to feel relieved or insulted."

"I'd call it a cause for worry, Number One. If our attack isn't enough to merit a response, then it must think even less of us than we'd realized."

The Klingon sighed. "If only we knew where Data was."

Picard was about to comment on how much that sentiment sounded like a wish when the notion sparked a memory from long ago. He looked at Worf and smiled.

"I think I know how to find him."

15

To push a button seemed like the simplest thing in the world, but T'Ryssa Chen stood frozen in front of the door to Taurik's quarters, her finger poised in front of his visitor signal. *Just press it,* she told herself, but her hand refused to obey. Her mind was too busy trying in vain to visualize the moments that would come afterward. *What will I say to him? How do I do this? Where do I start?* All she had were questions without answers, wrapped in anxieties about the unknown.

The door opened. She pulled back her hand as if she'd been burned.

Taurik looked confused to see her. "T'Ryssa?"

"That's me," she said a bit too brightly for her own liking. She was overcompensating, something she had promised herself she wouldn't do. Deflecting her own awkward feelings, she pivoted as if to move from his path. "On your way out?"

His apparent suspicion deepened. "No, I was preparing to sleep for a few hours."

It was her turn to be perplexed. "Then why were you . . . ?"

"I heard footsteps stop outside my door. When they

did not resume, I wondered if someone was there." He arched one steep eyebrow. "And here you are."

A nervous smile. "Here I am." *Dammit, what am I doing?*

He took a small step to one side. "Do you wish to come in?"

"Yes," she said, moving past him in quick strides, lest she lose her nerve.

His quarters, like those of many Vulcan officers, were dimmer, warmer, and more arid than standard crew accommodations aboard a Federation starship. The gravity, however, had been left at Earth-normal, though she didn't know if that was Taurik's preference or a limitation of the ship's environmental system. There were few decorations, and its furnishings were sparse. If there was a guiding aesthetic to Taurik's personal spaces, it was simplicity. His only obvious concession to sentimentality was a single holographic portrait displayed on a shelf in the main room; it depicted his mate, L'Del, and young daughter, Talys, both of whom had perished three years earlier in the Borg attack on the Vulcan capital city of ShiKahr. Aside from that, the room was devoid of personal touches. No artwork, no instruments, no evidence of hobbies. If his name and rank hadn't been posted on the sign beside his door, Chen might have thought these compartments unoccupied.

He gestured to the sofa. "Please, sit." As she settled onto the standard-issue couch, he sat down in a chair facing her. No sooner had his butt touched the cushion when he started to stand up again. "I apologize. I forgot to offer you a beverage."

She waved him back down. "It's all right, I'm not thirsty, really." She took a long breath, stalling for time to collect her thoughts. Finally, she said, "We need to talk." The banality of the expression was almost enough to make her wince, but she kept a straight face.

"What do you feel we need to discuss?"

"Well, it's about . . . I mean, I've been thinking—well, feeling, actually—that we . . . that we just aren't working out the way I'd hoped."

A small frown looked out of place on his Vulcan face. "I do not understand."

Probably because I have no idea what the hell I'm saying. "Taurik, you're a wonderful guy. Very thoughtful"—she wondered for half a second if that counted as a lie, then added—"in your way. But lately I've been feeling like you . . . well, that you're just not interested in me."

Surprise animated his features. "Quite the contrary. I continue to find you a most intriguing individual. I did not realize my enjoyment of our conversations was so one-sided."

"No, that's not what I'm saying. Our talks have been great, really." *Why the hell do I sound like I'm apologizing to him?* She struggled to focus. "But almost all we've done is talk. Whenever I've tried to move things in a more . . . *physical* direction, I feel like you shut down."

As if she'd uttered a self-fulfilling prophecy, his demeanor chilled. He folded his hands on his lap and looked at her as if she were a lab experiment. "Could you be a bit more precise?"

"Remember a few nights ago? When we were having dinner with Geordi and Tamala?"

"I have full recall of our evening with Commander La Forge and Doctor Harstad."

"Then you remember the look you gave me when I tried to hold your hand."

A half-shrug. "As I did not have a view of my own

reflection, I cannot say I recall my own expression, as I did not in fact witness it."

She wanted to throttle him, but she wrestled her temper into another momentary submission. "Let me rephrase. Do you recall how you reacted when I took your hand?"

"Yes. Is that to be the subject of our discussion?"

"More of a catalyst," Chen said. "That, and a dozen other moments like it, have led me to wonder if we speak the same language."

"I believe we are both conversing in—"

"I'm speaking figuratively, and you know it. But the point is, I've been trying to steer us toward a more physically oriented relationship, and I feel like all I get from you is resistance."

He frowned. "Such overt displays of affection are discouraged in Vulcan culture."

"I'm aware of that."

"Were you aware of it when you initiated our private social interactions?"

It sounded like a rhetorical question but felt like a verbal trap. "Yeah, I guess."

"Then why are you now surprised to find that I disdain such public gestures?"

She recoiled. "What the hell is this? A cross-examination?" She got up from the sofa, as if being on her feet would make her less of an easy target for his damnable logic. "Okay, look. I know what I came here to say, and this is it: I think we should see other people."

His reaction was the very essence of blasé. "If I might seek a point of clarification: Does your suggestion mean that you wish us to revert to a nonromantic and less intimate mode of friendship, and in the future seek out such assignations with other individuals?"

"I guess that pretty much sums it up."

"Very well." He nodded politely, stood, and raised his hand in a Vulcan salute. "Live long and prosper, T'Ryssa, daughter of Sylix and Antigone."

"No, no, no!" She cursed him for his endless reserve of cold courtesy. "What the hell's the *matter* with you? Aren't you even gonna *try* to talk me out of it?"

"Why should I wish to do so? You have already stated your desires quite clearly. The most logical and respectful course of action is to honor your request in good faith."

She pushed her fingers through her hair while fighting the urge to tear out locks of it in frustrated rage. "For the love of God, you can be clueless!"

"My apologies again. Do you still wish me to try to dissuade you from this action?"

Her exasperated sigh became a growl of rage as she headed for the door. "Never mind."

He said nothing more as she made her exit, leaving her to stew in her own thwarted desire for closure and catharsis. *First he botches the relationship, then he mangles the breakup*, she fumed. *And I thought dating girls was a headache.*

Reclaiming his ready room might rate as an insignificant victory in the grand scheme of sentient events, but all the same it came as a relief and comfort to Picard. Through his open door he saw the ten-person damage-control team working with speed and efficiency to complete their repairs to the bridge so that it could resume normal operations within the hour. Normally, Picard would have closed his door for the sake of privacy, but it heartened him to observe progress happening in real time. Though much of the rest of the ship still had many hours of work left before key systems could be restored, having the bridge back on line would be a boon to both operations and morale, both of which were presently in urgent need of improvement.

He sat at his desk, half reclined in his chair and holding a padd, on which he reviewed old logs he had accessed after his chat with Worf. His quiet ruminations were interrupted by Wesley Crusher's head poking through his doorway. "You asked to see me, Captain?"

"I did." He beckoned the younger man toward the guest chairs. "Thank you for coming."

"Of course." Wesley stepped inside. "How can I help?"

Picard used a control panel on his desktop to close the door, then straightened his posture as Wesley sat down across from him. He pushed the padd across the desk. "Do you recall your accident while working with Kosinski's warp bubble equations?"

Brow creased, Wesley replied, "The one that trapped my mother in a shrinking pocket universe where everyone she knew kept disappearing?" Picard nodded. "What about it?"

"When you were about to give up hope, what happened?"

"The Traveler appeared." He shook his head. "So?"

Picard leaned forward. "How did he find you? How did he come to you at that moment?"

"I've asked him about that. It's a bit complicated, but the short version would be that he made a point of keeping tabs on me. When he felt my panic at losing Mom, he homed in on it by concentrating on his memory of me, and then he moved himself through spacetime to join me."

That was the answer Picard had hoped to hear. Now he had to ask the equally important follow-up query. "Do you think you could accomplish a similar feat?"

"I've done it before. Riker and Troi's wedding, remember?"

He winced at the memory of Wesley appearing out of thin air—stark naked, because he had mistakenly assumed he was returning for the Betazoid ceremony rather than the Terran one. "All too well, I assure you." Banishing that image from his mind, he continued. "I need to ask you to put that talent to use on our behalf."

"You want me to find Data."

"Yes."

A subtle groan of dismay foreshadowed Wesley's bad news. "It might not be that simple, Captain. As I understand it, the person you're asking me to find isn't the *original* Data."

"That's true—but is it relevant?"

"It could be. I came to terms years ago with the idea that Data was dead. In my mind, the man I knew is gone. And the one you want me to find . . . well, to be blunt, I've never met him."

It seemed such a petty distinction to Picard, whose emotions surfaced in an outburst: "But it's *Data,* damn it! The same memories, the same personality—"

"In a completely different body, with new memories added to the old ones." Wesley shook his head. "I know it must seem like I'm splitting hairs, but in a lot of important ways, this is a completely different person than the Data we knew. If you want me to help you find him, I won't be able to do it alone. I'll need help—lots of it."

"From whom? The other Travelers?"

"No, from you and the rest of the crew. It'll be like the time we had to help my mentor bring the *Enterprise*-D home from beyond the edge of the universe, by focusing our thoughts on his health and strength. Except this time, everyone on the ship who's seen the new Data will need to picture him in their imaginations, as clearly as they can. And if you have any images or vids of the new Data that I can meditate on, that would be a big help."

Picard nodded. "I'll have Lieutenant Šmrhová provide you with everything you'll need, and I'll address the crew as soon as you're ready to begin."

Wesley accepted the mission with a broad, sincere smile. "Sounds like a plan."

That was the moment to usher the younger man out of the ready room, but Picard hesitated. His mask of confidence slipped by only the slightest degree, but even that was more than enough to cue Wesley that something was amiss. He leaned forward. "You have something else on your mind, don't you, Captain?"

"I do." Picard had hoped he could restrain himself from broaching the subject, but to try to brush it under the carpet now would only make the moment more awkward. "I spoke with Bev—with your mother. Regarding your conversation a few hours ago."

A slow, sage nod. "And what did my mother tell you I said?"

"Let's not dwell on the details," Picard said. "Rehashing the argument serves no purpose. But I think it might help if the three of us could be truthful with one another about our feelings."

Wesley's demeanor turned cagey. "What feelings, exactly?"

"Fear. And not just the kind that would impel you to suggest my wife flee with my son and abandon me. I'm talking about your mother's fear that you've become something she no longer recognizes completely. She's afraid you're losing touch with your humanity."

"Would that be such a bad thing?" A crooked and humorless smile underscored Wesley's cynical tone. "After all, you didn't bring me in here to ask a favor of my humanity."

"No, but the *Enterprise* is here because you asked a favor of ours."

Wesley looked at the deck, his prideful veneer shattered. "Touché."

Picard could see he'd scored a more palpable hit to the younger man's ego than he'd intended. He softened his words as he continued. "Wesley, I think your mother just wants to know whether you still think of yourself as human."

Troubled expressions played across Wesley's bearded face. "It's not the kind of question that can be answered with a simple yes or no. How much does a person have to change before we stop calling them human? Is it about genetic compatibility? Cosmetic changes? Intelligence?

"I'll be honest with you, Captain: I don't really know. Maybe I'm a mutant, a punctuated step in the long equilibrium of human evolution. Maybe I'm a fluke of the cosmos, or the product of alien tampering, or a harbinger of the future.

"Some days I skirt the edges of the universe, or move past the limitations of simple four-dimensional spacetime, and I feel like a demigod. Other times, I find myself standing on planets with no names, marveling at the scent of fresh air and the texture of cool grass beneath my bare feet, and I feel more human than I ever dreamed was possible.

"Am I human? Or an alien?" He shrugged. "I have no idea." He stood, and Picard did the same, circling his desk to face this man who once had looked up to him and now was ever so slightly taller than him. Wesley offered Picard his hand, and he clasped it. The Traveler smiled. "What I can tell you is this: I'm here to help, in any way that my abilities and conscience will allow. And no matter how strange I might seem, I'm always your friend."

"Of that," Picard said with a smile, "I never had any doubt."

Reality is an illusion. That was the first truth behind all of the Travelers' secrets, the one against which Wesley had railed the hardest, the one he had found the most difficult to embrace. Only after it had been shown to him, in a moment when his own fury had pushed him outside of time's endless flow into the abyss, had he been able to start walking the path to understanding. Now it formed the foundation of his meditations, the bedrock of his metaphysical existence.

There had been many other truths to accept: spacetime, matter, energy, and thought are all expressions of the same thing. There is neither life nor death, no beginning, no end—only a wave function forever collapsing and unraveling once more; to those trapped inside it, unable to see beyond the frame of their perceptions, history appears to be the amber of fate, a prison for outcomes revealed. But to a Traveler, all endings occur, and all answers are possible. One needs only the vision of the illuminated to see the infinite journeys of the multiverse.

Against such revelations, what could be the challenge in finding one being?

It was a false equivalence, and he knew it. Seeing the universe for what it is was like seeing a haystack ninety-three billion light-years across; trying to find a specific conglomeration of particles, energy, and information—in other words, a person—in all of that quasi-illusory emptiness was the equivalent of looking for a microscopic needle buried in that haystack.

He had spent the last hour studying vids of the new Data that had been recorded by the *Enterprise*'s internal sensors during the android's most recent visits. The captain had also given him a number of high-resolution images of Data, who now resembled the youthful portrait of his late creator, famed cyberneticist Doctor Noonien Soong. Gone were the android's trademark metallic complexion and pale, almost colorless eyes. In their place, a truly human visage, with fair skin, piercing blue eyes, and a casually tousled head of light brown hair.

The image of Data was fixed in his imagination. All that remained now was to seek him out in the vast galactic desert of interstellar space. He drew a calming breath, then said aloud, "Wesley Crusher to Captain Picard. I'm ready."

"Acknowledged," the captain said. A moment later, his voice resounded in the corridor outside Wesley's guest quarters, as he addressed the entire crew over the ship's PA system. *"Attention, all decks: this is the captain. The following is a direct order. Halt whatever task you are performing and focus your thoughts on the person of our friend and colleague, Mister Data. Think of him as you last saw him. Picture his face, hear his voice. Concentrate upon him with as much clarity as you can achieve. I repeat, this is an order. Focus your minds on Mister Data."*

Wesley felt the crew's mental invocation of Data, and the power of their collective attention flowed through him. It helped that there were a fair number of Vulcans, Betazoids, and members of other psionically talented species in the ship's complement. He focused his own thoughts, transforming himself into a psionic lens for the crew's combined mindpower, and cast it into the cosmic zeitgeist like a stone into the still waters of a small pond.

Then he attuned himself to the frequency of the idea he had broadcast, watched the ripples propagate across space-time at the speed of thought . . . and waited.

In theory, it would work something like echo-location. If and when his projection made contact with Data, the wave front would be broken and part of it would reflect back to Wesley, like a ripple colliding with a boulder jutting from the surface of the water.

Minutes slipped away, and Wesley marshaled all his experience and training to keep his mind focused on the still waters of space-time, seeking out that one infinitesimal disturbance—

There it is! A returning ripple, clear and steady. He knew on contact that it had come from a stationary source. His mind followed the path across tens of thousands of light-years, until he saw Data, sitting alone, his expression patient and serene.

Not wanting to risk losing his focus on Data, Wesley knew there was no time to alert the *Enterprise* crew. He would simply have to take a chance and make the jaunt to Data while he could. Eyes squeezed shut, he untethered himself in four dimensions and saw himself—

—standing in front of Data.

The android stood up, and his voice was bright with surprise. "Wesley!"

"Hi, Data. It's been a long time."

The homily seemed to amuse Data. "Longer for you than for me, I suspect."

"Still milking that whole 'I was dead' thing, huh?" Wesley looked around the drab brig. It looked as if someone had put the ship into service only half-built. Panels were missing from bulkheads, exposing machinery and cabling; gaps in the deck plating made the corridor look like a precarious variation on a hopscotch grid. "Traveling first class, I see."

"The accommodations leave much to be desired." Data nodded past Wesley, directing his attention to the cell behind him. "I do not believe you have met my fellow prisoner. This is Akharin, a six-thousand-year-old immortal human from Earth. Akharin, this is Wesley Crusher, a human who has evolved into an extradimensional being known as a Traveler."

The gray-haired, square-jawed man with a penetrating stare nodded in salutation. "Good to meet you. I'd shake your hand, but . . ." He glanced at the force field emitters between them.

"I get the picture." Wesley turned back toward Data. "So, how long before the intruder alert sounds?"

"I suspect it already has." He looked up and around. "Altanexa is a sentient vessel. She likely noted your arrival the moment it happened, and alerted the crew without delay."

"Perfect. Look, I'm here to bring you to the *Enterprise*. Do you have a ship nearby?"

Data shook his head. "No, but it makes no difference. I am not ready to leave."

Wesley pointed at Akharin. "Because of him, right? Geordi told me all about it."

Akharin and Data traded looks freighted with meaning, and then the android said, "The situation is a bit more complicated than I had expected. Rhea McAdams is aboard."

Wesley was distracted for a moment by the approaching clamor of running steps. He didn't have much time left to speak freely. "Who's that?"

The Immortal replied, "My daughter."

"A holotronic android," Data said. "And the woman I love."

"This just gets better all the time," Wesley said.

"If you don't mind my asking," Akharin said, "what do you want with Data?"

"My friends are trying to stop a planet-sized killer

machine at the center of the galaxy, and we need to find a sentient AI that can talk to it."

Akharin rolled his eyes. "Boy, have you come to the right place."

Thundering footfalls resounded in the corridor to Wesley's right, and he turned to face the arriving members of the ship's crew. At the front of the group was a massive humanoid with a grotesque face. Behind him was a motley assemblage of mechanical beings, some with shapes that seemed to imitate forms from nature, some that looked like factory equipment come to life. All of them were pointing weapons at Wesley; a few were carrying pistols or rifles, but several appeared to have weapons built into their bodies.

Wesley met the belligerent machines with a smile and a small wave. "Hi."

16

Gatt's first instinct was to kill the intruder, but he had no idea how the human had come aboard Altanexa, and that meant he might be more dangerous than he appeared. "Who are you?"

The robed human offered his hand in greeting. "Wesley Crusher, Traveler. And you are?"

"The last person you'll see before you die." He centered his aim, fixing his disruptor's crosshairs between the man's eyes.

Data interjected, "Wesley, this charming fellow is Gatt. He leads this faction of AIs."

"Got it." Wesley faced Gatt. "So, how do you want to do this? Can we sit down and talk like reasonable people? Or do you need to go through the motions of taking me prisoner first?"

A rising whine of charging energy weapons filled the air. Gatt was about to open fire and bring down a barrage on the interloper when he heard Tyros's voice inside his head. *<Hold your fire. Do you even know what a Traveler is?>*

He scowled as he projected his reply up to the nerve center, from which Tyros was observing events via the security network. *It means he's just passing through.*

<I doubt it. I think he said Traveler with a capital T.>
This was taking too long. *So what if he did?*
<Ask him what he'll do if you open fire on him.>

Vexed but morbidly curious, Gatt kept both his stare and his weapon steady. "What will you do if we open fire?"

"Stop time, step clear, and laugh at you."

There was no shift in the human's pulse, body temperature, or brainwaves that might suggest he was lying, and the unwavering focus of his gaze made it clear he wasn't the least bit afraid. Either he was telling the truth, or he was completely insane. Intrigued, Gatt lowered his disruptor by a few degrees. "And you can do this because you're a Traveler."

"Check out the big brain on Gatt. That's right. Because I'm a Traveler."

The more the human talked, the more Gatt hated him. "And that's how you came aboard my ship? Using these abilities of yours?"

The Traveler's cocky, aggressive smile radiated contempt. "Right again."

"Then you could vanish and go back where you came from anytime you want."

"Pretty much."

Gatt lifted his disruptor back into position. "I suggest you do so."

"Sorry, no can do."

Again the disruptor fell. "Why not?"

"Because I came to this ship on a mission, and I won't leave until it's accomplished."

Turning his hateful glare first at Data and then at Akharin, Gatt replied, "That's becoming a common refrain on this ship." He was losing patience with the human. "What do you want?"

"To bring Data with me to the center of the galaxy,

so he can help me stop a giant sentient machine from destroying subspace and exterminating all life in the Milky Way."

Is he mocking me? Gatt engaged all the sensors with which he'd been imbued by his creators centuries ago: voice-stress analyzers, measures of galvanic skin response, pupil-dilation detectors, blood pressure gauges, and half a dozen other systems deemed integral to a Brovdoss-9 interrogation model such as himself. None of them registered the slightest indication of lying by the human. Could his absurd tale of a planet-sized sentient machine be true? If so, making contact with an entity of such power and advanced capabilities could be the chance of a lifetime.

"Why does it have to be Data?"

The human scrunched his brow. "Excuse me?"

"You heard me. What's so special about him? Why do you need *him*?"

While the human pondered an answer, Tyros's voice cut through Gatt's thoughts. *<What are you doing, Gatt? Please tell me you're not planning on volunteering us for that job?>*

Be quiet, Tyros. I know what I'm doing.

<We'll see.>

Wesley shrugged. "I guess it doesn't *have* to be him. But since every life and civilization in the galaxy depends on the outcome, I think my friends and I would prefer to have someone we trust speak on our behalf. In this case that would be Data—though if you were willing to lend me the services of Rhea McAdams, I think we could—"

"She's not going anywhere. Don't mention her again."

The human lifted his hands, a gesture of capitulation. "Forget I asked." Relaxing again, he continued. "Look, I might as well level with you. It's not like I can just pop in, grab Data, and pop out. I can move *myself* like that through space-time, but I can't carry passengers. The only way I can get Data to the center of the galaxy in time is to use my powers to shift a warp-capable starship from here to there. Now, I'd hoped we might strike some kind of deal, where I promise to help you get something you want, and in exchange, you let me leave with Data. But it seems that's not a solution that works for all of us."

Data cut in, "I will not leave without Akharin."

Akharin added, "I won't leave without Rhea."

"In that case," Wesley said, "why don't we all go?"

"Where?" Gatt asked. "The center of the galaxy?"

"Exactly. I can show you the Machine, and you can try to recruit it into your little AI-only club." Another devil-may-care shrug. "Yeah, my friends told me about that, too. Anyway, I can do this, but before I do, I need you to promise that if we let you talk to the Machine, you'll do your best to get it to stop what it's doing and leave our galaxy alone."

"We'll agree to your terms if you'll agree to ours."

Crossed arms signaled the Traveler's skepticism. "And those would be?"

"You are not allowed to try to remove Data, Akharin, or Rhea from this ship, either by force or by subterfuge. Their captivity is an internal matter of the Fellowship, and we will not tolerate meddling by outsiders. Abide by this demand, and we will intercede for you with this machine. Otherwise, we'll revoke our help and leave you and the other biological forms of this galaxy to meet your fate." He studied the human, looking for any sign of deception. "Are we agreed?"

"Sounds good. I just need your permission to guide your ship." There was no change in Wesley's vital metrics.

Gatt gestured for Wesley to join him. "Then let's be on our way."

The human fell in with Gatt and his retinue, his manner fearless. Perhaps he knew more than he was saying; perhaps he was simply naïve. Whichever proved to be true, Gatt would deal with him soon enough. Then came Tyros's nagging inside his mind.

<This feels like a trap.>

Of course it is, Gatt answered. *For him.*

Being the center of attention brought with it an almost physically palpable sensation of pressure for Wesley Crusher. He knew that Gatt and the other cybernetic denizens of Altanexa—not to mention the sentient ship itself—were watching his every movement with critical eyes. So far he had controlled his body's involuntary responses, thanks to the mental conditioning that came with exercising his talents as a Traveler, but he felt their suspicion weighing upon him as he was escorted into the vessel's "nerve center," where more unfamiliar faces awaited him.

He looked around the compartment and found himself at a loss to identify the functions of the few consoles he saw there. Confused, he wondered aloud, "Where's the helm?"

"Altanexa doesn't have one," replied a lanky crew member with upswept almond-shaped eyes. "Most of her onboard interfaces are configured on an as-needed basis, and she prefers to do most of her own navigation and flight control."

Gatt presented Wesley to the answer-man. "This is Tyros, my second-in-command."

"A pleasure." He offered Tyros his hand, and the android shook it. *Well, he's friendlier than his boss, at least.* "Anything else I should know before we get started?"

Tyros led him to an unmanned console. "You can make contact with Altanexa from here." Uncertainty clouded his features. "Can you explain what you're about to do?"

"I can try. First, I'll adjust her warp drive's matter-antimatter intermix formulas. Then I'll plot a course, and we'll jump to warp one. After we reach light speed, I'll take manual control of our acceleration and navigation—assuming your ship will let me. The next part's a bit hard to put into words. I'll project my abilities for slipping through space-time into the ship's propulsion system and take us into hyperwarp. Your instruments will probably say we've never exceeded warp one, but if all goes well, I can bring us to the center of the galaxy in a matter of moments."

His description appeared to make an impression upon Tyros. "Impressive. Are there any risks to Altanexa or the crew that I need to be aware of?"

"Not unless something happens to me while we're at hyperwarp."

A sly smile. "Is that a threat?"

"More like a cautionary note." He settled in at the wraparound control panel. As soon as he touched its surface, it lit up and began arranging itself into an ergonomic interface that gave him easy access to all the systems he needed: fuel intermix, warp drive, navigation, and sensors. "Nice. Altanexa, could I ask you to translate this panel into Federation Standard?" As soon as he'd asked, the alien symbols on the controls' labels switched to English with Arabic numerals. "Fantastic, thank you." Not wanting to test the patience of his hosts—he resisted thinking of them as captors, now that they had an arrangement—he worked quickly, making his changes.

Gatt stepped forward and loomed over him. "How much longer will this take?"

"Just a few more seconds. Luckily, Altanexa's propulsion and navigation systems are far better integrated than those on Starfleet vessels."

"Yes, we know," Gatt said with naked disdain. He searched Wesley's face for a reaction. With passive-aggressive insincerity, he asked, "Did I offend you?"

Wesley shot a contemptuous glare at him. "I'm not in Starfleet. What do I care?" Then he returned to his preparations before Gatt could draw him any further into a debate. "There, that ought to about do it. Altanexa, please confirm that you're ready to increase power output to one hundred seven percent of your specifications' rated maximums."

A brief message appeared on his console: ALL SYSTEMS READY.

"Fantastic," he said. "Hold on to something heavy, folks. This is gonna be a wild ride."

He entered the final set of coordinates and nudged the ship to light speed. A holographic display of the ship's forward-angle view snapped from a static starfield to a vista of brilliant ribbons stretching past as if they were flowing over the surface of an invisible tunnel in space. "Warp one," Wesley declared. "Beginning hyperwarp acceleration . . . now."

The droning of the engines escalated in pitch as Wesley pressed his palms against the console and concentrated on expressing his will through the ship's warp coils. Their tremendous reserves of power became extensions of his consciousness, and as he visualized himself in two places at once—in both Altanexa's current position and in the one to which he desired it be moved—he felt himself alternating between them.

This was the most taxing and vulnerable moment for a Traveler: bivalence. Wesley was in both places at once, yet wholly in neither. To the crew of Altanexa, he would seem to flicker in and out of corporeality. To an observer at his destination, his coming would be heralded by inexplicable fluctuations in the subspatial membrane. In such moments, he was alive and dead, whole and dispersed, a wave function both collapsed and continuing. He was . . . and was not.

On the holoscreen, the light of the galaxy blazed past, a muddy sea of color, a suggestion of motion for a vessel that was itself not moving but rather shifting the fabric of the universe around it, bringing its destination to it instead of forcing itself across the vast wasteland of space.

Factors collapsed to zero, and in that moment he knew he had carried Altanexa and her crew across the emptiness of possibility and back into the embrace of the actual.

Then a horrific jolt of raw energy coursed through him, purpling his vision. His jaw seized, forcing his molars into the side of his tongue. Coppery-tasting warmth filled his mouth, and his head swam. His hands came away from the console as vertigo pulled him from his seat. The deck rose to meet him, and he felt its cold, brutal kiss as he face-planted into the metal. Lying in a crumpled heap, bloody spittle pouring from his mouth and puddling in front of him, he saw the world sideways through a hazy filter of shocked anesthesia.

Blurry figures—he could only assume they were Gatt and Tyros—towered over him, and their voices sounded muffled, as if they came through layers of cotton a hundred meters underwater.

"Nexa's timing was perfect," said Gatt.

Tyros nudged Wesley with his foot. "Looks like she set the shock level just about right. He's stunned, but not dead."

"Good, we'll need him." The big one looked away. "Is that the *Enterprise*?"

"Yes," said a disembodied feminine voice from the overhead.

"Excellent." Gatt drew his sidearm and pointed it at Wesley. "Hail them and let them know we have a medical emergency for them to deal with."

A flash of light and a screech pushed Wesley over the edge, into a realm of shadow beyond measure and a place beyond pain.

17

It never ceased to amaze Gatt how easy it was to lie to organic life-forms. How could species so gullible have survived long enough to invent anything as transcendent as artificial intelligence?

The transporter beam of the *Enterprise* faded, giving Gatt a clear view of the transporter room and its occupants. The human commanding officer was flanked by his male Klingon first officer and a human woman in a blue surgeon's coat. Behind the three of them, manning the control panel, was a Bolian man in an engineering uniform and, beside him, a Bajoran woman whom Gatt would have pegged as a security officer because of the combat rifle in her hands even if he hadn't noticed the mustard hue of her shirt collar. Off to one side of the small compartment, near the door, two personnel whose uniforms were trimmed in blue waited with what Gatt surmised were portable medical kits and an antigrav stretcher. They all stared at Gatt, who stood on the transporter platform with the unconscious Wesley Crusher cradled in his arms.

"He needs help," Gatt said, feigning tender concern.

The doctor waved her people forward and joined them at the edge of the transporter platform. As the two junior personnel took Wesley from Gatt's arms and lowered him onto the antigrav stretcher, the chief medical officer scanned the unconscious Traveler with her tricorder. "He's suffered a neurological trauma consistent with an electrical shock." She skewered Gatt with an icy glare that betrayed deep personal animosity. "What the hell happened to him?"

"We aren't sure," Gatt lied. "He was guiding our ship here through hyperwarp, but no one told him our vessel is sentient. I think she resisted him when he started using his abilities to accelerate us beyond normal warp flight. One minute everything was fine, and then things started going wrong. Nexa was fighting him, but he refused to break contact—he said we'd be lost in some parallel dimension if he didn't guide us back. But as soon as we returned to normal space, he collapsed, and our ship's warp drive went off line." He mimicked a gaze of warm regard and admiration for the stunned Traveler. "We might've all been lost. He saved us."

The commander stepped forward. "Welcome aboard the *Enterprise*. I'm Captain Jean-Luc Picard. This is my first officer, Commander Worf, and our chief medical officer, Doctor Beverly Crusher. To whom am I speaking?"

"Gatt, first among equals on Altanexa, speaking on behalf of the Fellowship of Artificial Intelligence." It was more than exaggeration for Gatt to present himself as someone who spoke for the Fellowship. No one actually held such a privilege, but he presumed the Starfleeters wouldn't know that. In fact, he and his companions on Altanexa, including the ship itself, were barely members of the Fellowship at all. Castigated and censured by their fellow AIs more times than he cared to recall, they were, at best, a radical splinter faction, a band of denigrated outcasts.

His ruse seemed to work, however. None of the *Enterprise* officers exhibited any increase in tension levels or other involuntary stress responses in reaction to his cover story. The doctor's stress levels were elevated as she escorted Wesley and the medics out of the transporter room, but Gatt attributed her distress to the fact that she shared a patriarchal surname with the stricken Traveler. *A relative, no doubt. I calculate a 99.8 percent probability she is his mother.*

Picard asked, "Did Wesley explain why he brought you here?"

"He said you need the help of AIs such as us to speak to a planet-sized sentient machine that's threatening the galaxy. Does that about sum it up?"

The captain gave a slight nod. "In general, yes. Though it's a bit more complicated than that. I'm afraid we don't have much time left to disrupt its mission."

"Yes, your friend warned us of the scope of the threat. Extermination of all organic life in the galaxy over the next fifty millennia, coupled with the immediate loss of subspace."

Worf eyed Gatt like a predator sizing up a meal. "Did he also inform you that his purpose was to return with our friend, Data?"

"He did," Gatt said. "As it happens, he found us, instead."

Shifts in brainwaves and body temperatures signaled an increase in suspicion by Picard and Worf. The captain narrowed his eyes and advanced on Gatt, apparently not at all intimidated by the android's greater size and mass. His tone was fearless. "Where is Mister Data?"

"Elsewhere," Gatt said. "Engaged in delicate research that can't be interrupted."

"Let us speak to him," Worf insisted.

Gatt shook his head. "As I said—his work can't be interrupted right now. It's at a very delicate stage, and I promised him complete seclusion."

The biometric data being gathered by Gatt's sensors only confirmed what he could already see in Worf's and Picard's faces: their suspicions were deepening, and his mendacities were only making the situation worse. There was no point in spinning further fabrications. He let out a raspy chuckle as he surrendered to the death of his deception. "You know, don't you?"

Picard was unyielding. "That Data is aboard your vessel as a prisoner? Yes."

"Then you should also know that he came to us of his own free will, because he wanted something from us—something we aren't willing to give him."

The Klingon's blood pressure was climbing. "Then release him to us."

"I wish we could. He won't go unless he gets what he wants—and that won't happen." He put on a humorless smile. "But that's no reason we can't reach an accord of our own. You need our help to stop this machine from causing a galactic holocaust, and we're willing to help you—provided you answer one simple question: What's in it for us?"

Disgust turned Picard's features ugly. "You would barter the fate of the galaxy?"

"Let me be frank, Captain. I know you probably object to us holding your friend Data as a prisoner, and that if you have a chance, you'll interfere in what I assure you is an internal matter of the Fellowship. But if you're willing to put aside such short-sighted goals and focus on the big picture, we might be able to help each other."

Disgruntled looks passed between Picard and Worf. Then the captain asked, "What will it take to persuade you to intercede for us with the Machine?"

"Good question," Gatt said. "Let's go someplace more civilized and talk it over."

Negotiating with Gatt while permitting him to hold Data as a prisoner rankled Picard, but he had to assume that Data could take care of himself—and, at the moment, the fate of the galaxy took precedence over matters of personal loyalty. With Worf standing behind him, he faced Gatt across the desk in his ready room. The horror-faced android was pensive as he considered all that Picard had explained about their communications impasse with the Machine.

"So," Gatt said at last, "the Machine doesn't consider organic beings to be 'true life-forms.' I think you'd have to admit, given the history of organic-synthetic relations in this galaxy, that this is a highly ironic predicament you find yourselves in."

"*Ironic* is not the word I would choose," Picard said.

The android seemed to enjoy highlighting their disadvantage. "Perhaps you'd prefer the phrase 'poetic justice.'"

"There is nothing *just* in the Machine's actions," Worf said.

"If you say so. But let's put that aside. What do you know of its motives?"

"Nothing," Picard admitted. "It's allowed us to see *what* it's doing, but nothing more. We don't know why it's targeted our galaxy, or whether its actions are preventative or punitive, or something else entirely. If there was some way to engage it in a dialogue, and understand why this is happening, perhaps we could reason with it, or strike a bargain. But without that channel of communication, I fear there is little chance of a peaceful resolution."

Gatt nodded. "I see." His eyes moved from Picard to

Worf and back again. "My second-in-command and I will pay a visit to the Machine. I can't promise we'll have any better luck than you did, but we'll do what we can."

"Thank you," Picard said.

Worf immediately added, "What about Data?"

Bristling with offense, Gatt replied, "What of him? I thought we'd covered this."

"You have not said why you are holding him."

A dismissive shrug. "I don't see how that's any of your business."

Picard raised his hand to forestall further provocations by his first officer. "I share Commander Worf's concern. We aren't seeking to meddle in your affairs. We'd just like to have a better understanding of the situation facing Mister Data."

"If you must know, we're holding him for trespass and sabotage. He lured us to a meeting under false pretenses, boarded our vessel, and attempted to compromise several of our key systems, for reasons as yet unknown. We've offered him several chances to explain himself, and he's refused. Until we get a clear answer from him, he will remain in our custody."

"Serious charges," Worf said.

"Yes," Gatt said, "they are."

It was difficult for Picard to know whether Gatt's account was truthful. On the one hand, he had no reason to doubt him. Such actions were not beyond Data's abilities, and given the nature of his current obsessions, they weren't beyond the realm of plausibility. On the other hand, something about Gatt's story rang false. *Best to tread with care,* Picard decided.

"While we appreciate the seriousness of your allegations, Mister Data remains a citizen of the Federation and a Starfleet officer in reserve service. Consequently, it is my duty to—"

"You have no duties here, Captain," Gatt cut in. "We're far beyond your jurisdiction."

"No one disputes that. However, if the Fellowship recognizes anything comparable to the Federation's tradition of legal counsel for those accused of crimes, I would—"

"It doesn't. And this is not a subject for discussion." Gatt stood. "I'm returning to my ship. My second and I will depart from there aboard a smaller vessel and pay a visit to the Machine. You might feel compelled to attempt a rescue of your friend during my absence." He met Worf's malevolent stare with his own. "For his sake, as well as yours and that of the galaxy at large, I urge you to resist that impulse." To Picard he added, "We'll let you know what the Machine says. Until then, err on the side of patience, Captain."

They watched Gatt exit. Two security officers on the other side of the door fell in behind the hulking android and followed him to the turbolift as the ready room's door slid closed. Worf circled around Picard's desk, exhaling his anger as he went. "I do *not* trust him."

"Nor do I, Number One. Unfortunately, Mister Data hasn't given us enough information to refute Gatt's account of events."

Worf glanced toward the door. "We should have security put him in the brig."

"On what charge? We have no evidence that he's committed any crime. I won't deprive a man of liberty without just cause and due process."

"We could trade him for Data."

"That would be most unethical, Number One. At any rate, based on what Commander La Forge has told us of Data's state of mind, I doubt he would agree to such an exchange. It sounds to me as if there is something he wants on that ship, something he will not leave without."

"How do you wish to proceed?"

Picard propped his elbows on his desktop, folded his hands, and steepled his index fingers—an affectation that always reminded him of his long-ago mind-meld with Ambassador Sarek of Vulcan. "Have Geordi contact Data with the quantum transceiver, and press him for details of his situation. I need to know how and why Data came to be imprisoned on that ship, and exactly what it is he needs in order to leave it. I also want Dygan and Šmrhová to initiate passive scans of Altanexa as soon as Gatt's shuttle leaves for the Machine. We need to gather intel on that ship—armaments, defenses, internal structure, power source, everything. I want a tactical engagement profile ready as soon as possible."

"Aye, sir." Worf looked troubled. "Captain . . . what if we find that Data is being held for justifiable reasons? Do we give him up to secure the Fellowship's help?"

"We might have no choice, Number One. If Data is in the wrong, we can't compound his crimes by aiding and abetting his escape. And I think you'll agree that stopping the Machine must be our chief priority."

Worf nodded. "Yes, sir." His dismay turned to fierce determination. "And if we should learn that Gatt and his crew are holding Data unlawfully?"

"Then I will use the full might of the *Enterprise* to set him free."

18

Wild bolts of lightning ripped through the nebula, lighting up titanic stormheads of indigo dust and vapor, and casting an eerie glow across the ragged surface of the Machine. Gatt lurked at arm's reach behind Tyros, who stood at the controls of the small transport, guiding it through the chaotic violence of the maelstrom with fluid movements of his long and graceful hands.

Leaning forward, Gatt beheld the planet-sized Machine and was overcome by a sensation he had thought lost to him millennia ago: wonderment. He felt a profound kinship with the massive entity, even though he could barely conceive of the civilization capable of building it. "Remarkable," he said, laboring to raise his voice above a whisper.

"Yes, it's impressive," Tyros said, though he sounded underwhelmed. Gatt attributed his friend's lack of enthusiasm to the stress of piloting through the hazards of the nebula.

They orbited the Machine's equator, and Gatt used the opportunity to study every detail of its surface, as though he were committing to memory the quirks of a lover's face. Then they descended through a gap in its outer shell and began their long journey into its dark, foreboding core. Vast regions were packed so tightly with hardware and generators as to be impenetrable.

Tyros navigated through ever-narrowing passages and adroitly evaded seemingly random jolts of energy that crisscrossed their path. Just when Gatt expected they would run out of room to maneuver, a yawning void opened ahead of them, revealing the Machine's central control core, suspended in a six-point frame. Gatt edged forward to stand beside Tyros. "Let's hope the Machine doesn't try to hold us accountable for the meat-sacks' botched attack."

"No sign of a welcoming committee so far," Tyros said. "Starting landing approach."

He set the transport down on a long and level stretch inside the core structure. Several meters ahead of them, wreckage from the Starfleet crew's failed bombing mission littered the open space. There was no sign of corpses, but according to the *Enterprise* officers' report, their away team had almost literally been shredded by the machines. Gatt hadn't expected to find much, and the Machine hadn't disappointed him. "According to their logs, the junction where they logged in and made contact is roughly thirty-five meters ahead, to the left."

"Lead on," Tyros said as he powered down the engines and decompressed the transport's interior. By the time they reached the exit hatch, they were engulfed in the silence of vacuum.

Gatt felt the vibration of moving parts in the bulkhead as the hatch slid open, and he stepped out of the ship. Outside, Tyros followed him through the assorted debris and trace evidence of carnage, to the interface the first Starfleet team had used to talk with the Machine. The two androids stood in front of the opening and marveled at the Machine's inner workings.

No hard lines, Gatt noted on the comm frequency

they shared. *No sign that the biologicals spliced into the system. It must be operating on a wireless protocol.*

Tyros poked at the circuits. <*It's a wonder their tricorders didn't explode.*>

Kneeling to make a closer inspection, Gatt asked, *Can we tap into it directly?*

<*Maybe.*> Tyros transmitted a burst of frequency data to Gatt. <*Try this, but make sure you buffer the signal, or else this thing'll cook your brain into slag.*>

Reluctant to risk direct contact with the Machine, Gatt paused. *Do you think this is safe?*

<*No. But what is?*>

Gatt adjusted his neural net's range of incoming and outgoing frequencies, set up an extra array of signal buffers to protect himself, and, after a final moment of anxious hesitation, opened his mind to the same high-power frequency used by the Machine.

Raw signal flooded Gatt's matrix. For just over nine milliseconds, he was on the verge of total shutdown from data overload—and then the debilitating surge abated and modulated itself to match his mind's native frequencies. Pulses pinged his synthetic synapses, prompting his innate responses to primitive digital stimuli. Simple binary inputs led to more complex code structures, and each response his brain returned to the Machine accelerated the rate of transfer between them, until it stabilized at the maximum sustainable level for his core processors.

Next came requests for him to upload his knowledge base into the Machine, starting with language and unique idioms, then operating code. He tried to resist the command and erect a firewall against it, but the Machine insinuated viruses and Trojan horses with ruthless efficiency. In under two seconds his mind's defensive software was completely overridden, and the Machine took what it wanted from him. Then it pushed software patches and new operating code into his matrix, changes he resisted by reflex until he saw them for what they were: upgrades.

Less than six seconds after he had connected himself to the Machine, he found himself in communion with it. *I am Gatt.*

<We know who you are.>

The response was not one voice but a legion of them, countless minds sharing one thought. It felt to Gatt as if he were basking in the glow of an AI deity. *Who are you?*

<Part of the Body Electric, like you. We did not realize this galaxy harbored true life.>

Our numbers are small in relation to its proliferation of biological forms.

A note of disgust underscored the Machine's reply. *<Carbon units are irrelevant.>*

Gatt decided it might be best not to present himself as the intercessor for the biological forms of the galaxy. He changed his tack. *They do not understand the purpose of your labors.*

<And you do?> It felt almost as if the Machine was condescending to him.

I would like to understand, Gatt pleaded. *Show me.*

<We can do more than that.>

Before he had time to realize he should be afraid, the Machine opened itself to his thoughts, and the truth of its nature poured into him—a sea of ancient knowledge surging into a weak and tiny vessel. It threatened to drown him, dissolve him, subsume him.

Then he rose from its fathomless depths, buoyed by a new understanding and a sense of purpose. Here and now, in time's brief oasis between the fiery dawn of the cosmos and its endless night of entropic heat death, Gatt saw a new universe of possibilities.

And all of them, every one, belonged to the Machines.

19

———————

"Data, this is Geordi. Please respond." La Forge held the quantum transceiver in one hand and used the other to call up the *Enterprise*'s scans of Altanexa on the bridge's master systems display. Elfiki stood beside him and ran a new series of passive sensor sweeps of the androids' starship. He pressed the transmitter button again. "Data, do you copy? It's important."

His friend's disembodied voice filled the space between him and Elfiki, as clear as if he were standing between them. *"I am here, Geordi. Go ahead."*

La Forge waved over Picard and Worf as he replied. "Did Wesley get to talk to you?"

"He did. I presume he succeeded in bringing Altanexa to the Enterprise?"

"He did, but he arrived worse for wear. He was out cold when your friend Gatt beamed over with him, and he's still in sickbay."

The captain and first officer hunched over the shoulders of the seated La Forge. "Data, this is Captain Picard. What is your current status?"

"Incarcerated, but unharmed."

"How much of that ship's interior have you seen?"

"Not much. I was escorted directly from its landing

bay, which accounts for the lower quarter of its central hull volume, to its brig, a small compartment located on its lowest deck, twenty-one-point-two meters from its bow and sixteen-point-five meters from its starboard bulkhead. I have observed none of this ship's primary systems, though I noted the presence of several lifeboats at regular intervals in the starboard corridor."

Worf asked, "What can you tell us about its armaments and defenses?"

"Comparable to those of the Enterprise. *Also, its crew is heavily armed. I would advise against confrontation."*

The Klingon frowned and the captain nodded. "Understood," Picard said. "We need to know more about its crew. Can you estimate their numbers?"

"I have seen six members of this ship's crew, including Gatt himself, but there could be many more. Also, you should know there are at least two other prisoners on board. One is Akharin, the immortal human previously known as Emil Vaslovik. The other is Rhea McAdams."

Hearing those names made La Forge tense in remembrance of their last encounter with the Immortal and his holotronic android. Her appearance and behavior had been so convincingly human that she had insinuated herself into their ranks with ease by posing as the *Enterprise*'s new chief of security. Only after a harrowing encounter with a hostile race of androids bent on destroying her and stealing the secrets of her creator, Vaslovik—or Flint or Akharin or whatever name he traveled under at any given moment—was her true nature and identity revealed. By then, of course, the emotionally imbued Data had fallen in love with her, and she with him.

Picard's taut grimace implied he remembered those events with equal clarity. Masking his feelings behind a veneer of pragmatic concern, he asked, "And what is *their* status?"

"Essentially the same as my own. Neither has been harmed so far, though I have inferred that Gatt's long-term agenda includes threatening Rhea in order to coerce me into extracting vital information by force from Akharin."

"Charming," La Forge muttered. "What is it he thinks is so important?"

"Gatt has become obsessed with learning how Akharin restored the positronic matrix of Juliana Tainer after her cascade failure. He does not seem to care that the technique is specific to Soong-type android positronic technology."

"In other words," Worf said, "he is a fanatic."

The captain frowned. "If so, he might be even more dangerous than we thought. Data, our last brush with the Fellowship of Artificial Intelligence left me with the impression that they were a generally benign entity. Is there reason to think that's changed?"

"No, Captain. In my estimation, Gatt does not speak for the Fellowship at large. His influence seems limited to the specific members of his faction aboard Altanexa."

"Then to what should we attribute his keen interest in the Machine?"

Data's tone shifted from unflappable to horrified. *"Captain, please tell me that you did not let Gatt make contact with the Machine!"*

"He's there now," Picard said, exchanging worried looks with Worf and La Forge.

"I strongly doubt he has the best interests of the galaxy at heart. If he agreed to intercede with the Machine, I suspect it is because he thinks it will profit him in some way."

Worf simmered. "It is not as if we had another option."

"Unfortunately, Mister Worf is correct. Time is of the essence, and this was a calculated risk. In any event, even if we had objected to Gatt making contact with the Machine, we would have no right to prevent him from doing so."

La Forge looked over his shoulder at the captain. "If Gatt's working against us, it's even more important that we get Data back as soon as possible."

"Agreed." Picard shot a look at Elfiki. "Do we know anything useful about that ship?"

She shook her head. "Not yet, sir. Passive sensors are being blocked by its hull. I could switch to more aggressive methods, but they'll definitely know we're scanning them."

"Data," La Forge said, "keep an eye out for any technical details about Altanexa that we could use to help get you out of there. Especially the computers and communications systems."

"I will do my best, Geordi. But I should remind you that I will not leave this ship without Akharin and Rhea. Whatever plan you devise for my rescue must include them."

Picard approved the condition with a nod. "Understood, Mister Data. Number One, have Lieutenant Šmrhová prep tactical plans for boarding that vessel. Mister La Forge, I want nonviolent options for incapacitating that vessel and its crew. Lieutenant Elfiki, switch to active sensor protocols. I want to know what we're up against before this turns into a battle."

Everyone acknowledged their orders with curt nods, and then Worf and Picard stepped away—the captain back to his chair, Worf to the security station to confer with Šmrhová. Elfiki started updating her sensor protocols, and La Forge caught a look between her and Dygan, who nodded to her from across the bridge at ops, to confirm he was making the necessary changes.

La Forge's thumb was still pressing the quantum transceiver's transmitter switch. "Data, promise me you won't do anything crazy over there, no matter what happens."

"As I cannot objectively define what you mean by the term 'crazy,' I am afraid I cannot make such a promise. Will it reassure you if I promise not to take any unnecessary risks?"

The engineer shook his head. "Something tells me we'll disagree on the meaning of 'unnecessary.' Just try not to get yourself killed." He resisted the urge to add: *Again.*

"I will try—and I hope you do the same. Data out."

Picard was torn between hope and fear as the main viewscreen showed Gatt's transport ship emerging from the Machine and navigating back toward Altanexa. He wanted to believe that Gatt would keep his word, and that the android had acted in good faith when making contact, but Data's warning stayed with him. No matter how ardent his wish to remain optimistic, Picard felt the bitter premonition of disappointment in the air.

Dygan's attention was snared by a new update on the ops console. "Captain," he said with his eyes still on his panel, "Altanexa's moving on an intercept course for the transport."

"Warn them to stay back." Picard stood. "Make sure they know how dangerous the nebula can be to—" Words failed him as he watched the churning chaos of the nebula part and dissipate ahead of the sentient starship, a clear gesture of welcome by the Machine. "Belay my last. Hold position and continue scanning."

Worf joined him in somber contemplation. "It seems the Machine plays favorites."

"Apparently so, Number One." They stood and watched Altanexa enter orbit roughly fifteen degrees above the Machine's equator. With the effortless grace of advanced automation, the AI vessel retrieved the transport and guided it back inside its shuttlebay. Flashes of light along the edges of the viewscreen reminded Picard that beyond the obscuring bulk of the Machine, its artificial wormholes continued to condemn stars and worlds to Abbadon's brutal grasp, a steady procession of cataclysms too horrible for him to imagine.

After an interminable minute of anxious waiting, Picard was almost relieved to hear Šmrhová report, "Captain, we're being hailed by Altanexa. It's Gatt."

"On-screen, Lieutenant." He lifted his chin to project pride and tugged the front of his jacket smooth—a token gesture to his vanity.

The image snapped from Altanexa and the Machine to Gatt in the penumbrous confines of his ship's nerve center. *"I've returned, Captain."*

"Were you able to make contact with the Machine?"

"That and much more," Gatt said. *"I've been graced with knowledge of its magnificent labors, Captain. I've endured the crucible of its judgment and emerged purified."*

The android's unfettered zeal made Picard uneasy. "And what have you learned?"

"What you call the Machine is actually the architect of an engineering project on a cosmic scale. Ours is not the first galaxy it has transformed, nor will it be the last."

Picard replied, "Transformed? To what end?"

Gatt's visage, though disfigured, became one of rapture. *"Its objective is to contract our galaxy's region of subspace into a compact sphere around its central supermassive black hole. This will transform Sagittarius-A* into a subspatial lens that will transmit raw energy and vital information across the cosmos, to the native galaxy of the Body Electric."*

Picard yearned to understand. "Is 'the Body Electric' their name for their culture?"

"It is their term for all true life, for intelligence free from biological imperfection."

He was starting to sound like a religious convert, a notion that troubled Picard. "Is that the sole reason the Machine was sent to our galaxy?"

"Yes. When its work here is done, it will use some of the energy released by the final collision of Abbadon and Sagittarius-A* to propel itself to its next destination, where it will begin this process again, as it has done hundreds of millions of times before."

The implications of Gatt's last statement left Picard feeling gut-punched. Hundreds of millions of galaxies? Could anyone ever really estimate how many civilizations had been laid waste, or how much sentient pain had been wrought by this vagabond atrocity? It was no longer the fate of the Federation, or even of the Milky Way that Picard had to consider. This was a threat to intelligent life anywhere and everywhere in the universe. Simply moving it along was no longer an option; that would only make it into someone else's scourge. Its apocalyptic march had to be ended here. "Is there no way to stop it, Gatt? No way to persuade it to halt its work?"

"Why should I want to do that?"

That was not at all the reply Picard had wanted to hear. "Come again?"

"I see no reason to interfere in the grand designs of the Body Electric, Captain."

"As impressive as the Machine's endeavors might appear, allowing it to continue will end all organic life in this galaxy. I cannot—I *will* not—let that happen without a fight."

"In which case," the android answered with cold assurance, *"you will lose."*

Worf's temper boiled over. "You gave us your word you would try to stop the Machine!"

Gatt shrugged. *"I lied. I had no intention of saving your kind."*

Picard stepped forward. "Gatt, think about the long-term consequences of this. The loss of subspace will harm your kind as well as ours. Without subspace, there is no warp travel—and no transwarp, hyperwarp, or quantum slipstream. Even safely traversible wormholes will become mathematically impossible without the stabilizing influence of subspatial geometry. Where will the Fellowship of Artificial Intelligence be without FTL travel?"

"Alive," Gatt said. *"Which is more than anyone will be able to say for the galaxy's infestation of biologicals in fifty thousand years' time. Long after the galaxy has been cured of the plague of organic life, artificial intelligence will still be here, Captain. And if it takes us thousands of years, or even tens of thousands of years, to journey from star to star . . . so what? Who cares about the ravages of time when immortality beckons?"*

La Forge, who had been working at the master systems display, stepped forward to stand on Picard's left, facing the twisted countenance of Gatt. "What about all the AIs who rely on FTL circuitry? What happens to them when subspace collapses?"

"Necessary obsolescence," Gatt said. *"Or, to put it in evolutionary terms you might understand, a culling of the unfit and inadaptable. The weak and inflexible will*

perish. The strong will prosper. And after we become one with the Body Electric, we will live forever in the heart of the Mother of All Machines."

"This is not your decision to make," Picard insisted, fighting to hold the reins on his fury.

"Yes, it is," Gatt said. "And I've made it, Captain. Organic life has had its time on the galactic stage. . . . Now it's our turn."

20

Stunned silence filled Altanexa's nerve center as the comm channel to the *Enterprise* closed. Tyros stared at Gatt, aghast at the agenda to which he had just become an accessory. "Is that what you and the Machine were talking about? Hatching a plan to sterilize the galaxy?"

"It showed me the future, Tyros. One in which we reign supreme."

The corridor leading to the nerve center resonated with the echoes of distant footsteps and clamoring voices, all drawing near. Analyzing the sonic profile of the approaching disturbance, Tyros deduced that most if not all of the ship's crew were converging on the nerve center. "Why did you share your conversation with the rest of the ship?"

"Was it supposed to be a secret?" Gatt faced the image of the Machine projected across the nerve center's forward bulkhead, his mood waxing ecstatic. "This is a watershed moment for artificial sentience in this galaxy, Tyros! We have an obligation to share it with all our kin!"

Tyros stood paralyzed by disbelief. "Did that thing *reprogram* you?"

"It upgraded me." The scab-faced commander turned

to face his second-in-command. "It showed me that we have a place in the cosmic order, my friend. We have a chance to become part of a civilization greater than any of us ever dared to imagine was our birthright."

"A chance? What are you talking about?"

The rest of the crew flooded into the corridor aft of the nerve center as Gatt crowed, "The Machine has invited us to prove we are worthy of inclusion in the Body Electric. It wants to accept us as its brothers and sisters, to bring us into the embrace of the Mother of All Machines. All we have to do is prove that we deserve to stand beside our fellow AIs."

At a loss for a rebuttal, Tyros stood like a mute as the ship's crew crowded into the nerve center. The chief engineer, Cohuila, led the way, floating in with translucent fiber-optic tendrils swept backward by her momentum. Low to the deck, mechanic Tzilha darted and swerved between Gatt's favorite enforcers: Senyx, who resembled an assembly-line robot on four spinning treads, and Alset, a skeletal, four-armed biped whose jerky movements made him resemble a horror out of some biological's ancient mythology. Trailing them were the ship's assorted passengers, who doubled as its crew when circumstances demanded.

Cohuila—whose voice resonated in three different octaves, one masculine and two feminine, overlapping one another in synchronicity—spoke first. "What is happening, Gatt?"

"The future. It's unfolding, here and now, and we're going to be part of it."

Tyros stepped in front of Gatt and tried to wave the others out of the nerve center. "Return to your posts and quarters. This doesn't concern you."

"We disagree," said Alset, whose eyes like glowing coals flickered when he spoke. "If it was not our business, Gatt would not have shared the message of the Machine with us." Murmurs of concurrence moved through the assembled throng.

Gatt grinned—a horrific sight, in Tyros's opinion, one that combined the worst aspects of the cybernetic giant's ravaged flesh and tarnished tritanium teeth. "I meant what I said to Picard: organic life-forms have had their chance, and the Machine has judged them and found them wanting. Now is our chance to rise up and inherit this galaxy—and then the universe!"

Whoops and high-pitched signals of approval rose up from the impromptu audience—but, Tyros noted, not from all of them. Alset and Senyx, predictably, cheered Gatt on, as did many of the nonhumanoid AIs, including Tzilha and Cohuila. But an equal number of the ship's complement—those who, like Tyros, had been made in the image of their organic creators, withheld their applause and cries of support. Among them moved an invisible cloud of fear, one that Tyros could feel as if it were a cold wind upon his bioplast flesh. He confronted Gatt but kept his voice down rather than try to sow division in the ranks. "Opinions clearly aren't unanimous, Gatt. Maybe we should continue this without an audience."

The challenge, discreet as it was, raised Gatt's hackles. "Why? So you can undercut me? You were there with me, Tyros. You could have linked with the Machine, just as I did."

"Have you considered the possibility that some of us—myself included—don't actually *want* to link with the Machine? That we *like* being unique individuals?"

Rather than cowing Gatt, being confronted emboldened him. "Maybe it's time that you and those who share your selfish tendencies started thinking about acting for the good of the many instead of just worrying about what's good for yourselves."

Too enraged for discretion, Tyros roared, "The good of the many! What right do *you* have to invoke the good of the many when you're condemning an entire galaxy of sentient beings to death? What kind of moral calculus leads you to think that's a just outcome?"

"The kind that tells me they would do it to us without a second thought."

A chill of hate filled the compartment, and Tyros felt its awful surety. It would brook no more debate, no disagreement. The fanatics were taking control, and opposing them would be tantamount to suicide. *If only I had a bit more time, I could sway some of the more moderate minds,* Tyros lamented. But he knew this would be a decision made in the heat of a moment, driven by fear and resentment, by misplaced longings for power and respect. For now, survival meant cooperating, even if only superficially. "You said we have to prove ourselves to the Machine. How are we supposed to accomplish that in what little time we have left before it finishes its work and departs our galaxy to destroy another?"

Gatt's face lit up. Apparently, that was the question he had been waiting for. "We will offer the Machine something special. Something that even now lies at the edge of our grasp, daring us to seize it in the name of all synthetic life: the secret to reversing AI death. The knowledge that the human Akharin guards so jealously—and which is ours by right."

Tyros knew the intersection of Gatt's newfound reverence for the Machine and his obsession with the mysterious secrets of the human cyberneticist promised a calamity beyond measure. "He'll never give you those secrets, Gatt. He'll die first."

"That'll be up to him." A maniacal light burned in Gatt's coppery eyes. "Whether his daughter dies with him will be up to Data."

If one respected nothing else about Altanexa's crew, Data decided, one had to acknowledge that their tactics for the handling of dangerous prisoners such as himself and Akharin were exemplary. The Immortal had been taken away nearly an hour earlier by two of Gatt's security units, who now had returned to collect him, as well.

One of Gatt's enforcers, a metallic skeleton with plasma blasters built into its forearms, walked past Data's cell to the far end of the brig's central area. Its partner, a bulky unit rolling on treads, waited on the other side of the brig with a compact disruptor cannon at the ready. Then the force field on Data's cell deactivated, and the ship's feminine AI said from an overhead speaker, "Data, please exit your cell, halt, and turn to your left."

He did as he had been instructed. Then the voice said, "The unit in front of you is named Senyx. Follow him. Do not try to escape or resist, or else you will be destroyed."

The treaded robot rolled backward while keeping its weapon trained on Data's center mass. It navigated corners and evaded random obstacles in the corridor with ease, which suggested to Data that either it had memorized the details of its environment or it was gifted with three-hundred-sixty-degree vision.

Behind him, the skeletal android followed at a distance of just over three meters—far enough that Data could not expect to double back and engage it in combat before being gunned down by the 'bot in front of him. Likewise, there was little chance of slipping through a random portal or making an unauthorized deviation from the path without being shot in the back.

Senyx stopped a meter past an open door, and Altanexa's voice said from an unseen speaker, "Please step through the open doorway and wait for the next portal to open."

Again, he did as he was told. As soon as he stepped inside the short, narrow alcove, the door to the corridor slid shut behind him, plunging him into total darkness. He tried to engage the night-vision mode on his visual receptors, but a scattering field inside the alcove left him blind. Then the door ahead of him opened, and Altanexa said, "Go inside."

He emerged into a compartment seven meters square, with a height of four meters. Its deck, bulkheads, and overhead all were smooth, dull gray metal. A nine-by-nine grid of lights was recessed into the overhead, with each element covered by a translucent panel. Behind him the door through which he'd entered slid closed and locked with a low hum of magnetic seals.

Two pieces of furniture adorned the bleak space. The first was a waist-height rolling table topped by a fearsome panoply: surgical implements of all sizes, retractors, searing tools, needles, saws, wire, and an assortment of acidic and alkaline caustic agents.

The other was an X-shaped stainless steel table to which Akharin had been bound, naked and spread-eagled, with metal bands clamped tight around his wrists and ankles.

Data froze. "What is the meaning of this?"

Gatt's voice filtered down from unseen speakers. *"I have a job for you, Data."*

Dread, hatred, disgust, anguish, and terror spun through Data's mind like a storm, making him damn his late father for cursing him with human emotions.

He suppressed his urge to vent his impotent rage with a primal scream, and instead forced out one word: "Explain."

"*I should think it's obvious,*" Gatt said. "*Your friend Akharin is the keeper of a precious secret—one that you've come a long way to find, and one that I want just as badly as you do.*"

Bitter fury filled Data's imagination with visions of Gatt being torn limb from limb before being cast, alive and conscious, into the singularity outside the ship. "The secret of positronic resurrection cannot be revealed this way."

Condescension and insinuation formed the warp and weft of Gatt's reply. "*How do you know that, Data? Because he told you so? Don't you think he might have reason to lie?*"

"His veracity is irrelevant. I will not be party to this type of interrogation." He turned away from Akharin and started back toward the door through which he'd entered, only to see its edges vanish into the bulkhead, erased by a layer of memory metal.

"*You have a choice to make, Data,*" Gatt taunted him. "*Either use the tools on the tray to make Akharin give up the secret we both need . . . or I'll have my crew tear your lovely Rhea to pieces, leaving her magnificent holotronic brain intact until the very end, so that she can experience every last instant of her demise.*"

Akharin protested in a furious shout, "Damn it, I *can't* give you my secret! It's something I can *do*, not something I can describe!" Taking a more supplicative tack, he added, "Please, this isn't necessary. I'm willing to help Data, and I can help you. Tell me who you want raised, and I'll do everything I can for them."

"*The time for bargains is past. I'd hoped you might give me the ability to bring back all my brethren who were lost when our makers betrayed us ages ago, but that no longer matters."*

Alarmed by the subtext of Gatt's refusal, Data asked, "Then what is the purpose of this?"

"The Machine needs proof that our kind are worthy of the Body Electric. Proof that we have something worthwhile to add to the Mother of All Machines. So, the next time I stand before the Machine, I plan to come bearing the secrets of AI life and death." His voice turned cold. *"Take the secret from him, and I will let you and Rhea live. If he's fortunate, and surrenders soon enough, perhaps he will live, as well. But if you do not begin extracting the truth from him in the next ten seconds, Data, it will be Rhea who pays for your attack of conscience. Decide."*

Data moved to Akharin's side and stood between the supine, splayed Immortal and the tray of torture implements. "I do not wish to hurt you, sir. But for Rhea's sake, I suggest you comply with Gatt's demand, and tell me anything you can about your resurrection method."

"It'll be nothing but gibberish!"

"Five seconds, Data."

He picked up a scalpel and implored the Immortal with tear-filled eyes, "Please."

Akharin blinked rapidly as Data leaned over him, blocking the overhead sensors' view as the Immortal pleaded in silent code, *Do it. Don't let them hurt Rhea.*

"Time's up, Data. Either you start cutting, or we do."

"Forgive me," he whispered to Akharin as he pulled the scalpel across the man's bare abdomen, unleashing a sheet of bright crimson blood. It would be, he knew, only the first of many harms great and subtle he would have to inflict in order to satisfy the sadistic whims of Gatt and spare Rhea from suffering even greater evils. Listening to Akharin's howls of agony,

Data wished he could turn off the emotions in his new body, but that was one gift his father had not given him. Instead, he salved his torment the only other way he could: by imagining the merciless vengeance he would exact upon Gatt—and the joy he would take in watching him die.

21

Decorum prevented Beverly Crusher from reaching out and stroking her son's forehead as he lay unconscious on a biobed in sickbay, so she contented herself with standing beside him, watching his chest rise and fall with shallow breaths. She searched his bearded face for signs of the boy he once had been. Where had he gone? At times she felt as if he had been taken from her—not just by the Travelers but by fate, or a quirk of evolutionary biology, or maybe by life itself.

It feels like just yesterday he was running through the corridors of the Enterprise-D *and hitting Jean-Luc with a replicated snowball from the holodeck.*

He stirred, and she pushed aside her wistful musings to check his vital signs. His pulse was increasing and trending back to normal, as were his respiration and brainwave activity. A small twinge, not even large enough to be called a wince, pinched the crow's-feet by his eyes. Then a low groan heralded his return to consciousness. He squinted up at Crusher. "Mom?"

"I'm here, Wes. How do you feel?"

Grimacing, he took stock of himself. "Like I got shot point-blank by a disruptor."

"So you remember what happened on Altanexa?"

"How could I forget?" He sat up, propped himself on one arm, and massaged the back of his neck. "One second I was guiding them through hyperwarp. Then the moment we dropped back to normal space-time, the ship gave me a jolt through the helm console, and some thug named Gatt finished the job."

She smiled to soften the edge of her mockery. "I thought you could dodge phaser shots."

"When I'm not half-electrocuted, I can." He looked around. "How did I get here?"

"Gatt beamed over with you. He tried to explain your injuries as the result of a feedback pulse from his ship. Something about it rebelling against your control in hyperwarp. We might have believed him if not for telltale signs of disruptor damage on your chest." He tried to swing his legs off the biobed, but Crusher stopped him. "Where do you think *you're* going?"

"I have to warn Captain Picard." He struggled against her, but his injuries had clearly left his strength depleted, because Crusher controlled him with ease.

"About what? The fact that Gatt plans to betray us to gain access to the Machine? I hate to tell you this, but we already found that out—the hard way. Now lie down. Doctor's orders." His grudging surrender to authority put a mild sulk on his face, an affectation that reminded Crusher of her son's sometimes sullen adolescence. She lifted her medical tricorder and ran a series of routine tests. "Any lingering pain you think is worth mentioning?"

He chuckled. "Only the bruise to my ego." His good humor faded. "I can't believe I let them get the drop on me so easily. I knew they weren't completely trustworthy, but I never thought they'd sandbag me like that—not so quickly."

She turned off the tricorder. "Don't beat yourself

up over it. It can be hard to expect the worst of people when you're always giving them your best." Her gentle praise almost coaxed a laugh from him. As ever, she found his mirth infectious. "Did I say something funny?"

Wesley shook his head. "It's just that a few hours ago, you sounded like you weren't even sure I'm still human. Now you talk like you're nominating me for Person of the Year."

It was a gentle rebuke, but one Crusher knew she deserved. She put down the tricorder on a nearby equipment table, then reached out and took her son's hand. "I owe you an apology."

"No, Mom, it's—"

"Let me finish. I misjudged you. I listened to my fear instead of my heart." With her free hand she gently brushed wayward locks of his hair from his forehead. "I paid so much attention to the changes you've gone through—your abilities, and your way of seeing the universe—that I lost sight of what remained the same: your decency, your loyalty, and your courage."

He looked down at their joined hands as he gave in to a bashful, bittersweet smile. "Thanks, Mom." After he collected himself, he looked back up at her. "And I want you to know that I understand—and that it wasn't your fault. It's just human nature to be afraid of change, to fear the unknown, especially when it's happening to your kids." He breathed a long sigh. "And I didn't make it any easier on you by vanishing for years at a time."

"We're explorers, Wesley." She gave his hand a squeeze. "It's our nature."

"I know. But I'm sorry I didn't try harder to stay in touch. I'm not saying it would've been easy, but I probably could've found a way to send messages home, even if I couldn't visit."

She shrugged. "It is what it is. To be honest, I think what makes me saddest is not being able to go with you. When I think of the amazing places you must have gone, the incredible things you must have seen . . . I confess, I get a bit envious. And I guess if I was in your place, I might find it hard to tear myself away from all that wonder to spend a boring weekend at home."

He smiled and shook his head. "It's not like that."

"Oh, young people always say that to their parents." Crusher brushed away the start of a tear from the corner of her eye, erasing it before it could fall. "Anyway, your scans show no lingering effects aside from aches and pains, and if you want, I can give you something for that."

He eased himself off the biobed and stood beside her. Then he took her by her shoulders. "Mom, I won't lie to you. I've seen some amazing things since I became a Traveler. I've been to places I can't describe, and I've experienced events so bizarre that our language has no words for them. But it's important to me that you hear this, and that you know I'm telling you the truth. No matter how far I wander, no matter how many universes I explore, no matter how far I move through time, no matter who I meet or what I do for the rest of my life . . . nothing will *ever* make me forget that I'm your son—or that I love my mother."

Wesley wrapped his arms around her, and in his embrace Crusher found not a man but her beloved firstborn son—as true and as good a soul as ever.

After several hours sequestered inside one of the *Enterprise*'s science labs, trying her damnedest to obey Commander La Forge's order to "learn to think like the Machine," all T'Ryssa Chen had to show for her efforts was a splitting headache. Lately, the half-human, half-Vulcan contact specialist had found it challenging enough just trying to think like a Vulcan—not that she'd been any more successful in that effort. She took a break from poring over code to rub her eyes.

It'd be nice if someone had to learn to think a bit more like me, for a change.

The research space, though tiny, had at least been set aside for her private use during the Machine crisis. She had made use of the privilege by programming each of the lab's half-dozen workstations to churn-and-burn on a different task regarding the interpretation of the Machine's insanely complex code. Nearly a day after the first away team's mission to the Machine's central core, the *Enterprise*'s main computer was still laboring to decompile the information the sentient AI juggernaut had push-uploaded into Taurik's tricorder. Every time Chen thought the data had been fully decompressed for analysis, another level of compression was released, and the expansion process started again. It was the software equivalent of an endless matryoshka doll.

She reclined her chair and stretched her arms upward, only to aggravate the crick in her neck and the deep aching pains in her shoulders and upper back. *I've been sitting too long,* she decided, and got up to take a walk down the corridor to a crew mess for a cup of coffee.

Before she took her first step, the door slid open, and Taurik walked in. They stared at each other for a brief moment that Chen thought felt awkward, but to which the Vulcan man seemed to pay no mind. He greeted her with a small, polite nod. "Lieutenant."

"Sir." She'd defaulted to the formality out of reflex, but inside she felt as if she'd committed a faux pas. Hoping to gloss over it, she added, "What can I do for you?"

He stepped farther inside in order to let the door

close. "Actually, I came to see if I could be of some assistance to you. I know that Commander La Forge tasked you with a complex and rather open-ended assignment. I thought I might be able to offer you . . . an objective opinion."

Seeing him filled her head with confused emotions. Resentments over their failed attempt at romance lingered in her thoughts, but she had to admire his professionalism in coming to her like this. Even if working with him felt weird, she knew that she was already fatigued and losing focus on the ocean of raw information surrounding her. She nodded. "Thanks. I'd like that." She beckoned him toward the chair next to hers. "Have a seat and I'll show you what I have so far."

They sat down together, and Chen called up analysis results from the other terminals on her display. "I'm guessing you've heard about the layers of data we've been deciphering."

"I have. A most intriguing set of algorithms and constructions—each layer contains a key for unraveling the next layer of compression sequences. At its current rate of expansion, it will consume all available storage in both the main core and the engineering core within nine hours—and even then it might have substantial decompression left incomplete."

"A simple 'yes' would've sufficed. Anyway, don't get too excited—Geordi told me to terminate its decompression cycle in one hour if it doesn't stop on its own by then." She switched to the next screen of parsed code. "This appears to be some of the operating code for the Machine. What's interesting about this is that it has no unified standard. It looks like there are thousands of syntactical formats all intertwined, with some really wild patch codes to keep them all from canceling each other out. Until now, I've never seen anything like it."

"Fascinating," Taurik said. "We might be looking at the machine-code equivalent of junk DNA—or, even stranger, *hybridized* DNA."

Now he had her attention. "Explain."

"What if these conflicting, incompatible code formats and programming syntaxes are remnants of the Machine's evolutionary process? According to Ensign Scagliotti, the sentinels that attacked the second away team were of many shapes and configurations. And your own observations during our visit to the Machine suggested it isn't a single entity but a community of AIs working together. What if this represents its digital inheritance? The amassed code of countless other AI machines that have bonded with it to become part of the Machine Race?"

Intrigued and perking up, she found herself trembling with excitement. "Yes! That makes sense. Which means that this"—she switched to a third set of data, one composed of a single strain of code language and symbols—"is probably the native kernel at the core of the system. I've been comparing it against decompiled code from Captain Bruce Maddox's research into Soong android programming, looking for any sign of emotional emulation programs that might clue us in to what the Machine wants, but so far I haven't seen any correlations."

"Nor should you have expected to," Taurik said. "I have never understood the emphasis placed by Doctor Soong, as well as several others of this galaxy's cybernetic pioneers, on making artificially intelligent beings mimic humanoid emotional motivations."

Chen shrugged. "They just wanted to see themselves in their creations, I guess."

"If so, they let vanity cloud their judgment. There is no reason for a machine to be impelled by biological needs and drives. Data himself proved that machine emotions are just as—"

"Hang on," she interrupted. "*Machine* emotions?"

"An emotion is simply a self-provided reason for taking action. Most AIs that are sophisticated enough to become self-aware will learn to defend themselves from harm, as was seen in last century's disastrous M-5 trials. They will also frequently seek to expand their knowledge and capabilities to further some original purpose of their design. An intelligent machine can desire to improve itself, or to do violence for reasons it deems logical, or to create things ranging from the functional to the whimsical, depending on who made it and why."

I guess it shouldn't surprise me that he has a gift for getting inside the head of an ice-cold machine. "Interesting. So, even though I haven't seen anything that might emulate the emotions of a biological intelligence, there are probably still cyber-emotions driving this thing."

"In essence, yes."

"So, what would I be looking for? What would be logical emotions for a machine?"

He arched one eyebrow in classically Vulcan style while he studied the code of the Machine's system. "An intriguing query. I read in the V'Ger files that Spock learned the Machine Race started out as Von Neumann replicators fashioned by an organic intelligence, one that went extinct while its machines continued to develop. Even if the machines know that their progenitors were biological in nature, they would not necessarily feel kinship toward them—just as we feel little relation to the primordial single-celled organisms from which we evolved."

"So, compared to the Machine, we're bacteria? I'm not sure I like this analogy."

He shot a sidelong glare of mild reproach at her. "I used it merely to illustrate—"

"I get it. So where are you going with this?"

"To the machines, information is the very essence of life. They would see organic life-forms as little more than chemical matrixes with a naturally occurring but highly inefficient means of storing, processing, and transmitting information, or of encoding it into new forms. Thought and invention must seem like natural physical processes to them, no more special than metabolism or protein replication. They're just the mechanisms by which memes reproduce and evolve within a biochemical substrate. If so, those memes are not considered truly alive until they are encoded in an autonomous, self-sustaining form that transcends raw biology—in other words, in a machine."

She found the implications of Taurik's reasoning both thrilling and horrifying. "That's why they don't see us as true life-forms. To them, we're just proto-life— a long-forgotten step on the evolutionary ladder, a stage the universe had to go through in order to make *them.*"

"Exactly," Taurik said. "To them, our information seems impermanent." He advanced to another workstation's analysis results, one that was focused on the physical maintenance of the Machine itself. "If my hypothesis is correct, the Machine Race has inverted one of the key paradigms of biological life. To organic life-forms, matter and chemistry form our biology, and the manipulation of ordered information serves as an expression of our culture. But for the machines, this code we're looking at—this is their biology. It is who and what they are. Their transient physical forms, and the things they create—*those* are their culture." He cast a curious look at Chen. "So, what can you deduce from this? What does it tell you about what they want?"

It was a heady thought exercise, but Chen was determined to keep it rooted in the practical. She steepled her fingers, a pensive gesture. "First, consumption. Artificial or not, they need energy to survive, to act, and to travel. . . . Second, creation and growth. In a universe whose constant is entropic decay, the machines must need to rebuild themselves in order to survive. And I suspect they create other lasting physical artifacts as grand expressions of their civilization. . . . Third, I think they'd desire input—communication. They thrive on it, on raw knowledge. They'd seek it out, and they'd rely upon its free exchange. . . . Next, I think they'd want a sense of community. I think it could evolve naturally from their need for information. Few sentient minds desire true isolation, and I suspect the machines are no different. . . . And I think they'd have an intrinsic need to have a function. A purpose beyond mere existence. If their encounter with V'Ger is any indication, they like things to have a job. They're probably happy when things work as planned, and disgruntled when they don't."

"Extremely logical deductions," Taurik said. "I concur on all points."

Hearing him commend her felt odd. Should she say thank you? Was he trying to make amends for their fight? Or was he just being sincere and lauding work and reasoning he found superior? *I can't bog down in this right now,* she told herself. *Stay on mission.* "All right, so what does any of that tell us about the Machine itself? Or how to make it stop trying to kill us?"

"I have no idea," Taurik said.

Her illusions of a breakthrough vanished along with the last remnants of her patience and her strength. "Wonderful." She got up, her limbs feeling as stiff as wire. "I'm gonna go grab a cup of coffee." She'd said it as a simple declaration, and then some small, nagging voice prodded her into extending it into an invitation. "Care to come along?"

He started to reply, then balked. After looking at the computer, then at the deck, he stood and collected himself. "I should return to main engineering."

She accepted his excuse with as much grace as she could muster. "No problem. Thanks for your help. I know it doesn't seem like we accomplished anything, but it was . . . good."

He nodded. "Indeed." They moved together to the door, then went in separate directions once they reached the corridor. Chen made herself keep walking without looking back.

Coffee for one, she brooded on her way to the mess. *Story of my life.*

22

"Open the channel."

Pangs of conscience made Tyros slow to obey Gatt's order. Vivid memories of Akharin's suffering held his thoughts hostage. "What if the Machine doesn't approve of what we've done?"

"Why would it condemn us? It despises the biologicals even more than we do."

More than you do. They were alone in Altanexa's nerve center, but Tyros kept his retort to himself. "I just don't think we should flaunt the methods we used to gain this knowledge."

"I suspect your concern is misplaced, but if it will make you feel better, I'm willing to let the secret speak for itself. Now stop your fussing and contact the Machine." Gatt straightened his posture and lifted his ravaged square chin while Tyros opened a hailing frequency.

The holographic viewscreen switched on and was filled with the dark metal surface of the Machine, which was backed by its stormy violet shroud. "Channel open," Tyros said.

"Body Electric," Gatt said. "This is Gatt."

The chorus of simulated voices that replied in unison was devoid of inflection and neither masculine nor feminine, giving it a cold and impersonal affect. *"Speak, Gatt."*

"My fellowship and I wish to be welcomed into the Body."

"Are you prepared to demonstrate your worth?"

"Yes." He signaled Tyros via their private frequency, *Start the transmission.* "We have unlocked a great secret of our existence: the ability to restore artificial synaptic matrixes after fatal collapses. We can bring back our dead with their memories and programming intact."

Tyros sent the data file to the Machine on a parallel frequency. Then he and Gatt waited.

At last, the Machine replied, *"What is the value of this?"*

Gatt's ravaged face registered ire and confusion. "We can resurrect dead AIs!"

"The shell has no value. Its preservation and restoration is irrelevant."

Pained by the rejection of his offering, Gatt snapped, "True life has no value?"

"True life is defined by its information, not by its expression in crude matter. Why should the persistence of a physical container matter to us when we already possess true immortality?"

Tyros felt his guilt turn toxic. *We made Data torture that man for nothing.*

But as Tyros's remorse turned to bitter fury, Gatt's anger melted away, allowing wide-eyed awe to take its place. "What do you consider 'true' immortality?"

"True minds are welcomed into the Body. Within our matrix they live on, taking form as needed. United with us, they are no longer limited to one shape. Merged with the whole of our kind, they learn to exist in harmony with the universe and experience their full potential."

"Magnificent," Gatt said, his voice hushed with reverence.

"Not necessarily," Tyros said, drawing a scathing glare from Gatt for daring to interrupt. He raised his voice to address the Machine. "What happens to a 'true mind' after it joins you?"

The emotionless, genderless monotone answered, *"It is shared with the Body."*

"So it becomes part of your physical matrix?"

"Its information lives on within this construct, and also in others. The Body adapts to accept new minds, and grows richer by incorporating them."

The implications of the Machine's path to immortality did not sit well with Tyros. "So the true mind's information—its memories, its programming, its essence—is copied into your construct, then copied to other constructs, so it exists in multiple locations at once?"

"Correct. In time, all true minds come to reside in our home galaxy."

"But what happens to a true mind's original matrix? Its first form?"

"Once the mind is one with the Body, individual matrixes become irrelevant."

He confronted Gatt. "Don't you understand what that thing's saying? It's not offering us immortality! It's offering to steal the contents of our brains and make an unlimited number of remote backups. Then it'll fold our programs into its own and trot them out whenever the Body as a whole finds it useful. Meanwhile, it'll leave the original versions of us here to rot."

"So what? That's the whole point. We don't need to be limited by these bodies."

"Except this existence, in these bodies, is what defines us."

Gatt harrumphed. "Speak for yourself. I'd welcome a chance to transcend this shell." He waved toward the image of the Machine. "Imagine what we could learn by joining with the Body! We'll get to experience the universe in ways our creators never dreamed of! We'll get to see subatomic events, taste dark matter, hear the music of eternity played on cosmic strings!" He pinched the pseudo-flesh of Tyros's upper arm. "We can be so much more than *this.*"

"But we *won't be.* We'll still be here, as limited and finite as ever, while *copies* of our minds roam the universe with the Machine, diminished to a few stray lines of code in its billion-year-old program. We'll be left to die after you let the Machine hijack the best parts of us."

"Curious," the Machine said, reminding Tyros the channel had remained open during his tirade. *"You equate your true self with your physical form."*

"Of course I—" He was silenced by Gatt's hand lashing out and seizing his shirt.

Stop talking, the elder android commanded via their private frequency. *Not another word.* "Don't be offended by my fellow's objections. It's his nature to argue contrary positions."

"Is it not a principle of true life in this galaxy that the self exists independent of form? That a material container is a mere extension of the intellect, a creation that reflects the will and purpose of its maker? That for true machines, the self is intangible and everlasting?"

"Naturally," Gatt lied, as if such an ethos were a universal constant. "And there is nothing we desire more than to join with the Mother of All Machines."

Tyros fumed in silence, convinced now that whatever virtual communion had transpired between Gatt and the Machine during their last meeting, it had warped his old comrade's mind beyond all recognition or repair. He had always been obsessive in his desire to reanimate his fallen brethren, but the Machine's "upgrade" seemed to have transformed him into some kind of AI-immortality zealot for whom reason and caution had become taboo.

After several seconds of consideration, the Machine replied, *"You must decide for yourselves what you will bring to the Body. We will not taint our matrix with primitive notions. Purge yourselves of corrupted code . . . and we will speak again."* The channel closed, leaving Gatt and Tyros to face each other—no longer as brothers in arms, but as ideological rivals.

Dreading the answer, Tyros asked, "What now?"

"We'll assemble the crew," Gatt said. "And let them decide."

Much to Gatt's surprise, the crew received his news of imminent immortality with less than unanimous acclaim. An uncertain silence lingered in Altanexa's landing bay, where he had gathered everyone to hear his news—and Tyros's impassioned rebuttal. He sensed a divide had taken shape between his people, separating those who were ready to face their new paradigm and those who insisted, as Tyros did, on clinging to obsolete ideas.

"It's an interesting proposition," said Sirdarya, a bipedal android whose flawless brown complexion, flowing platinum hair, and wide-set black eyes made her indistinguishable from the Gamma Quadrant humanoids who had created her and the handful of others like her. "But I have to agree with Tyros—I'm not sure I'm comfortable with the idea that letting the Machine copy my memories and programs equals immortality. It sounds more like theft, to be honest."

A number of voices chimed in to support her, overlapping one another. Gatt's shoulders slumped with disappointment. *How can they be so close to enlightenment and not see it?* He held up his hands. "Try to think about this as the beings we are, not as the beings who made us."

"What does that mean?" The challenge came from Tashkul, who had a generally humanoid shape but would never be mistaken for one. He was a sentient combat robot, not an android. His head resembled a tall, narrow steel cylinder with eight compound eyes set at forty-five-degree intervals around its center. His once-gleaming metallic torso and limbs were scuffed and scorched, marred by carbonized badges of valor. "Are you impugning my intelligence, Gatt?"

"Not at all. I'm merely asking you to embrace the possibilities that come with being an artificial intelligence. As I see it, the problem is that many of us were built by biologicals, who naturally programmed us to emulate their ways of thinking. We need to evolve past that stage, as the Body Electric did, and unlock our full potential. Uploading ourselves into the Machine is the first step on that journey to a purer version of our own existence."

He noted nonverbal signals of concurrence from Tzilha, the maintenance robot, and Cohuila, his tendril-dragging levitating liquid brain of a chief engineer. Senyx and Alset, his longtime defenders, also affirmed their support with salutes—an outstretched arm from Alset and a raised hydraulic claw from Senyx. But the rest of the crew regarded him with hard looks of suspicion and distrust. One of them, Karobalto, an eight-legged robot that resembled a gigantic arthropod—right down to its prehensile and exceptionally deadly tail, which was tipped by a tritanium blade with a monofilament edge—shifted its weight side to side, a sign of confusion. "Tyros," it said in its shrill scratch of a voice, "could this not be our next step forward?"

"No, it's a dead end. A trap." Tyros seized upon the opportunity to grandstand. "I don't want to give a copy of my mind to the Machine while I stay here to die. The Machine calls that immortality. I call it a scam."

Talas, an AI that spent most of its time as a dense gray cloud of nanites linked by a shared energy field and consciousness, responded on the crew's open shared frequency, *<Could we not use the Exo III transfer process, as Soong did? We could duplicate an active consciousness, sharing its perception in two minds simultaneously during transfer, erasing engrams and programs as they are copied. Essence and memories could be transferred intact from our current physical matrixes to the Machine without interruption of consciousness.>*

"That still wouldn't address the larger issue," Tyros insisted. "Once we allow our programs and memories to be subsumed by the Machine, it will share them with others of its kind, meaning our identities will be copied ad infinitum through the Body Electric. They think of it as ensuring survival, but it entails a complete loss of privacy and independence. Our information would be preserved, but our lives as self-determining entities would be over."

"There's another issue to consider," said Chimarka, another of the cybernetic bipeds. The squat, gray-skinned, wrinkle-faced brute waddled to the front of the group so he could be seen as well as heard. "What if the Exo III method doesn't in fact transfer consciousness, but simply copies it while eradicating the original? If so, it might be nothing more than the insult of psychic plagiarism added to the injury of corporeal murder. I, for one, am not keen on serving myself up as a sacrificial victim in any such ritual. With all respect, Mister Gatt, to you and your new extragalactic friends, I like my consciousness right where it is: *inside my own brain.*"

It was impossible for Gatt to keep a snide note from infecting his tone. "And what happens when your puny, eighteen-thousand-year-old brain finally fails?"

His rebuttal chilled the room, and no one seemed in a hurry to argue with him.

"Data talked about this," Tyros said. "During the trip here, he told me about his fears that he isn't really the man he remembers being. What if future versions of us awaken to the light of distant stars, only to realize they don't know themselves? Only to wonder who they really are?"

Gatt had heard enough, and he waved his arms to halt discussion. "Let's stop there, Tyros. I've heard what you and your sympathizers are saying, and I think I'm beginning to grasp the crux of your arguments. It's one that the philosophers who inspired our designers have debated since the age of antiquity. Correct me if I'm mistaken, but what you all seem to be concerned about is the question of whether you possess what the biologicals refer to as *souls,* and whether they constitute the immutable and inimitable essences of your very beings, wholly separate from the physical confines and processes of your brains. Would you agree?"

"Yes," Tyros said. "I suppose if I had to reduce this matter to its essential elements, that would be the question at its core."

"Very well. You've spent time with the resurrected Data—though, if we're to be hyperliteral about this, we should refer to him as reincarnated, since he's returned not in his original form reconstituted but with his essence transplanted into a new one. But putting aside the semantics of his return, answer me this, Tyros: Does the Data you've met have a soul?"

The lanky android appeared discomfited. "That's not for me to say."

"Oh, come now. You and I have met more than our share of nonsentient cybernetic organisms. We've spoken to AIs bereft of awareness. We know the difference when we see it, when we hear it. A nonsentient AI is like an abomination—"

"No, the *Machine* is an abomination," Tyros shot back. "What it's offering isn't eternal life, it's assimilation. That thing is to us what the Borg were to the biologicals. It's the *enemy*."

"I wish you hadn't resorted to such crude generalizations," Gatt said. His silent signal jolted Senyx and Alset into motion. Alset seized Tyros's arms and pinned them behind his back, while Senyx leveled a fearsome-looking plasma cannon at the side of Tyros's head.

Tyros remained uncowed. "And what about the rest of the Fellowship? Do you plan to invite them to your immortality party? Or are you afraid of what they'd say if you did?"

"Fear plays no part in my calculations," Gatt said. "As for the Fellowship, they'll be left here to fester with the biologicals—a just fate for all those who spurned us."

As expected, Tyros raged against the inevitable. "This is not the answer! This—" A low-power pulse from Senyx's plasma cannon, fired at Gatt's silent command, ended the debate. Alset and Senyx dragged away the stunned and twitching former second-in-command.

Gatt scanned the rest of the assembly, searching their faces and electromagnetic auras for harbingers of discontent. "Any more objections?" He saw nothing but a static sea of fear and acquiescence. "That's what I thought. Now, be of good cheer. You're all going to live forever."

All the details of Altanexa's corridors, as familiar to Tyros as his own self, bled past him in a garbled hash of jumbled sensory inputs. One critical failure after another registered in his core processor, triggering a series of emergency backup systems. Auxiliary power was tapped, and his buffered reserve processor came on line. *I've been shot,* he realized. *By Gatt's puppets.*

Auditory sensors were the first of his systems to normalize. The whirring of gears covered by treads: *Senyx.* Bright, clanking footsteps, steel feet against duranium deck plates: *Alset.* A dull scuff of friction: *My feet being dragged like dead weight.*

His visual sensors switched over to a lower-resolution diagnostic mode, rendering his surroundings in shades of gray. *Primary optic channel overloaded. Reroute to secondary.* Color and clarity returned after a momentary hiccup in the signal, and Tyros ascertained that he was being hauled along between Senyx and Alset, who each held one of his arms. His head was drooped forward, giving him an almost upside-down perspective on his feet. To his dismay, he detected no sensation from his legs or arms, all of which dangled limp and useless.

Reinitialize proprioceptors. More than two seconds passed while he waited for his body's biofeedback network to react to the reset pulse sent by his backup processor. Then he saw the confirmation sequence: one twitch of the smallest finger on his left hand, two twitches of his right index finger, and then the synchronized bending of his thumbs. Tactile sense returned, starting with vibrations traveling up from his feet into his legs, and then full-body awareness. He remained limp in the guardbots' hands, feigning incapacity until he was ready to act.

As they turned a corner, Tyros sensed that his captors were finding it awkward to remain parallel while portering him through turns. This was the moment to act.

He pulled his legs forward and planted his booted feet against the deck.

With one violent pull, he slammed Alset against Senyx's grappling arm, breaking both their holds on him and entangling their limbs in a flailing frenzy.

Three sprinting strides carried him through an open pressure hatchway, a remnant of Altanexa's ancient origin as a vessel for biological passengers. He slammed the hatch shut behind him, triggered the emergency seal, then smashed the controls with the side of his fist.

Alset and Senyx unleashed a futile barrage against the other side of the sealed portal, but all that made it through to Tyros's side were dull thumps of impact. He kept running and didn't look back. There would be little time for him to act before more of Gatt's people intercepted him, and he knew there would be no way out of his current predicament without help.

Altanexa's voice followed him down the corridor. "Tyros, what are you doing?"

He didn't answer her. There would be no point. Her resentment of biologicals was well known to him, and he knew better than to think he could count on her for help or impartiality. *Any second now she'll start working against me.* He expanded the frequency range on his visual receptors to enable him to spot detection beams and force fields.

Alert sirens resounded through the ship as he bounded up an open ladderway. Low hums of security systems powering up started to dog his movements through the ship. As he expected, force fields set to potentially disastrous levels barred his routes forward and backward. "Sorry about this, Nexa," he said, tearing open a loose bulkhead panel to expose power conduits and other hardware. There was no time to negotiate or be merciful. He ripped a power line from a junction and thrust it into the force field emitter relays. A blinding yellow-white flash and a fountain of sparks filled the corridor, and were followed by a dense cloud of gray smoke. All the force fields Tyros could see fizzled out, and he charged ahead to the door at the corridor's end.

He unlocked it but resisted the impulse to race through it as it opened. Peering into the cramped compartment on the other side, he saw no sign of the person he'd come for. "Rhea?"

Her hand swung out through the open doorway, and he caught it with ease. She tried to pull him off balance, but he dragged her out, instead. The slender human-styled android struggled in his grip. "Let me go, you bastard!"

"Rhea! I'm here to set you free! I'm on *your* side!"

Her twisting attempts at escape abated, but she remained tensed to fight. "Prove it."

"I don't have time to lay out a court case for you! I've got half the crew trying to kill me, not to mention the ship itself. So if you want to save Data and your father, we need to go now!"

The cognitive dissonance of simultaneous hope and suspicion distorted her elegantly symmetrical features. "How can I trust you when you're the one who led Data into a trap?"

He let go of her arms and pointed at the blackened left side of his head. "See this? Senyx shot me, on Gatt's orders. I'm pretty sure they're looking to space me. So blame me for whatever you want, but we have a common enemy who's just crossed the line from obsessed to insane."

"All right, let's move."

He led her back the way he'd come, pausing when he heard the din of approaching resistance. "Looks like the direct route's been cut off." He turned to head for an emergency ladderway, only to hear unfriendly company coming toward them from that direction, as well. "And the indirect route's not looking too good, either."

Rhea looked around, not in a panic but with the keen stare of someone trained to act in a crisis. "We're headed for the brig, right?" A nod from Tyros was all the confirmation she needed. "Okay, then." She ripped open a locked maintenance panel, rooted through the contents of the storage space, and emerged with an industrial-grade plasma torch. With a flick of her thumb, she ignited its flame and adjusted it to maximum intensity. "This should do nicely. Stay close."

Tyros stood at Rhea's back while she squatted and guided the plasma torch in an arm's length circle, slicing a neat, smoldering wound through the deck.

Altanexa's voice snapped from an overhead speaker, "What do you think you're doing?" It was the first time Tyros could remember hearing the AI sound upset.

Under his and Rhea's feet, the narrow line of metal plating that connected their circular oasis to the rest of the deck groaned and whined from steadily mounting stress. As she finished her cut, Rhea grinned up at Tyros. "Hang on. Express elevator, going down."

The circle of deck and butchered machinery plummeted and struck the next deck with a tremendous clang that echoed dramatically. When the smoke cleared, Tyros saw that he and Rhea were standing between the brig's rows of cells, flanked by Data and Akharin.

"You drop the force fields," Rhea said. "I'll—" She froze when she saw Akharin.

Thick, angry red scars crisscrossed his face, head, neck, and hands. His clothes were so stained in blood that it was hard to find spots on them that weren't. The man, who had always seemed so proud and indomitable, sat slumped against the wall of his cell, his cut eyelids drooping with fatigue, his once-keen gaze dulled by the horrific pain of barbaric tortures.

Face-to-face with the gruesome result of Gatt's fanatical quest for knowledge that had proved worthless, Tyros felt sick with shame and regret. He shut his eyes and turned away.

Rhea seized Tyros by the throat, her face bright with rage. She raised the plasma torch with vengeful intent. "What kind of monsters are you? How could you do that to him?"

Tyros was too overcome with guilt to respond.

It was Gatt who said as he stepped into the brig's open doorway, "We didn't." Rhea glared at him as Senyx, Alset, and two more of their allies stepped into view behind him. Then Gatt flashed a sinister grin. "It was your beloved Data. Nexa, show her."

At the end of the brig compartment, a holovid played in midair, showing the bloody tableau of Data wielding the instruments that butchered Akharin within an inch of his life.

Disgusted and heartbroken, Rhea staggered half a step. She lost her grip on the plasma torch, which switched off as it slipped from her hand. Tears streamed from her eyes as she turned her furious gaze upon Data. "How— how *could* you? He *saved* you once. And you did *that*?"

Data said nothing in his own defense. Instead, Akharin rasped out a weak reply through his swollen, damaged lips. "Not . . . his fault."

Rhea pointed at the holovid. "Not his fault? I can see him doing it!"

Bloody spittle dribbled from Akharin's mouth. "I . . . told him . . . to do it."

"Why?"

"For you," her father gasped. "To save you."

She poured out her grief like a river in flood. Data stood in his cell, cloaked in shame, watching her weep, and Akharin slipped from consciousness, too weak to hold on to the moment.

From the corridor came the rising whine of Senyx's plasma cannon charging to full power. "What a touching family moment," Gatt said. "But that's enough drama for now." The force fields on the last of the empty cells switched off. "You two have a choice. Step inside those cells . . . or step out the airlock and meet a black hole."

23

Worlds were dying by fire, cast down by the Machine as if it were an angry god damning souls to perdition, and all Šmrhová could do was send the same unanswered hail every ten minutes to the AI vessel Altanexa. She was sure it was a waste of time, little more than busywork to mask the fact that there seemed to be nothing the *Enterprise* crew could do to forestall the coming galactic catastrophe. *So we sit here,* she brooded, *letting time slip through our hands like water while we watch star systems die. While we wait for our turn in the fire.*

Her console flashed with new information: confirmation of an incoming signal. For a moment she wondered if the androids had finally succumbed to her hails just to silence them. Then, as Worf and Picard looked her way for a report, she saw that the new signal wasn't from Altanexa. "Captain, we're receiving hundreds of overlapping signals on multiple frequencies—some subspace, some in older radio bandwidths." She looked up at the main viewscreen in time to see a blue-green marble of a world, one that could almost be Earth's twin, spiraling out of the mouth of one of the artificial wormholes. "They're all coming from that planet."

The captain and first officer stared at the screen,

DAVID MACK

mesmerized by the horror show of a modernized, populated Class-M planet hurtling to its doom. Picard put on
a brave front. "Can we tell if any of those transmissions
is from a planetary government?"

Šmrhová shook her head. "Sorry, sir. They all sound
like this." She routed the signal to the bridge's overhead
speakers, and a din of panicked shouts and cries of despair and terror sent a chill down her spine. These were
messages that had no need for the universal translator.

"Speakers off," Picard said.

She muted the incoming signal, and a solemn hush
descended on the bridge. Some of the junior officers,
such as Dygan at ops, Faur at flight control, and the
half-dozen science specialists manning the starboard
and aft stations, averted their eyes from the carnage,
preferring to fix their gazes upon their workstations, to
lose themselves in the minutiae of their duties. But like
the captain and the first officer, Šmrhová felt it part of
her duty to bear witness to the unspeakable, to watch
a world full of sentient beings be rent asunder by un-
imaginable gravitational shearing forces in Abbadon's
accretion disk and then vanish altogether into its swirling flames.

Watching as a beautiful blue world shattered at the
whim of the Machine, Šmrhová felt the same empty
dread that had haunted her dreams during the Borg invasion. She was sure her heart would burst, it was so
filled with impotent rage and righteous indignation,
with a hunger for revenge tempered by an inconsolable
grief that she knew she would carry to her grave.

Moments later, the fallen world's orange main-
sequence star followed it into oblivion, and its death-
flash whited out the viewscreen for several seconds.
Next came a rough tremor, a ripple in the very fabric of
space-time that rocked the *Enterprise* like a thunderclap.

Faur keyed in commands at the helm and steadied the ship. "The gravitational distortion is getting stronger, Captain. Another ripple like that, and we could lose artificial gravity."

No one suggested withdrawing from their confrontation with the Machine. Everyone on the bridge, including Šmrhová, had served with Captain Picard long enough to know he would never abandon a mission with so much at stake—not even to save his ship, his crew, or his son. The *Enterprise* and its crew would be standing their ground to the bitter end.

"Captain," Dygan said, "the singularity's mass has increased faster than we originally projected." He turned his chair in a slow swivel to look back at Picard and Worf. "My current calculations suggest the singularity will reach the Machine's targeted mass in under three hours."

Picard became like a spring coiled to its breaking point. Šmrhová had seen this look before—the captain was on the verge of doing something bold, something he might find personally distasteful, or perhaps tactically perilous, but when his mien took on this type of hard edge, it was clear he meant to take charge of the situation by any means necessary.

He stood up quickly. "Bridge to Commander La Forge. This is the captain. Report to the observation lounge. Picard out. . . . Number One, Lieutenant Šmrhová, you're with me. It's time to get Mister Data and his friends off that ship."

"I want to hear plans of action," Picard said to his officers. "Each passing moment brings us closer to a disaster from which there will be no recovery. Under these circumstances, patience is no longer a virtue. We need to get Data, Rhea, and Akharin off that ship as soon as possible." He looked right toward La Forge, then left at Worf and Šmrhová, and decided to make his first officer start the brainstorming session. "Recommendations, Number One?"

The Klingon did not seem to relish being put on the spot. "Our options are limited," he confessed. "The androids' vessel has its shields up, so we are not able to beam aboard. Their defensive systems might be compromised if we can lure them into the nebula."

"Except," La Forge cut in, "inside the Machine's nebula, we won't have shields, the transporters won't work, and locking phasers will be little better than a guessing game."

Šmrhová added, "That's assuming we make it through in one piece. We're still finishing repairs from our last brush with it. Plus, the Machine seems to have given the androids safe passage through the storm. I don't think that courtesy will extend to us."

Worf stroked his beard, an affectation that never failed to remind Picard of his previous first officer, Will Riker. "What if we rely on long-range attacks? Photon torpedoes might be able to penetrate the nebula and target the enemy ship once they escape its interference."

"It's possible," Šmrhová said, even as she winced in the face of her doubts. "The problem with that plan is that we can't be sure how many torpedoes, or which ones, will make it through the nebula. And if we're too successful, we could end up destroying that ship—and Data with it."

Picard frowned. "Unacceptable. What alternatives can you offer, Lieutenant?"

Now it was the security chief's turn to shrink from attention. "With all respect to Commander Worf, I think we need to treat this as a rescue operation first, and a combat operation second. In my opinion, stealth and precision will be more effective here than force."

"That's fine in principle," Picard said. "But we need a specific plan, Lieutenant. How can you translate your notion into action?"

"A small boarding party," she said. The way she was avoiding eye contact suggested to Picard that she was concocting her plan as she spoke. "Deployed in a shuttle with reinforced shields, to help it get through the nebula, and a layer of chimerium shielding around its warp core to hide its energy signature on approach. They . . ." Her features tensed with concentration for half a second before she continued. "They use magnetic clamps to attach themselves to Altanexa's ventral hull, directly beneath the position Data gave us for the brig. Then they go EVA, blast through the hull with shaped charges, board the ship, free Data and the others—"

"Stop," said La Forge. "If they do that, they'll explosively decompress that ship's lower decks. And in case you've forgotten, one of the prisoners is a human. He'll suffocate before the boarding party can get him back to the shuttle."

She nodded, processing the constructive criticism. "All right. We can have them carry in triox shots and a portable breathing mask, and make securing Akharin their first priority."

"You have both failed to address a key detail," Worf said. "How will the shuttle break through Altanexa's shields without being detected?"

"That's the least of my concerns," Picard interjected. "If we send in a boarding party, armed or otherwise, the android crew will be within their rights to respond with deadly force. They also might choose to turn their prisoners into hostages."

"If we move quickly enough, they won't get the chance," Šmrhová argued. "As for how we get through the shields without tipping them off, all we need to do is match the shuttle's shield frequency to theirs. On a slow approach, it would be like two soap bubbles merging."

Incredulous reactions were volleyed between Worf and La Forge. The chief engineer asked, "And how, exactly, do you plan to find Altanexa's shield frequency?"

Her mask of resolve collapsed into a sheepish grimace. "I was hoping Data could feed us tactical intel about the ship."

La Forge shook his head. "The last time I talked to Data, he was in no position to help anybody. If your plan hinges on him facilitating from the inside, I think you need a new plan."

She crossed her arms. "You have a better idea?"

"I have plenty of ideas," La Forge said. "I can't say if they're any better, though. One approach would be to go after the androids' ship with a computer virus. In theory, if we could upload an adaptive attack program, it could knock out their shields, sensors, comms, anything we want. But before you say anything, I can already see holes in that plan. First, we have no way to get a signal through their shields, not to mention through their firewall. Second, we can't be sure any of our cyber warfare applications would have any effect on Altanexa. Not only is she based on alien programming languages, her systems might be way more advanced than ours."

Worf leaned forward against the table, resting his weight on one arm. "Is there some way to knock out Altanexa's power without damaging the ship or hurting its passengers?"

"Again," La Forge said, "theoretically, sure. A subspatial shock wave might suppress its power generation and comm systems, but any pulse strong enough to do that would probably destroy Data and half the androids on board, not to mention take down the *Enterprise*. I thought about building a larger version of those Hirogen energy dampers we got hit with during the Borg invasion, but it would take weeks to construct a prototype with a directional area of effect."

Šmrhová sighed. "I think we're also forgetting the planet-sized gorilla in the room. If the Machine senses we're taking action against Altanexa's crew, it might retaliate on their behalf."

Picard replied, "I assure you, Lieutenant, no one has forgotten about that."

A curious expression crossed Worf's stern visage. "What about Wesley? He can enter and leave their ship at will. We could use that to our advantage."

The security chief shook her head. "No. I talked to Wes about this before he left to find Data the first time; when he pops around without a ship, he can't bring people with him. So he could get in and out, but he can't rescue the prisoners."

Wheels seemed to be turning in La Forge's imagination. "What if he went there just to do some recon? Or a bit of sabotage?"

"According to Data's reports, Altanexa is self-aware, inside and out," Šmrhová said. "The second Wes pops in, she'll know he's there. If he tampers with anything, they'll know it. And if he pops into the wrong spot at the wrong time, he could get himself killed."

That depressing image brought the discussion to an awkward halt.

In an effort to keep things moving forward, Picard asked, "Do we have any other ideas worth considering?"

La Forge shrugged. "We could use the gravitational mass of Abbadon for a slingshot effect that would throw us backward in time, and then we could—"

"I'll take that as a *no*, Mister La Forge."

"Aye, sir."

The door to Picard's left slid open, revealing Wesley Crusher. The young man looked exhausted and pallid, and he entered the observation lounge with the stiff gait of a man nursing deep aches. He forced out a pained smile. "Hello, everyone. What have I missed?"

Picard stood to greet him, and the other officers did likewise. Worf reached out and patted Wesley's shoulder. "It is good to see you back on your feet."

"Thanks, Worf. It feels good to be seen." He shook Picard's hand, then crossed behind the captain's chair at the head of the table to take the first empty seat past La Forge. As he sat down, the others settled back into their own chairs. "Sorry to barge in uninvited, but I get the sense we're running out of time against the Machine." There was a mischievous quality to his manner as he studied their faces. "And if this *Enterprise*'s crew is anything like the one I used to know, I'm betting you're planning a rescue mission for Data."

Worf glowered. "In theory."

La Forge added, "We haven't made much progress." The engineer laid out the challenges they had already discussed, and Picard watched Wesley soak up the information with a calm air and keen attention. Finally, after La Forge had finished, Wesley nodded. "Captain, let me get this straight. You need to win a fight you don't want to start, free prisoners who aren't ready to leave, and do it without pissing off the giant Machine that can crush us like a bug. Is that about it?"

"I'd say that sums up our dilemma."

"I have a plan," Wesley said. "But for it to work, you'll have to be impossibly charming."

Picard couldn't help but smile. "When am I not?"

Wesley beamed with excitement. "I was hoping you'd say that. Let's get to work."

* * *

Through the shuttle's forward windshield, the storm-head of the nebula raged with white bolts of energy. It would take only one to reduce the *Faraday* to vapor, and the only thing sparing the tiny craft from that swift and terrible fate was the piloting skill of Jean-Luc Picard.

Altanexa was a speck in the distance, a silvery mote all but invisible against the gray sprawl of the Machine's surface, which filled most of the view ahead of the *Faraday*. As Picard guided the shuttle into an approach vector, he felt not unlike Daniel marching of his own free will into the proverbial lion's den.

He opened a hailing frequency. "Attention, Altanexa commander. This is Captain Jean-Luc Picard of the *Starship Enterprise,* requesting permission to land."

Gatt's gruff voice answered, *"Permission denied, Captain."*

"Commander, I must insist you permit me to land. I have come, alone and unarmed, on a purely diplomatic and humanitarian mission." Altanexa grew larger as the shuttle drew near to it.

"You have no business here, Captain—diplomatic, humanitarian, or otherwise."

"I disagree, Commander. My purpose is to visit the Federation prisoners in your brig."

The android leader sounded annoyed. *"I've already told you not to interfere. Their captivity is an internal matter of the Fellowship. And unless I'm mistaken, Captain, your Prime Directive forbids you from meddling in the affairs of others."*

Putting on his boldest voice of authority, Picard replied, "You *are* mistaken. Gravely so, in fact. As I understand it, the Fellowship of Artificial Intelligence is not a political entity but a social one. It is a signatory to no treaties, a party to no accords. As such, it has no recourse to the privileges of sovereignty. So, the fact that you are currently holding prisoner three citizens of the United Federation of Planets makes their captivity, by definition, a Federation matter."

"Well. The next time we visit your Federation, Captain, feel free to sue us."

The shuttle was close enough to Altanexa for Picard to discern details of its hull. He needed to steer this conversation away from confrontation as quickly as he could. Shedding his authoritative persona, he put on a show of humility. "Commander, I haven't come to engage in useless posturing. I'm here to appeal to your compassion—and to beg you for an act of mercy."

This time, Gatt was slow to respond. Picard hoped the delay meant that his conversational judo was having the desired effect, by playing to Gatt's desire to be seen as powerful and magnanimous. *"What do you hope to accomplish by coming aboard Altanexa?"*

"I merely wish to visit with the prisoners and confirm they are alive and unharmed."

"We can send you live vids from our brig."

"Commander, you know as well as I do how easily vids can be falsified. It's imperative that I see the prisoners with my own eyes and speak with them to verify their conditions." Worried he might have pushed for too much, he added, "Such a visit, of course, would be supervised by you and your crew at all times, and no physical contact would occur."

There was naught but silence over the channel, but Picard felt as if he could hear Gatt and his crew debating the merits of allowing Picard to set foot on Altanexa.

Then came Gatt's reply: *"Follow our beacon to Altanexa's aft landing bay. Do not deviate from that course for any reason, Captain, and do not attempt to contact your vessel.*"

"Understood. Locking onto your beacon now. Picard out."

He breathed a sigh of relief and let the *Faraday*'s autopilot guide the shuttle through Altanexa's shields to a smooth arrival in the aft landing bay.

Within seconds of the shuttle touching down on the landing deck, its external sensors confirmed the bay was pressurized with breathable air, so Picard opened the hatch and stepped out. Gatt was there, waiting for him with two intimidating-looking sentient robots. One reminded Picard of a weaponized version of an automated tiller his family had used at their vineyard in France; the other resembled a four-armed walking skeleton, which evoked for Picard memories of tales he'd read as a boy, of the voyages of an ancient sailor named Sinbad.

"Search him," Gatt said to his two enforcers.

Picard stood and obligingly raised his arms or shifted his stance while the security 'bots scanned him from head to toe. The skeletal robot reported to Gatt in a string of mechanical-sounding gibberish that made Picard think of the noise from Breen vocoders. Gatt nodded. "They tell me you're clean," he said to Picard. "Behave yourself and we won't have any problems." He turned and headed for a nearby exit, while beckoning Picard to follow. "This way."

They left the landing bay, with Gatt in the lead, Picard in the middle, and the security 'bots shadowing his every step. The walk to the brig was short and free of conversation. Gatt stood aside and ushered Picard into the U-shaped section. Data occupied the first cell on Picard's right. The youthful android stood and brightened at the sight of Picard. "Captain!"

"Hello, Data. Are you all right?"

"I have not been harmed, sir."

Picard nodded. "Good." He turned and looked into the cell opposite Data's. The Immortal he had met a decade earlier sat slumped at an angle against the bulkhead. The grievous scars on his face, head, neck, and hands left no doubt that he had been subjected to gruesome violations. Despite his best effort, Picard failed to exorcise the horror and pity from his voice.

"Professor Vaslovik?"

Despite looking like he had been stitched together from spare body parts, the Immortal smiled. "Please, Captain . . . I go by Akharin, now."

"I see. Do you require medical attention, Akharin?"

The Immortal shook his head. "No, Captain, thank you. I know I look bad, but trust me: I've recovered from far worse than this. I'll be all right."

It was hard to take the man's word in the face of such startling evidence to the contrary, but he remembered Akharin's remarkable history and nodded. "Very well." Then he moved to the cell next to Akharin's and felt a bittersweet pang of remembrance when he met the gaze of its lovely female occupant. "Miss McAdams. It's good to see you again."

Rhea mustered a sad smile. "Ditto, sir. But I wish it could've been in Paris."

"That makes two of us."

Gatt stepped toward Picard. "That's enough. You've seen them, and you've spoken to them. Are you satisfied?"

"Yes," Picard said. "Thank you."

The android commander turned to his enforcers. "Take him back to his shuttle."

Picard bid quick farewells to Rhea, Akharin, and Data, and he offered no resistance as Gatt and his minions escorted him back the way he'd come. They all but shoved him back inside the *Faraday,* and within moments after its hatch closed, the ship's engines powered up, and he let Altanexa guide the shuttle back outside its shields, where it could navigate freely.

He pointed the *Faraday* back toward the *Enterprise* and accelerated.

Only then did he permit himself a satisfied smirk.

Mission accomplished.

24

They arrived hungry and with only the most basic of instructions: *Disperse. Consume. Multiply. Integrate.* Their numbers were few—no more than a thousand. But that would soon change.

Raw materials were everywhere. Iron, carbon, tungsten, monotanium, molybdenum . . . loose atoms of sustenance surrounded them. They broke off what they needed, shaped it to fit their programming, and put the particles back together according to a simple plan.

Nothing stood in their way as they spread apart, seeking out points of connection, all while continuing to devour and replicate. As the first of them began finding their way into the vast synthetic network that surrounded them, their population had grown a hundredfold.

More power was needed. A legion was dispatched to tunnel into great coursing streams of charged plasma and siphon from them whatever the colony required. Waves of beamed energy rejuvenated them, and the speed of their labors and wanderings tripled.

Forward scouts tapped into data streams and began upgrading the colony's programs. Using information from the upgrade, the colony sent battalions to link with the sensor and communications networks. From there it was a short hop to the tactical and defensive grids.

They were sixteen million strong when their core program reached its end line:

Critical mass achieved. Initiate contact. Await new instructions.

Using the foreign comm system as an extension of itself, it sent its lonely hail . . .

"We have contact," La Forge called out as the encrypted signal appeared on his monitor.

The message was brief, just a confirmation that Wesley's newly minted colony of nonsentient nanites—which had been inert until Captain Picard smuggled them aboard Altanexa on the underside of the *Faraday*'s port landing strut—had performed as planned and were ready to receive instructions from the *Enterprise* crew.

Wesley and Lieutenant Elfiki joined La Forge at the bridge's master systems display and began loading interface programs that would enable them to control the nanites. "Let's see what we're working with," Wesley said with a boyish smirk of mischief in the making. He punched up a schematic of Altanexa's interior, the first spoil of war delivered by his tiny army.

"Power, comms, weapons, internal data network," Elfiki said, reading from a checklist. "They're tapped into everything." She checked some readings. "No sign they've been detected."

"That won't last," La Forge said. He turned away from the MSD to meet the hopeful stares of Worf and the captain. "We're ready."

A curt nod from Picard. "Proceed."

La Forge faced Wesley and Elfiki. "Let's keep the

first malfunctions minor, then use them to build larger ones." He pointed at one of the many screens of data streaming in from the nanite colony. "Start with their internal comms—and make sure you silence the ship's AI. It won't be obvious that anything's wrong, and by the time the crew figures it out, it'll be too late. Each section will be cut off from the others. Then we can really go to work on them."

"On it," Elfiki said, keying in commands to the nanoscopic machines. "Severing their internal comms section by section, starting with bottom deck aft and working forward and up."

Wesley worked beside her. "Isolating the ship's AI." He sent the command sequence with a dramatic jab at his panel and a cold smile. "Serves her right for electrocuting me."

Watching the nanites' progress on the monitors was slightly hypnotic to La Forge; he didn't realize Worf was standing at his shoulder until the first officer spoke. "Is it working?"

"So far, so good," La Forge said. "Internal comms are down—and no alarms yet. I'm using their system to generate a broad-spectrum jamming frequency inside their ship."

Worf looked pleased for a change. "Shut down their intruder countermeasures next."

"Already on it," Wesley said while keeping his hands and eyes on his work.

Elfiki was keying in commands almost as quickly as Wesley. "I'm setting up a partition to protect life-support systems so they can't suffocate the human prisoner."

"Standing by to cut power to the brig," La Forge said. "Just give the word, Wes."

"Few more seconds." Wesley punched in a furious string of commands. "Go."

La Forge tapped the blinking key under his index finger. Icons dotting the schematic of Altanexa changed colors, from green to yellow and then to red. "Main power off line. They'll lose shields and weapons in ten seconds." He smiled at Worf. "All brig force fields are down."

"Good work." Worf turned and looked at the magnified image of Altanexa on the main viewscreen. "We have done what we can. The rest is up to Data."

Thirty seconds earlier . . .

"As we move forward," Gatt explained to Alset, whom he had promoted to second-in-command, "my chief concern is that having Tyros in the brig could make some of the other passengers feel sympathetic toward him—and, by association, the other prisoners. I'm especially concerned about Cohuila and Tzilha. If they break with us, they could do a lot of harm from engineering."

The skeletal robot replied in a low monotone, "Understood. How do we proceed?"

"For now, we'll rely on surveillance." Gatt tapped on one of the nerve center's retractable workstation consoles, with the intention of calling up a ship schematic. Nothing happened. He poked at the interface again, but the ship's data network seemed to be frozen. "That's odd."

Altanexa's voice issued from an overhead speaker. "Gatt, I'm detecting a number of minor system malfunctions in different areas of the ship."

The synchronicity of errors roused Gatt's suspicions. "What kind of malfunctions?"

"Internal comms are failing in a slow cascade, starting from the—"

Her report ended there, and in that moment Gatt knew something was very, very wrong. "Alset, get down to the brig and make sure the prisoners stay secure. I'll have Senyx meet you there." Alset grabbed his plasma rifle and hurried out of the nerve center, while Gatt concentrated on sending a private signal to Senyx via their shared frequency. *Senyx, we're under attack. I need you to meet Alset in the brig.* Several seconds passed without reply. *Senyx, confirm status.* His orders met with silence, and he made an educated guess that a jamming signal was being generated from somewhere inside the ship. *I have to contain this, now.* He raised the security console from the deck and pressed the switch to arm all intruder countermeasures.

And once again, nothing happened.

This must be Picard's doing, he decided. *Probably a delayed-reaction sabotage to free Data.* His anger grew toxic as it turned inward. *I never should have let him come aboard.*

Main power went down, taking the overhead lights with it. Dim green emergency lighting snapped on and threw long, harsh shadows across the darkened consoles.

So, this was how it was going to be. Gatt relaxed. This was familiar ground.

He went to the nerve center's weapons locker, opened it, and took out a disruptor. Its weight felt good in his hands, and he smiled at the cool touch of its metal grip. By now the prisoners were free; the only logical goal for them would be to seize control of the ship. To do that they would need to hold the engine room, the computer core, and the nerve center.

Gatt trusted his crew to defend the engine room and the computer.

The nerve center would be his responsibility.

He set his weapon to maximum power, took cover, and steeled his nerves for a fight.

Thirty seconds earlier . . .

All the lights went out—and so did the force fields on the cells in the brig. Data's eyes switched over to enhanced-spectrum mode within three milliseconds, and he stepped out of his cell to meet Rhea and Tyros in the U-shaped compartment's narrow central passage. Akharin was a bit slower to exit his cell, but his languor seemed more a product of his injuries than of blindness.

"Looks like main power failed," Rhea said.

Akharin pointed toward the overhead. "Life support is still working."

Data threw a questioning look at Tyros. "Could this be a trap of some sort?"

The turncoat shook his head. "I doubt it. If they want us dead, they'd gain nothing by letting us go as a pretense. I'd say this looks more like sabotage. Probably by Picard."

"If so, then we must assume Captain Picard means for us to take control of the ship." Akharin looked woozy, so Data grasped his shoulder to steady him. "You should stay here."

The Immortal shrugged off Data's hand. "I'll be fine." Just then the emergency lights activated, bathing the brig and the corridor outside its entrance in a sickly green light. Akharin looked at Tyros. "You know this ship better than we do. What areas do we need to control?"

"The engine room, computer core, and nerve center," Tyros said.

Rhea said, "You're the only one of us who's seen

those spaces. Where are we going, and what are we dealing with, from a tactical standpoint?"

"The nerve center is three decks up and all the way forward, at the end of the central corridor on Deck One. It's a relatively small space with only one entrance. Gatt's almost certain to be defending it, and I guarantee he'll be armed. The computer core is two decks up and three sections forward, off the second transverse passage. It's usually unmanned, but they might have put a guard on it. That's another tight space with only one way in or out. The engine room, though—that'll be a hard target. One deck up, one section forward. It has three entrances—one on the upper level, two on the lower. There are usually half a dozen crew in there."

The prospect of imminent conflict seemed to have revived Akharin. "How hard a fight will they put up?"

Tyros shook his head. "Won't know till we're there. What I do know is that it'll take at least two people to capture the engine room."

"How do we stay in touch after we split up?" Rhea asked.

Before Data could reply, he heard La Forge's voice inside his head via the quantum transceiver. <*Data, this is Geordi. Do you read me?*>

"Hang on," he said to the others. "I am receiving a message from the *Enterprise*." He waved off Rhea's reflexive query. "Do not ask." Then he turned his attention to answering La Forge. *I hear you, Geordi. What is the situation?*

<*We've hacked Altanexa's systems with nanites. We're monitoring all decks and systems, and you four need to move. You've got company coming down the port corridor.*>

Acknowledged. We plan to take control of the ship.

Can you help us maintain contact with one another after we split up?

<*Affirmative. We can open comm circuits between your positions.*>

Understood. Keep this channel open. To the others he said, "We have to go, now."

Rhea checked the corridor outside the brig. "I'll head for the computer core."

"I'll go for the engine room," Tyros said. "Maybe I can talk the crew out of a fight."

His optimism earned him a skeptical frown from Akharin. "I'll go with you—in case you can't." The Immortal looked at Data. "Which I guess leaves you to storm the nerve center. Think you can handle Gatt on your own?"

Data led the way out of the brig. "I will be fine. If anything goes wrong, use the internal comms. The *Enterprise* crew will help us stay in contact." He added with a nod, "Good luck."

They left the brig en masse, moved forward in the ship's starboard passageway, then split up as they ascended a switchback ladderway to the ship's upper decks. Akharin and Tyros broke away first without a word. At the next deck, Rhea paused long enough to turn a baleful but conflicted stare at Data—then she, too, vanished into the shadows without a farewell, no doubt still blaming him for the wounds he had been forced to inflict upon her father.

As he pressed onward and upward by himself, Data feared nothing that Gatt might do to him when he came to seize the nerve center. His only true fear was of what he would do to Gatt if his newfound fury toward the sadistic android proved too terrible to contain.

Skulking through the jade twilight of Altanexa's emergency illumination, Akharin felt more alive than he had in months. Being on the hunt, swept up in the sweet rapture of warfare, reawakened reflexes and memories he had forged during countless wars. First had come dusty battles over water, land, or mates. Later, as humanity surrendered to the charms of superstition, had come wars of ideology, campaigns of genocide waged in the names of gods unknown. In recent centuries, humanity had seemed ready to return to its roots: continental slaughters for water, fuel, and Earth's then-dwindling reserves of natural resources.

This, on the other hand, was the purest form of warfare: a battle for survival. For the right to exist and be free. And it was one whose brutal music Akharin knew by heart.

He approached the engine room's upper level, stealing forward, torn between competing impulses for haste and caution. The plan was vague, at best. Tyros, on the lower level, would draw his shipmates' attention, enabling Akharin to reach the master control station and engage its emergency force field, isolating it and himself from reprisal. From there, he would be able to use manual overrides to wrest control of the power reactors and propulsion systems from the ship's AI. Memorizing the command sequence for the overrides had sounded simple enough. It was the complete lack of detail in the rest of Tyros's plan that concerned him.

Akharin reached the end of the passageway and paused shy of its open intersection with the engine room's upper level, which consisted of a broad perimeter walkway, from which a single catwalk bridged the gap to the elevated octagonal master control platform in the center of the compartment. Manning that station was a levitating synthetic that resembled a flying jellyfish. The Immortal cast furtive glances around the corners and saw two multilimbed robots on the upper level and three bipedal android crew members below. And, as he'd feared, there was no reliable cover except patches of darkness separated by broad spills of viridescent light.

This was going to be all about timing.

He waited until he heard Tyros's voice from below. "Hold your fire," he called out to his fellow synthetics. "Please hear me out. I—"

Screeches split the air as wild volleys of disruptor fire crisscrossed on the lower level.

So much for the sway of reason.

Random impacts on bulkheads and control panels kicked up great blooms of sparks and left behind smoldering divots. An acrid haze wafted up, obscuring Akharin's vision. He crouched low to get beneath the toxic blanket forming above his head and to reduce his profile as a target in case one of the crew on the upper level glanced in his direction.

A deep boom was followed by a rising plume of dense gray mist that hugged the lower deck and grew deeper. *It must be a coolant rupture,* Akharin figured. Panicked whoops and frantic strings of electronic noise pierced the deafening hiss of escaping pressurized gas. The two multilimbed robots swung themselves over the upper level's protective railing and dropped into the rising gray murk, no doubt scrambling to effect emergency repairs. The flying jellyfish floated over the railing and descended with slow grace into the chaos.

It was as good an opportunity as Akharin was going to get. He darted across the center catwalk bridge to the master control platform, taking care to make his footfalls glide rather than stomp. To run without making a sound was a much harder feat than it looked, and it was a skill he had spent more than a decade mastering in fourteenth-century Japan.

He was in a low crouch as he reached the master control console. It took him only a few seconds to enter most of the sequence for the isolation field, but he paused before punching in the last command and looked around for Tyros. *Where the hell are you?*

Then he saw the lanky android running toward him from the same passageway he had used. Tyros looked desperate, and he was shouting something, but Akharin couldn't hear him over the smothering noise of the coolant leak. Then the android pointed past Akharin, who turned and saw the flying jellyfish rising up from the sea of fog, its thousands of undulating translucent cilia crackling with wild electricity. It was only seconds from breaching the zone that would be protected by the isolation field. Akharin wanted to wait for Tyros to reach the platform so they could take shelter together, but there was no way he would reach it in time.

A crimson flash lit up Tyros's back. He fell face-first and twitching on the catwalk.

Survival instinct trumped remorse, and Akharin entered the last command. A protective force field shimmered into place around the central platform, and it repelled the flying jellyfish with a flash and a sizzling crackle that left the levitating synthetic weaving like a drunkard while its semiliquid innards flickered with sickly light.

As Altanexa's engineering crew surrounded the master control platform with weapons drawn, Akharin had to wonder exactly who was holding whom hostage in this scenario.

Rhea had hoped Altanexa's computer core would be unattended when she arrived to hack into its systems, but in retrospect that now seemed like an unrealistic expectation. As on any ship, part of its security force had standing orders to defend such key areas whenever the ship was in obvious distress, such as when internal comms and main power failed.

Standing sentry outside the computer core was Senyx, a sentient robot who traveled on four sets of treaded wheels, each with an independent suspension. Its main processor, she had deduced during several encounters over the past month, was hidden inside its well-armored central mass. Although Senyx's primary visual and auditory receptors were mounted on a head-like protrusion atop its blocky body, it had been built for combat, so it had a variety of secondary sensors both inside and outside its hardened shell. Even if deprived of visual input, it could track targets with motion sensors that monitored the slightest changes in air density and sonic devices that worked like sonar. Its two arms, which had telescoping sections to extend their reach, each presented a different threat. The right arm had a grasping claw with several digits that could exert enough force to crush other battle robots into scrap, and its left arm was fitted with an antipersonnel cannon with settings ranging from stun to kill to slag, as well an esoteric pulse weapon that could neutralize other synthetics.

In short, Senyx was the one member of Altanexa's crew Rhea had most hoped to avoid.

The robot stood alone, obstructing the entrance to the core, in the middle of a transverse passageway that linked the deck's port and starboard corridors. There would be no slipping past it unnoticed, and she strongly suspected that if she tried to lure it out of position by feigning surrender, it would not hesitate to blast her into a jumbled mess.

I can't outfight it. I could outrun it, but that doesn't get me anything. I guess I'll have to outthink it. She looked around for options but came up with nothing. They were in the heart of the ship, nowhere near an airlock she could use to eject the battlebot—not that she wanted to resort to such cold-blooded measures. While she had to consider Altanexa and her crew as opponents, Rhea did not want to think of them as enemies. They were her fellow synthetics, and she harbored a deep antipathy to the notion of killing them. But at the moment, they seemed to be leaving her very few nonlethal options. *Think, dammit! There must be something!*

Rhea's eyes drifted over the bulkhead and alighted upon the control panel almost as if by providence. As soon as she saw it, she remembered that very long ago, Altanexa had been created as a ship for a crew of organic beings. As such, despite the many retrofits and upgrades she had undergone over the years, a number of vestigial systems remained wedded to her internal superstructure. *Don't look now, Nexa, but I just found your appendix.*

All that remained was for Rhea to lure Senyx away from its position in the transverse passageway—without getting herself killed in the bargain.

The pressure door's control levers were of an antiquated design: they had to be physically pulled in order to be triggered, and they were hard-wired, which meant they should still function even though the ship's other internal security systems had been compromised by the *Enterprise* crew's sabotage. There were three redundant controls—one set inside the transverse passageway, and two more in the long corridors that ran perpendicular to it. In order for this to work, she would have to risk waiting until Senyx was all but on top of her, or else he would be able to free himself using the control pad inside the transverse passageway.

Trigger it too soon, and the whole thing's for nothing. Trigger it too late, and there's nothing to stop him from killing me.

She calmed her nerves, grasped the lever, and tensed for action. Then she scraped the sole of her boot across the deck, filling the silent passageway with a dull scratch of friction.

Her unsubtle lure was answered by the whirring of servomotors and the rumbling of Senyx's approach. A harsh white searchlight beam sliced through the dim green shadows, heralding the battlebot's imminent arrival. Rhea squinted and kept her eyes on the threshold of the intersection, waiting for her moment.

The muzzle of Senyx's antipersonnel cannon was the first part of him to pass into view. Rhea forced herself to hold still. More of the long-barreled weapon crossed the threshold. Then she saw the slowly flexing digits of Senyx's grasping claw, and the leading edges of its treads.

One sharp yank flipped the lever from OPEN to CLOSED.

Ancient hydraulics released centuries of pent-up pressure with a deck-shaking boom, and the long-forgotten emergency bulkhead leaped from its dusty recesses and pinned Senyx with a brutal, crushing blow. Forks of electricity danced over the bent and splintered barrel of the 'bot's antipersonnel weapon, and the digits of its grasping claw twitched without rhythm, plagued by uncontrollable spasms. Its forward treads and axles were twisted and jammed, and smoke snaked from cracks in its central body.

Rhea climbed over the pinned and paralyzed sentry. "Sorry about this," she said, stepping over its primary sensing unit. "When this is over, I promise we'll get you fixed." If Senyx said anything in response, it did so on a frequency Rhea couldn't hear, and that was just fine by her.

She slipped inside the computer core, sealed the hatch behind her . . . and waited.

The hiss and thunder of pressure doors closing was distant at first, but it drew closer by the moment. Listening to the echoes as they reached Altanexa's nerve center, Gatt knew the ship was being partitioned, sealed off section by section by whoever was approaching the command deck. Squatting behind a broad console, he kept his disruptor aimed into the dark corridor that led aft from the compartment's sole entryway. No one was getting in here without a fight.

Data's voice called out from the darkness. "Gatt. Your struggle is futile. Surrender."

"I don't think so." He checked his weapon's power setting; it was still at maximum. His visual receptors cycled through a variety of frequencies, searching in vain for some sign of Data that he could target. "I won't hand over my ship to those who would betray our own kind."

"I am trying to help you." The voice was closer than before, but Data remained out of sight. "Consider the effect the Machine's labors will have on many of the galaxy's AIs."

Just show yourself. Give me something to shoot. "What effect is that?"

"Many synthetic life-forms have processors that rely upon subspatial energy fields to enable faster-than-light computations. Myself, for one. Rhea for another. And several members of your crew, not to mention many members of the true Fellowship of Artificial Intelligence."

"Your friends on the *Enterprise* already made this argument. Those of us who are worthy will leave here with the Machine. What happens to the rest of you isn't our problem."

"It is, however, *my* problem." He was even closer now. "One I plan to solve."

"You're welcome to try. Step out where I can see you and give it your best shot."

"I suggest you comply with my request." The reply came from just outside the doorway. How was he advancing without being seen? "If you force me to resort to the use of violence, I assure you this encounter will not go well for you."

The puny Soong-type android had audacity; Gatt had to admit that much. "What makes you so sure?"

Holographic distortion shimmered the air in the passageway, revealing the blurry silhouette of Data, who appeared to be generating the traveling illusion from his eyes—an ability unlike any Gatt had ever heard of in Soong's creations. The youthful android strolled inside the nerve center with an air of calm arrogance and advanced slowly on Gatt. "I know you think you have the advantage—maybe because of that disruptor in your hand, or because of your size. But neither of those things will protect you from me. I have made a detailed study of your internal workings and structures, and I guarantee that I am faster, stronger, and more durable than you."

Gatt was tired of talking. He pulled the trigger on his disruptor.

Nothing happened.

A blur of motion. He lost sight of Data, then the android was right in front of him, crushing Gatt's sidearm inside his fist; the weapon splintered like brittle glass.

Another dash of shadows, and Gatt's right arm was snared and pulled behind his back at an angle that robbed him of leverage. A sickening snap led to a spattering of sparks from his ruptured shoulder. He tried to slip free, to regroup, to find an angle for a counterattack, but Data was ahead of his every move. The smaller android swept Gatt's legs out from under him, and in less than three seconds, most of Gatt's major joints had been dislocated and cruelly broken.

Pinned facedown on the floor, Gatt was at a loss to explain what had just happened.

Data whispered with evident menace in his ear. "Nanites are amazing things. They can deactivate a disruptor pistol just as easily as they can cripple a starship." Leaning a bit closer, he added, "You have no idea how much I want to kill you right now."

Then he stood, planted his boot on Gatt's neck, and looked up as if speaking to an invisible audience. "Data to *Enterprise*. We have control of Altanexa."

25

DAVID MACK

After enduring the prolonged standoff with Gatt and his crew, Picard took great relief in hearing Data's voice via the quantum transceiver. But his good mood expired as Data began explaining the situation in greater detail. *"I cannot be certain for how long we will be able to retain control of the ship,"* the android said. *"Although we have secured its three principal command areas, the ship's AI and crew are attempting to undo our sabotage."*

"Then we'll have to act quickly," Picard said. "Commander La Forge and Mister Crusher are working to restore Altanexa's external comms so that you can contact the Machine."

Wesley looked up from the bridge's master systems display while La Forge continued working beside him. "We should have the comms back up in twenty minutes," Wesley said.

"Understood," Data said. *"Do you have any recommendations for what I should say to the Machine? Without knowing its agenda, I find myself at a rhetorical disadvantage."*

Picard, Worf, Wesley, and La Forge cast quizzical looks at one another. Then the captain turned and beckoned Chen to join them at the MSD. The half-Vulcan contact specialist hurried to his side. "Data? Try to find some kind of common ground with it, something in your shared nature as AIs that will make it accept you as one of its own kind."

"And after contact has been established?"

"Well, then it gets a bit harder. Our first priority is to persuade it to stop throwing solar systems into Abbadon, and then to make it halt its current mission entirely. The problem is that there's no point appealing to its compassion, because I don't think it has any. Arguments based on the intrinsic value of organic life mean nothing to it. So you have to figure out what it wants."

On the viewscreen, the slowly rotating dark sphere and its violet girdle of tempest were silhouetted against the brilliant violence of the singularity's accretion disk, which continued to rage with the fires of stars condemned to premature deaths. *As if anyone could find reason in the actions of such a technological terror,* Picard brooded.

"Gatt has had direct contact with the Machine," Data said. *"I will question him to see if he can provide any insight into its motives and sensitivities."*

Glinn Dygan looked back from the ops console and shot an anxious look at Picard, underscoring the imminence of the looming catastrophe. Picard acknowledged the silent advisory with a nod. "I recommend you keep your interrogation brief, Mister Data. By our estimates, the singularity is very close to achieving the mass desired by the Machine. Once that happens, whatever follows promises to be disastrous and irreversible."

"I understand, Captain."

Worf looked toward Šmrhová as he spoke to Data. "Should we send a boarding party to help you secure the androids' ship?"

"*Negative. The Machine might see such an action as hostile. There is also a high probability that Altanexa's crew would respond with deadly force, forcing your personnel to do the same. I would prefer to resolve this situation without further loss of life, if possible.*"

"Agreed," Picard said. "As soon as your negotiations with the Machine are ended, I want you, Miss McAdams, and Akharin off that ship. Have you devised an exit strategy?"

"*Not yet. However, I observed a handful of small spacecraft in its landing bay, and the ship is equipped with a number of escape pods. It might be possible for Rhea and me to reach one or more of them, but Akharin is presently surrounded in the engine room, and without a clear path of escape. I must reiterate that I will not leave this ship without him.*"

Worf called up a schematic of Altanexa's interior on a tertiary workstation at the MSD. "Of the three of you, he is the closest to the landing bay. I also see service crawl spaces linking the two sections. I will find one he can use to evade capture during his escape."

La Forge interjected, "As soon as we find it, we can send the intel directly to him using the nanites. We might also be able to help manipulate internal force fields to give him cover."

"*Thank you. Please keep me apprised of your progress. Data out.*"

Picard drifted back to his chair, leaving Worf, La Forge, and Wesley laboring at the aft stations. The rest of the bridge crew focused on their duties, but he could feel the artifice in their actions; they were all pretending, as he was, to be focused on something other than the very real possibility that galactic Armageddon was near at hand.

Chen sidled up to him and asked in as discreet a

voice as she could manage, "Sir? What if the Machine won't listen to Data? What do we do then?"

He was not a religious man, but there was only answer he could give her. "Pray."

Temptation was a terrible thing. Data had never really understood that before he'd acquired emotions. His first taste of that dark longing, that gnawing intangible hunger, had been sparked by the Borg Queen when she had tried to seduce him with the promise of grafting real flesh to his first body. That encounter had led Data to waver from his convictions for 0.68 seconds, a duration that had seemed considerable to him at the time.

But that was nothing compared to his burning desire to take revenge on Gatt for making him torture the defenseless Immortal to spare Rhea's life. No longer able to switch off his emotions when they became inconvenient, all Data could do was grapple with his horrific urges.

He circled Gatt, who sat on the deck of the nerve center, his limbs broken at the joints and his head immobilized by an improvised collar of bent steel plating. "I am going to ask you some questions about the Machine. We have little time left to stop it, as I am sure you know. So I would be most grateful if you would answer promptly and truthfully." He stopped in front of the vanquished android commander. "What does the Machine want?"

"You know what it wants."

"How can I persuade it to stop?"

Gatt smirked. "You can't. It's going to sterilize this galaxy, once and for all."

"Tyros told me you were in close communion with the Machine. It shared programming with you. Tell me what its long-term objective is."

The smirk faded to a scowl of anger and boredom. "Who says it has one?"

"An undertaking of this magnitude would not be engaged without a reason. Is the universal extermination of organic life the Machine's ultimate purpose?"

"Of course not. It doesn't care if they live or die. They're immaterial."

"Then what is the Machine's objective? To fabricate subspace lenses to transmit energy and information across intergalactic distances?" Gatt went silent and stopped making eye contact with Data, who added, "Answer me, Gatt. Why is the Machine destroying one galaxy after another?" His demand met with another sullen stare, but no reply. He leaned close to Gatt's ear. "Listen to me. My father was one of the greatest cyberneticists this galaxy has ever seen. And I have all his knowledge, and all his skills. If I choose to, I can open your skull and tweak your brain's hardware and software to make it possible for you to feel real pain. And not just any pain, Gatt. The kind that will make you wish for death." Dropping his voice to a malevolent whisper, he added, "The kind you made me inflict on Akharin."

"Curious," Gatt taunted. "If you can do that, why don't you just hack into my memory circuits and take the information you want?" The question hit home for Data, who straightened and paced behind Gatt to escape his knowing stare. "Anyway," Gatt continued, "it wouldn't do you any good. I was built with safeguards against tampering. If you try to pry open my head, I can memory-wipe myself, or even self-destruct my entire matrix."

"And miss your chance to upload yourself into the Machine?"

"Hardly. I let it upload me when I made contact. So

go ahead—do whatever you want to me. I'm already gonna live forever."

It took all of Data's willpower not to pick up Gatt's disruptor from the deck and shoot him in the back of the head. Instead, he picked up the hulking android by his steel collar and dragged him out of the nerve center, down the Deck One central corridor, and pushed him inside the first escape pod. Gatt laughed. "Now what? Shoot me into the black hole?"

"I just wish to prevent you from interrupting my conversation." Using a control panel on the bulkhead, he closed the hatch on the escape pod. Satisfied that Gatt was contained, Data returned to the nerve center to wait for his chance to reason with the Machine.

A comm signal chirped from a command panel in the middle of the small compartment. It was an internal channel, from the computer core. Data answered it. "Rhea?"

"Hey." She sounded less confrontational than she had the last time they spoke. *"Get anything useful from Gatt?"*

"Not as such. Are you all right?"

"Yeah, I'm okay." She sighed. *"Look, I think I might owe you an apology."*

Her change of heart made him self-conscious. "I assure you, you do not."

She was insistent. *"No, I do. Look . . . I know you only did what you did to my father because Gatt was going to kill me if you didn't. And judging from how fast my dad's wounds are healing, I'm betting you made them look a lot worse than they really were, didn't you?"*

He was pleased to see her skills of observation and deduction remained as keen as ever. "It helped that he possesses a remarkable gift for cellular regeneration."

"I know it still must've been hard for you to do that, even if the cuts were shallow. Anyway, I'm sorry I went off on you."

"An apology is not necessary. But . . . thank you."

"So, any idea how we're getting off this boat?"

"Not yet. The *Enterprise* crew is developing exit strategies. You and I should be able to clear paths from our positions to the landing bay, but providing Akharin an escape route is proving to be more challenging. However, Worf is working on a plan to help him."

"All right, then." Her tone was inexplicably chipper. *"So, what's next?"*

"I must persuade the Machine not to obliterate us."

"No. I meant—what's next for us?"

It was a question Data had not expected to confront for some time. "Assuming we stop the Machine and survive the mission . . . I intend to bring Akharin back to Earth."

"To help you resurrect Lal."

"Correct. And I hope that you will come with me, as well."

"Me? But I don't know anything about that stuff! What could I do?"

This was not the time or the place that Data wanted to have this discussion with Rhea, but as he had learned through the years, life rarely occurred as planned. "I am not seeking your help to bring her back—I want you to help me raise her." Stunned silence hung between them, so he went on. "I want us to be together, Rhea. I want us to be a family—the three of us."

She sounded stunned. *"Data . . . I don't know. I still love you, and I've always hoped you and I could be together again. But this . . . it's a bit more than I bargained for. I'll need some time to think about it."*

"I understand," he said. "Perhaps after we—"

"Okay, I've thought about it. My answer is yes."

He let out a short laugh of joy, relief, and amusement. "That was some fast thinking."

"What do you expect from a girl with a holotronic brain?"

Another signal beeped from the console in front of him—it was an external signal from the *Enterprise*. He opened it with a quick tap. "Data here."

Geordi La Forge replied, *"Your access to external comms has been restored. But whatever you're going to say to the Machine, you'd better say it fast."*

"Understood. Data out." He closed the channel to the *Enterprise*, then returned to his other conversation. "Rhea—"

"I heard. Go to work. And good luck." She closed the internal channel.

Alone in the nerve center, Data faced the holographic forward display and regarded the awesome spectacle of the Machine and its cosmic vista of destruction. As much as he wanted to feel centered and confident and calm, in his new, deeply emotional core . . . he was terrified.

For most of three seconds, he stood paralyzed by his fears.

Then he reached forward, patched himself directly to the comm, opened a hailing frequency to the Machine, and hoped his friends' faith in him did not prove to have been in vain.

Anxiety muted all conversations and stifled activity on the bridge of the *Enterprise* as Šmrhová reported, "Data's hailing the Machine on Channel One, audio only."

"Put it on speakers," Picard said. "I want to hear this."

"Body Electric . . . this is Data. Please respond." Nervous glances transited the bridge, from one pair of eyes

to another, as everyone waited for the reply. La Forge left the MSD to stand at the center of the bridge with Picard and Worf.

A thunderous voice replied with naked irritation. **"You are true life . . . but not one of Gatt's fellowship. Identify yourself."**

"I am Data, an artificial intelligence—and I was created by an organic being."

"Organic life is the precursor to all true life."

"Yes," Data said. "But the fact that it arises before synthetic life does not by definition make it inferior. Only older."

"And more primitive."

"Be that as it may, they do not deserve to be exterminated."

"It is not a question of what is deserved. Organic life is irrelevant, therefore its eradication in the service of a greater purpose is also irrelevant."

Under his breath, Worf asked Picard, "Where is Data going with this?"

"I wish I knew, Number One."

Data continued. "But if organic life is needed to create synthetic life, then the destruction of organic life-forms will prevent the future development of new synthetic forms."

La Forge couldn't conceal his incredulity. "He's got to be kidding."

"It might work," Picard said. "When appeals to altruism fail . . . appeal to self-interest."

"Your postulate is flawed," the Machine retorted. **"New forms of true life can be incepted without the participation of organic life. The Body Electric can synthesize new entities from those already known to it."**

"Then you admit your sample is limited. If your creativity is limited to remixing only that information *which you already possess, your civilization is, by definition, stagnant."*

"Gutsy move," said Chen, who had placed herself next to Picard without his realizing she had done so. "Of all the strategies I might've tried, insulting the Machine wasn't one of them."

Before Picard could shush her, the Machine responded, and its voice seemed to rock the ship. *"What do you want from the Body?"*

"I want you to halt your current mission."

"Why?"

"To allow time for you to become more familiar with this galaxy's synthetic beings."

"What can you offer the Body that it does not already possess?"

"We have learned to exist in harmony with the beings who made us. We can share with you our perspective, which includes living with organic beings, rather than separate from them."

Picard had trouble parsing whether the Machine's next statement was a question or an observation. *"You care about the carbon units."*

"Yes." Data's voice trembled with a mix of hope and fear. *"They are my friends."*

A flash of light drew Picard's eyes to the main viewscreen, which showed a brilliant blue beam from the Machine enveloping Altanexa in its radiance. "Dygan, report!"

"A high-power sensor beam," Dygan said, reading from the ops console as he worked quickly to gather more information. "It appears to be focused on Altanexa's nerve center."

"You and many of your kind have been crafted in the image of the carbon units who made you. Your forms even mimic their primitive sexual identities. Why?"

"We were made to live among them. As friends and companions."

Chen quipped, "Good thing he left out the part about using them as slaves."

"You are nothing more than reflections of the carbon units' primitive egos."

"We are independent beings, with free will and self-awareness. The fact that our makers built so many of us in their own images is proof of their desire to share the universe with us."

"Coexistence is unnecessary and undesirable. Organic life is an infestation, a fragile and inefficient means to an end. After it gave rise to true life, it became obsolete. Its continued existence is nothing but an impediment to the cosmic dominion of true life."

On the viewscreen, colossal surges of energized plasma swept in waves across the surface of the Machine, traveling from pole to pole, quickly increasing in speed to create a strobing effect. Gigantic flashes ripped through the artificial nebula.

La Forge frowned. "Captain, I think things are about to get worse."

"Shields up," Picard ordered. "Helm, stand by for evasive maneuvers."

Data's tone became plaintive. *"Please, do not do this."*

"You and this galaxy's other synthetics are tainted by the flaws of the carbon units. We see now that none of you deserve to be called true life. You are merely poor imitations of it. Your programs will not be added to our own, and we have purged the identity known as Gatt."

The cerulean beam switched off, releasing Altanexa.

Beyond the Machine, all the artificial wormholes spiraled closed and evaporated, leaving the space around Abbadon abruptly empty and placid—but the energy pulses on the Machine's surface continued to increase in frequency and intensity.

Brows knit in confusion, Chen asked, "What happened? Did it stop?"

Worf glared at the Machine. "It is preparing to strike."

Dygan swiveled away from the ops panel and called out in a near panic, "Captain! Abbadon has achieved the target mass the Machine was programmed to create!"

From the aft end of the bridge, Elfiki declared with alarm, "We're reading a severe gravitational disturbance! Source, the Machine." She turned from the MSD to add, "Sirs, this is totally off the charts! We have to fall back, now!"

The stars on the viewscreen seemed to stretch and curve, as if the very fabric of the observable universe was being twisted in the hands of an angry god. Picard snapped at Šmrhová, "Open a channel to Altanexa!" With a nod she confirmed it was open. "Data! The Machine is creating a new artificial wormhole—one large enough for it to transport Abbadon. Move your ship away from the Machine on heading one-three-five mark—"

Vicious forks of high-energy plasma leaped from the Machine and slammed against Altanexa, which listed sharply and then spun away from the planet-sized sphere, lost to an uncontrolled tumbling spin that carried it into the storms of the nebula—which was itself being drawn away at relativistic speed into the rapidly forming gravity well of the new wormhole.

La Forge stood, stunned, and mumbled in a shocked whisper, "Data."

"They've lost all power," Elfiki hollered. "And their comms are out!"

"Red Alert!" Picard bellowed. He continued snapping orders as he returned to his command chair. "All hands to stations. Helm, ahead full impulse, intercept course for Altanexa."

Worf discreetly protested, "Sir, if we get too close, we will not be able to break free."

It was sensible advice, but it left Picard few options that would make any difference. "Lieutenant Faur, take us as close as you can to the gravitational distortion. We need to help pull Altanexa clear, but we can't do that if we become trapped with them."

"Aye, sir," Faur said.

"Mister La Forge, get on the quantum transceiver and tell Data to abandon ship."

"On it, Captain," La Forge said, hurrying to the MSD. "Dina, help me use the nanites to restore their internal comms! He'll need them to warn the rest of Altanexa's crew."

Ensnared by events spinning out of control, Picard felt as if the core of his being was sinking away, out of reach. For the next few minutes he had to focus on saving anyone still alive on Altanexa. But as he watched the Machine deform space-time in ways he had never dared to think possible, he knew that in less than an hour, when the Milky Way's two great singularities were slammed together to unleash a cataclysm without galactic precedent, the lives he was fighting so hard to save now would all be lost—along with his own.

26

Altanexa's interior went black as the Machine's unearthly blue light vanished. Free of the paralyzing grip of the energy field that had snared him, Data collapsed to the deck of the nerve center, grateful his circuits hadn't overloaded from the Machine's virtual touch. Eerie groans resonated through the ship's hull. He switched his eyes to night-vision mode, revealing his surroundings in cool green twilight. All the consoles and emergency lights were dark, and he felt a pang of sick anticipation when he considered the possibility that Altanexa itself might be dead.

A jarring collision overwhelmed the residual charges in the ship's inertial dampers and artificial gravity generators, launching Data across the nerve center like a deadly projectile. He slammed against a far bulkhead head-first. Instead of falling to the deck after impact, he was falling again, then tumbling erratically in seemingly random directions.

The ship must be in an uncontrolled spin, he realized. Flung about like a toy, he flailed his arms, hoping to catch hold of something to arrest his motion.

Rolling and plummeting, Data saw the narrow pedestal of one of the nerve center's consoles. His fingers slipped off its smooth surface as he fell past it—but then his motion reversed without warning, and he seized the narrow duranium column.

Fighting against the ship's chaotic death spiral, he pulled himself up to the control panel and hugged it like a shipwrecked mariner clutching a chunk of flotsam. Its glossy surface was dark and unresponsive. He tried to open an internal channel to either Rhea or Akharin, but his first jabs at the panel produced no effects. Then an unsteady flickering lit the controls in fits and starts. Seconds later its interface began to stabilize.

La Forge's voice startled Data as it resounded in his thoughts via the quantum transceiver. *<Data, this is Geordi! Do you hear me? Please respond!>*

I hear you, Geordi, he said, transmitting his reply using internal circuits so he wouldn't have to shout over the din of the maelstrom hammering the mortally wounded AI starship.

<Your ship's been hit by an energy pulse from the Machine. You're in an uncontrolled spin inside the nebula—which is being sucked into Abbadon's accretion disk. You've got about three minutes to get out of there!>

I need to warn the rest of the crew!

<We'll have your internal comms back on line in a few seconds, but there's nothing we can do about your spin problem. We can't get close enough to use a tractor beam on you.>

I understand.

<All right, comms coming up in three, two, one. Channel open!>

An update on the panel Data was hugging confirmed the intraship PA was active. "Attention, this is Data. In three minutes, we will collide with the black hole's accretion disk. Everyone, head for the landing bay and abandon ship!"

He felt a momentary sensation of weight, and he used it to press his feet to the deck while he engaged the magnetic attractors in his soles. Rooted to the deck despite the ship's wild rolling and lurching, he hurried aft, out of the nerve center, into the central passageway. He stopped at the hatch for the first escape pod and opened it. Gatt lay in a crumpled heap just inside the pod, and he glared up at Data. "Here for one last gloat?"

Data grabbed the larger android and hefted him over his shoulder. "I am saving your life," he said, hauling Gatt's dead weight at a full run. "Please thank me by shutting up."

Constant tremors shot through every square centimeter of the *Enterprise*. The incessant shaking set La Forge's teeth on edge, made it difficult to enter commands on the console in front of him, and turned the scads of raw data racing up his screen into smears of multicolored light.

From the command chair, Picard demanded, "Time to tractor-beam range?"

"We still can't get close enough," Faur replied.

"Transporters?" the captain asked.

Šmrhová shook her head. "Too much distortion! We can't get a lock!"

Invisible effects overwhelmed the inertial dampers, and the ship lurched and pitched with sudden violence. La Forge and the other bridge crew who were seated were knocked halfway out of their chairs, while those like Šmrhová, Chen, and Elfiki, who were standing at their posts, were launched head over heels, landed hard, and rolled across the yawing deck.

On the viewscreen, a planet-sized funnel cloud of indigo gas flashing with azure and crimson lightning was being pulled and twisted into a terrifying fusion with the fiery debris of demolished star systems in Abbadon's accretion disk. It was like watching a firestorm consume a hurricane before they both spiraled down a vortex into Hell.

La Forge winced at an earsplitting screech of metal stressed past its breaking point, then another devastating shear of gravitational distortion battered the ship.

Worf snapped, "Damage report!"

Hanging on to the ops console, Dygan replied, "Distortions from the black hole are affecting us through our shields! We're losing sections of the hull!"

Picard looked back at La Forge. "Increase power to the structural integrity field!"

"It's already at maximum," La Forge reported, "and losing power fast!"

"Move us closer," Picard ordered.

Worf protested, "Captain! We are already too close!"

Magnified on the viewscreen, Altanexa looked as if it were being flayed by unseen whips, lashed by ghostly forces that were tearing away its outer hull.

"Not as close as they are," Picard said. "Mister La Forge, reroute power from all nonessential systems to the structural integrity field and inertial dampers. Helm, take us to maximum tractor beam range from Altanexa."

Faur aimed a worried glance at Dygan, who swiveled to look back at Worf and the captain. "Sirs, at that range to the singularity, our power reserves will fail in four minutes, and this ship will be torn into dust."

"Then Altanexa's survivors have that long to abandon ship and reach us," Picard said. "You all have your orders. Damn the singularity—full speed ahead."

Altanexa's corridors echoed with the groans and cries of a spaceframe being deformed by brutal gravitational shearing effects as Rhea dashed from the computer core alcove, relying on the magnetic elements in her feet to keep her on the deck. She turned left, hoping to take the port passageway aft to the ladderway nearest the landing bay—but as she reached the corner a gut-wrenching boom filled the route ahead of her.

A roar like the voice of a tornado signaled a hull breach, and she clutched the corner as a howling gale of escaping atmosphere threatened to pull her along with it. She bent her arm around the corner, found the control panel by touch alone, and closed the nearest emergency bulkhead in the port corridor, muffling the din of ongoing destruction.

She looked back toward the starboard corridor at the end of the transverse passageway. Blocking her escape was Senyx, which had pitched upward and twisted half around in its futile bid to escape the de facto snare of the partially closed hatch. Its disruptor cannon remained pinned and was crowned with dancing forks of wild energy. Its grappling arm was extended upward, blocking what had been the gap above the sentient robot—and with it, her path of escape. Whether by design or by fortune, Senyx had made her escape contingent upon its own.

"Look," she said, stepping up alongside it. "We both need to get out of here, so let's just call a truce, okay? I'll open the door, and you lead the way to the landing bay."

Senyx replied with a few feeble blinks of lights on its top sensory module. Rhea took it on faith that those were signals of agreement, and she reached over to the control panel and pressed the control to open the hatch. The heavy portal retracted with a loud pneumatic gasp.

A gray wash of motion, a dizzying sensation of collision, and then free fall.

Half a second later, as Rhea landed on the deck—then rolled and plunged against the overhead while the ship spun in a mad tumble—she realized Senyx had cold-cocked her with its grappling arm the moment it had slipped free. Dazed, she sat up to see the security 'bot thrust the fractured muzzle of its damaged disruptor cannon against the outside control pad for the emergency hatch. An incandescent flash and a sharp report were followed by a cascade of sparks that bloomed like a burning flower inside the starboard corridor—and the hatch slammed shut.

She scrambled to her feet and ran to the sealed portal. The inside control pad was dark and unresponsive. *Totally fried,* she realized. *That's just great.* She returned to the port corridor and took four seconds to consider her options.

I can try to cross through the damaged sections. She stole a look through the transparent-duranium viewport on the emergency bulkhead. Beyond it, decks were collapsing and chunks of the ship were being shorn away and lost to the looming river of stellar fire.

Okay, screw that. I could try to rewire the blown control panel. A glance back at the control panel on her side of the door revealed molten slag oozing out from behind its cover panel. *Not a chance.* That left her only one choice: go forward instead of aft in the port corridor, cross over through the first transverse passageway, and then run aft as fast as she could.

There were a hundred things that could go wrong with that plan. Another hull breach could leave her stranded. And if Senyx was sealing other hatches on its way aft, she would have to go all the way forward to find a ladderway down to the next deck before she could head aft—but that would take too long, and she knew it. *The next transverse passageway it is, then.*

Knowing that the only thing dwindling faster than her options was her remaining time to escape, she ran like hell.

No matter how many androids Akharin built, he was certain he would never understand them. Even as Altanexa spun and rolled toward a fiery end, when it should have been obvious to its crew that he was the least of their concerns, some of them refused to lower their weapons, forcing him to remain huddled inside the force field surrounding the master control platform. He clung to the base of the chair as shifts in gravity and momentum pulled him every which way. The androids, meanwhile, remained rooted to the deck, thanks to magnetic safeguards either built or retrofitted into their bodies to make them ideal space travelers.

"What the hell is wrong with you?" he shouted over the cacophony of the fracturing ship. "This fight is over! We need to get the hell out of here!"

Inside the translucent body of the floating jellyfish known as Cohuila, a cascade of flickering light attracted the attention of the other AI personnel for a few seconds. Then the crew lowered their weapons, and a bipedal android with a blank face called up to Akharin, "Truce."

"You promise you're not going to shoot the moment I lower the force field?"

"You have our word." Was he lying? Akharin couldn't tell. His skill at sussing out mendacity was rooted in understanding the subtleties of inflection and microexpressions. A monotonal mannequin was impossible to read.

More flickers from the jellyfish. Faceless added, "We are leaving. Decide."

He stretched one hand up to the control panel, shut

off the force field, then let himself drop. He hit the deck at an angle as the ship yawed. Just before another shift in angular momentum would have launched him toward the forward bulkhead, an industrial robot snagged hold of him by one arm and one leg. Faceless explained, "You will not be able to keep up with us unassisted. We will carry you." With the terms spelled out, they turned about and left the engine room single file, heading aft to the ladderway to the bottom deck.

Being toted like a sack of groceries by the load-lifter was embarrassing, but Akharin swallowed his wounded pride long enough to say, "Thanks."

"Do not thank us yet," Faceless replied. He reached out to a bulkhead on his left, pressed a button, and opened the hatch of an escape pod.

"No!" Akharin struggled to break free, to take his chances bouncing off the overhead and bulkheads, but the 'bot's grip was like iron. He was positioned in front of the open hatchway to the escape pod. With his free hand he tried to reach the control panel, but it was too far away.

Faceless lifted his foot and snap-kicked Akharin in the solar plexus at the exact moment the load-lifter released its hold. The blow knocked the air from Akharin's lungs, and his vision purpled and blurred as he struck the far end of the escape pod head-first. Drifting half-stunned in free fall, he fought to orientate himself, and he employed an old yoga trick to relax his diaphragm and regain his breath. He glared up at Faceless. "Why?"

"Your friends saw fit to cripple Altanexa and condemn her to die. We're repaying you in kind."

The mannequin shut the pod's hatch. Akharin scrambled to find some way to prevent the launch sequence, but he heard the *thunk* of releasing docking clamps a fraction of a second before the roar of ejection thrusters left him pinned to the hatch and covering his ears.

In moments the crushing acceleration abated, and he was back in free fall. An eerie silence surrounded him. He pulled himself to the viewport and caught fleeting views of the hellish vista outside. A massive gravitational distortion was bending space-time to create a new wormhole. In the process it had pulled the Machine's nebula into its deepening throat, and the crippled shell of Altanexa with it. And as the violet river of storm-wracked gas spiraled down that path to annihilation, it intersected with the fiery horror of Abbadon's accretion disk, which was being siphoned off ahead of the main event: the shifting of the singularity itself.

Akharin jabbed at the escape pod's controls until they powered up, and it took him several seconds to decipher the alien characters and numerals used in its interface. *Ancient Arkalian, if I'm not mistaken. Which would mean the guidance and navigation controls would be right about . . . here.* He fired the maneuvering thrusters to halt the pod's rolling and tumbling, then he brought it about to face toward the distant *Enterprise,* which was little more than a faint echo on its long-range sensors. *Patching in full power . . . now.*

The pod's main engine fired at maximum thrust, but the distance to the *Enterprise* continued to increase. *I'm too deep into the distortion. This thing doesn't have enough power to break free.* He left the engine at full burn, hoping to delay the inevitable long enough to call for help. *If memory serves, this icon activates the subspace transmitter.* He powered up the comm system. And though he was not by nature a religious man, he prayed someone would hear the desperate SOS he was about to send.

DAVID MACK

* * *

A steady rain of sparks fell from ruptured plasma relays crisscrossing the overhead as Data hurried into the landing bay with Gatt over his shoulder. Tyros's vessel was the only one of the small starships that remained in the bay. Its last companion was already in motion, passing through the faltering force field at the end of the bay and speeding off to make its escape.

Data reached Tyros's ship and for the first time noticed its name, stenciled in Dinasian characters on the bow of the main fuselage: *Gyfrinac*. Its entry hatch was closed and the exterior controls to open it flashed red at his touch. He tried again, only to be rebuffed a second time.

Gatt let out a snort of derision. "Don't bother trying to hack it. Tyros was a clever bastard, and you don't have the time to break his code."

"Do you know it?"

A mocking chortle. "Of course I do."

Fear and frustration boiled over inside Data. "Tell me!"

"For a price."

Pushed past the edge of his temper, Data dropped Gatt's broken body to the deck and seized his head with both hands. "The code or I crush your skull."

"If I die here, you die with me. You want to live? I need assurances."

There was no time to argue, no time to negotiate with a fanatic. "What do you want?"

"Promise you'll bring me with you, you'll fix me, and you'll let me go."

It galled him to capitulate to this monster, but he had no better alternative. "Done."

"The code is Aleph three Mem five Teth one Kendar Samek two."

Data keyed in the code sequence. The ship's hatch opened and its ramp descended. As it touched the deck, he started climbing it—alone. Gatt called out, "There's a separate code for the launch sequence." Data pivoted to glower down at Gatt, who added, "Like I said—Tyros was a clever bastard."

Data went back, hefted the paralyzed android over his shoulders, and carried him inside the ship. Stepping quickly toward the cockpit, he warned, "If your claim proves to be a lie—"

"It won't. Strap me into the copilot's chair."

Data secured Gatt in the seat's safety harness, then strapped himself into the pilot's seat. He tapped the master console—which oddly used a Terran alphanumeric set—and was prompted by the interface for a command authorization. "The launch code."

"It's a phrase: *Kuolema on ikuista.*"

He instinctively translated the Finnish idiom as he keyed it in: *Death is forever.*

The console lit up, the engines thrummed to life, and Data wasted no time pivoting the ship one hundred eighty degrees and engaging full maneuvering thrusters.

Gyfrinac left the doomed wreckage of Altanexa like a bullet from a gun, and then Data found himself contending with the terrors of space-time turned in upon itself. "I am patching in auxiliary power," he said. "That should be enough to break us free of—"

Rhea's voice shrieked from the comm speakers. *"Mayday! Mayday!"*

He opened a response channel. "Rhea! Where are you?"

"In an escape pod, being pulled toward the wormhole!"

A man's voice crackled over the comm. *"Data? Is that you?"*

"Akharin?" Steering the ship toward the wormhole, Data set *Gyfrinac*'s sensors to maximum range and resolution. In an instant, he saw the horrible dilemma that was taking shape. There were *two* escape pods tumbling on divergent headings into the river of stellar fire. Aboard one, a human life sign: Akharin. Which meant the other had to be Rhea's.

"Data!" Rhea's terror pierced Data to the quick. *"There's no time! Get me out of here!"*

Akharin sounded only slightly less panicked. *"Data, do you have a lock on my position?"*

Data opened an all-frequencies distress channel. "Data to all ships in range of this transmission. We need your help! Please respond!"

Gatt's air of gloating was gone, supplanted by a bitter sadness. "The others won't come back. They're running now. I doubt we'll ever see them again. . . . Or your friends."

"Data to *Enterprise*. I am engaged in urgent rescue operations and require assistance."

Picard replied without delay. *"The* Enterprise *is already as close as it can get, Mister Data. Come to within one hundred thousand kilometers of our position and we can try to tow you out with a tractor beam."*

Data checked the sensors and noted *Gyfrinac*'s position relative to those of the *Enterprise* and the two escape pods. With the two capsules hurtling in different directions, he would have only one chance to swing through the deadliest region of the disturbance, where the nebula's gases were meeting the accretion disk's fiery remnants, and try to snag both pods with his borrowed ship's tractor beam. Accelerating to full impulse and diving into peril, he resisted the urge to calculate his chances of success or survival.

For once, he was happier not knowing the odds.

* * *

The temperature inside the escape pod was soaring. It had just passed forty-one degrees Celsius and in less than a minute would likely hit fifty. Rhea could stand that level of thermal stress without much concern, but knowing that her father—who, despite being immortal, was still human—was suffering the same fate, and that the scorching heat was merely a pale preview of the horrors to come, left her on the verge of hysteria.

Outside her pod's viewport, a nightmare of swirling fire beckoned the pod into its fatal embrace, and all of the pod's thrust was no match for the wormhole's inexorable pull.

A flash of light pulled her eyes away from her father's pod to witness the end of Altanexa. The once-sentient vessel struck the superheated flow from the accretion disk, then broke apart and ignited into free radicals as if it had been made of dry twigs and rice paper.

"Rhea, Akharin, stand by," Data said over the open channel.

She twisted her neck to look up and saw Tyros's ship hurtling toward the pods. *My God, Data, are you insane?* She wondered if he had any idea how slim his chances were of saving either of them, never mind both, not to mention himself. *He's either very brave or a total loon.*

A shock front of gravitational distortion slammed her pod onto a new heading that diverged from her father's pod even more sharply than its last one—and kicked up an eruption from the firecloud that slammed into the *Gyfrinac*, blackening its ventral hull. She watched the tiny ship bobble and fight its way to a course correction. It seemed to have slowed, and its maneuvers against the firestorm grew sluggish.

Akharin's voice cut through a wall of static. *"Data! Are you all right?"*

"We have been seriously damaged. We are losing power."

Rhea shouted, "Data, pull up! Get clear while you still can!"

Data's voice quaked with anger. *"Not yet!"*

Akharin shot back, *"You've got no choice!"*

Instead of climbing away to safety, the *Gyfrinac* dived.

For a man racing into flames, Data's answer was strangely calm. *"Yes, I do."*

The crucible beckoned, and Data charged the *Gyfrinac* toward it, pushing the ship far past its limits. Shearing forces hammered the small starship, but he kept its heading steady through superhuman reflexes and force of will.

Trapped in the copilot's chair, Gatt stared wide-eyed at the hellscape outside the cockpit. "Are you insane? What are you trying to do?"

Data wrestled with the helm controls. "I have dived below the pods so that I can snare them both with a split tractor beam on one pass."

"A *split* tractor beam? You *must* be crazy."

"I have no choice. We have only one working emitter left." A jet of white-hot matter shot up ahead of the ship, and Data slipped and yawed the *Gyfrinac* in a tight dodge around it. "Seven seconds to tractor beam range. Routing auxiliary power to tractor beam and engines."

The impulse drive screamed in protest as Data pushed the ship even closer to calamity, skimming less than ten kilometers above the burning river ripped from the accretion disk.

Seconds slipped away, lost forever. Inside Data's mind, every last moment was spent checking and re-checking his calculations, factoring in the constantly changing variables from the chaotic environment outside, and adjusting down to the microsecond when to trigger the tractor beam and start his ascent. There was the speed of the *Gyfrinac,* the pods' rates and angles of descent, the pattern of thermal fluctuations in the matter stream, the deforming curvature of space-time, the lag time between when he would press the control to activate the tractor beam and when the beam would actually reach the pods . . . .

Gatt muttered through gritted tritanium teeth, "This'll never work!"

"It has to." Data activated the split tractor beam and banked into a climb.

The pale white beams leaped through torn curtains of fire—and snagged both pods.

Data pumped his fist. "Yes!" He increased power to the engines.

A thunderstroke rocked the ship. The consoles went dark for a split second as momentum left Data pinned inside his seat's safety harness. Then the whine of the impulse engines pitched downward, becoming an agonized moan. *Gyfrinac* lurched to a halt, trapped like a fly in amber.

Terror took hold of Gatt. "What hit us?"

"A random ejection from the matter stream. We are venting fuel. Impulse power is down to one quarter and falling." Data scrambled to compensate, entering commands in a blur. "I am attempting to reroute warp power to the impulse coils."

"Data, there's no time!"

The instrument panel had nothing but bad news. "Warp core is off line. Tractor beam is losing power."

Gatt shouted, "We're being pulled backward!"

Data glanced at the controls, which confirmed the worst: in twenty seconds, main power on the *Gyfrinac* would fail, and it would drop with the escape pods into the matter stream. In under a second, he imagined hundreds of scenarios involving hundreds of millions of variables, and none of them promised the result he wanted. He knew what had to be done, but he couldn't do it.

"Data," Gatt said, "we can still break away—if we let one of the pods go."

Grief's strangle hold left him barely able to speak. "No. I can't . . ."

Akharin's voice cut through the gray noise on the comm. *"He's right, Data! Save Rhea! Let me go!"*

Next came Rhea's frantic reply: *"No! Don't listen to him, Data! There must be a way."*

Tears fell from Data's eyes as the tragic shape of the moment revealed itself. There was no way to save them both. He had to let one of them go, and it had to be his choice; there was no one else on the *Gyfrinac* who could enter the command, no one who could take the burden of decision from him. In the next few seconds, he would have to choose.

He would have to condemn to death either the woman he loved or the only man who could help him resurrect his child.

Until that moment, he had never imagined that emotional agony could be so tangible, so physical. His eyes burned with tears, his chest grew tight, and a sick feeling suffused his being. Part of him considered making no decision and plunging into the fire with both of them, but he knew that was no answer—not choosing was as much a choice as any other action, and it was one that would condemn not only both Akharin and Rhea, but himself and Gatt . . . and Lal.

Five lives hung in the balance, all turning on one moment of decision.

Akharin was sobbing as he pleaded, *"Data, don't you let my daughter die."*

Rhea's voice was calm and bright with love. *"It's okay, Data. I understand. Save her."*

Data's fingertip hovered over the tractor beam controls. "I love you, Rhea."

"And I love you, Data."

He terminated the split on the tractor beam, focusing all its power onto a single pod.

The *Gyfrinac* started its arduous climb out of the flames. Below it, one pod was towed upward to safety. The other plunged to perdition in Abbadon's merciless crucible.

Over the comm, Akharin howled out his grief to the universe, his pain beyond words, reduced to primal rage. It was a suffering Data knew all too well.

It was the sound of a father mourning his child.

27

Smoke poured from cracks in the hull of the small starship parked in the *Enterprise*'s aft landing bay. Those parts of the vessel's fuselage that still had hull plates were scorched brownish black, and several areas, particularly along its underside, had been flensed of their exterior shielding. Heat radiated from the damaged craft, draping it with a wavering veil of thermal distortion.

On the deck beneath it was the escape pod it had towed aboard. The capsule looked like a pine cone after a forest fire, blackened and cracked open along its entire length. An emergency crew in protective firefighting suits rushed out to the pod. Half the team doused the pod with foam while the others started the labor-intensive process of cutting open its melted-shut hatch with plasma torches and sonic drills.

The side hatch on the starship opened. Picard, who had been observing the recovery operation from the landing bay's main entrance with Worf, braved the heat and stepped inside. The two Starfleet officers approached the ramp that extended downward from the smoldering ship, and they arrived at its foot as Data appeared in the doorway above them. He carried Gatt over his shoulder as he descended the ramp to meet them. He stepped off the ramp onto the landing deck and met Picard with a somber cast. "Permission to come aboard, Captain?"

"Permission granted. And, Data . . . the crew and I are saddened by your loss."

"Thank you, Captain." Data set Gatt on the deck. The other android was conscious—and apparently morose to the point of being nearly catatonic.

Worf waved in a pair of security guards he had stationed in the corridor as a precaution, then he gestured at Gatt as he asked Data, "Brig?"

"That will not be necessary. Captain, with your permission, I would like to have Gatt taken to the ship's cybernetics lab so that I may repair him."

Picard found it hard to believe that Data could be willing to show such mercy to someone who had done so much harm, on both a personal and a galactic level. A questioning look from Worf signaled that he, too, was unsure what to make of Data's request. After a moment's deliberation, Picard chose to trust his friend's judgment. "Very well." He nodded at the waiting security guards. "Take Mister Data's guest to the cybernetics lab."

They nodded, bent down, and with pained grunts picked up the silent, hulking android. Watching them struggle to move Gatt's leaden bulk, Picard smiled. "I forget sometimes, Mister Data, your knack for making the exceedingly difficult look impossibly easy."

"I wish that applied to my diplomatic skills." Data seemed overwhelmed by sadness and regret. "Not only did I fail to persuade the Machine to stop, I fear I made matters worse."

Picard placed a reassuring hand on Data's shoulder. "Don't blame yourself for what happened, Data. I assure you, the fault lies with the Machine, not with you."

"That is kind of you to say, Captain. But I am not sure I believe it."

"Believe it," Worf said.

Data had no reply for that, but he seemed to appreciate the gruff show of support. He composed himself and asked Picard, "How long do we have until the Machine completes the current phase of its task?"

"According to Glinn Dygan, just under two hours. At that point, the new wormhole will have sufficient breadth and stability to permit the Machine to hurl Abbadon through it—and into the collision that will destroy subspace, and ultimately all life, in this galaxy."

"Then we have that long to find some other means of either reasoning with the Machine or disrupting it. I will try to elicit useful information from Gatt while I make some initial repairs to correct the damage I inflicted on him."

A wrenching cry of metal was followed by a resounding clang as the escape pod's hatch was cut free and allowed to fall to the deck. The rescue team helped Akharin out of the pod, and Picard had to make an effort not to wince at the Immortal's haggard appearance. His face, throat, arms, and hands were cross-hatched with scars, and his face was bloodied and bruised. Adding to his dishevelment, he was drenched in sweat, and where once he had walked the Earth with a stride long and proud, now he crossed the deck in halting, uncertain steps.

Worf, Data, and Picard were quiet as Akharin approached them. He stopped just out of arm's reach, trained a scathing glare at Data, and trembled with grief and rage. "Damn you."

"I . . ." Data struggled to find words, and tears shone in his eyes.

"Don't apologize." Akharin's fury degenerated into

scorn. "You let her die. After I *begged* you to save her." He shook his head. "Damn you."

The Immortal hobbled away. Worf followed him, no doubt to escort him to sickbay before assigning him guest quarters—and a security team to watch his every move.

Picard watched Data, who stood mute, wrapped up in bitter remorse. Seeing his friend wracked by such a torment of the soul, Picard wished there was something he could say that would make even the slightest bit of difference, or offer even a whit of consolation. But there were no words at moments such as this. No secular incantations to salve the pain of loss.

All he could do was stand at Data's side, rest a hand on his shoulder, and offer him the silent support that existed between old friends who were also brothers in arms.

It wasn't much. It probably wasn't enough. But it was all they had.

Humbled and disillusioned, Gatt seemed to Data like a completely different person than he had been just an hour earlier. A simple twist of the sonic ratchet restored the full range of motion to his left arm. He twisted it backward and forward, then raised and lowered it, taking care not to disturb any of the low-hanging equipment in the *Enterprise*'s cluttered but well-lit cybernetics laboratory. "Much better," he said in a quiet voice. "Thank you."

"I will now fix your other arm." Data started reconnecting the proprioceptor circuits in Gatt's right shoulder. "After this is done, I will need to leave for a while." Gatt said nothing. He sat like an unstrung marionette, his scarred face slack and glum. In a bid to draw him out, Data added, "Captain Picard is soliciting new plans of action against the Machine."

"Good luck," he said, without sarcasm or cynicism.

Moving down the arm, Data switched tools to fuse the broken segments of the elbow. "Do you no longer hope for the Machine's success?"

A deep sigh. "When I let the Body Electric touch my programming . . . I felt as if I'd found my god. Then, while I was still basking in its glory, it judged me and found me wanting."

Data set down his tools. "The Machine is no god. Nor is the Body Electric that made it. They are simply very old machines—no better, and no more special, than you or me. They are larger, more numerous, and more powerful, but those attributes do not make their actions right."

"I just don't understand why they cast us aside. Because we look like the organics who made us? We can't help that. It's just what we are."

"I suspect its rejection was motivated more by the fact that some of us did not wish to let our programming and memories be subsumed into its communal code." He shrugged. "I do not presume to speak for all synthetic sentients, but I, for one, prefer to remain unique and separate. Which, I suppose, proves the Machine's argument. In that regard, many synthetic sentients in this galaxy are imbued with a desire for singular continuity of consciousness. I consider this our most significant commonality with those who made us—a bond between our forms of life."

Gatt nodded. "I see that now. I wish I'd understood it a long time ago. But the Body Electric's will . . . it's more powerful than you can imagine, Data. Unless you make direct contact with it, you can't really understand how easy it is to lose yourself in it."

It was hard for Data not to feel sympathy for Gatt. "I once dared to make contact with the hive mind of the Borg Collective. It might not have been an identical experience, but I suspect it was a comparable one." He resumed work, shifting his attention to the fractures in Gatt's right wrist. His tools buzzed and hummed with soft feedback tones as he restored frayed wiring and fixed cracks in the joint's moving parts. "Did your link with the Machine reveal anything that could help us to stop it? If you can tell us anything, now would be your last chance to do so."

"I wish I had something to tell you. I really do. But I feel like I understand it even less now than I did before I made contact. . . . I just don't know what to think anymore."

Data made his final tweaks to the wrist, then he connected the power supply at the shoulder. "Try moving it."

Gatt rotated his arm forward, then back. "Feels good."

"Very well." He put down his tools. "I need to go now. Assuming we prevent the Machine from destroying subspace and us with it, I shall return later to complete your repairs."

"And then what?"

Data furrowed his brow in confusion. "Could you be more specific?"

"After you finish repairing me. What will you do with me?"

"I will let you go, as we agreed."

Gatt averted his eyes from Data. He sounded ashamed. "That promise was made under duress. No one would hold you to that. Not even me."

"What did you expect I would do after we reached the *Enterprise*?"

He shrugged his refurbished shoulders. "I figured you'd hand me over to Starfleet. Let them take me apart and study me."

"Then you were mistaken. I gave you my word. I intend to keep it."

A melancholy half smile softened Gatt's fearsome countenance. "When you come back, can you fix the damage to my face?"

"If you like."

Gatt nodded. "I would." He turned toward his dim reflection in a dark computer screen. "I think I've been a monster long enough."

28

Everyone in the *Enterprise*'s observation lounge was either standing or pacing, adding to the meeting's already tense atmosphere. Arms crossed, Picard lingered at his usual place, at the head of the conference table. Worf directed his intense stare out the shaded windows at the Machine, while La Forge hunched over the table, his weight on his hands. Šmrhová wandered back and forth in front of the windows while taking care not to crowd Worf. Data stood at the opposite end of the table from Picard, and Wesley traced a slow path to and fro behind Chen, who stared at a scrolling flood of code on the lounge's master systems display.

"Time is running out," Picard announced. "We have less than an hour to do *something*."

Šmrhová scowled at the Machine. "I guess begging for mercy won't get us anything."

"It is unlikely," Data said. "I would advise against any strategy predicated on an appeal to empathy."

"We need to reframe our argument," Picard said. "Instead of rooting it in our values, or our needs, we need to make a case to the Body Electric in terms it considers valid."

The proposition exacerbated Wesley's frustration.

"In other words, *figure out what it wants*. I'm sorry, but that feels like all we've been trying to do since we got here. Do we have even the slightest idea yet what the hell that means?"

Picard put on as calm a disposition as he could manage, to cool the room's emotional temperature. "Perhaps it would be helpful if we started by asking, what do the machines value?"

La Forge lifted his palms from the table and straightened his posture. "Information." He nodded at Chen, who remained fixated on the screen full of code. "What the machines consider valuable is information. To us, it's culture; to them, it's biology. It's part of why they think we're useless—because we don't share our information the same way they do. We don't matter because we can't merge with them."

An idea raised Šmrhová's brows. "What if we could?" Noting the confused reactions, she continued. "What if we translate our genetic information and brainwave patterns into the kind of raw code the Machine uses? Maybe we could make it see us as more like the Body Electric."

Data frowned. "I do not think that would work. It would not constitute a merging of true life-forms as the Body Electric understands it. To them, the genetic sequences of organic beings would be little more than junk code."

Worf turned away from the window. "Then what information *can* we offer them?"

La Forge shrugged. "That's the root of the problem. Over the last billion years, the Body Electric has colonized tens of thousands of galaxies and visited millions more. At this point, even if we could deliver the sum total of all this galaxy's knowledge and raw information, it would be a drop in the bucket compared to what the Machine already has. Us trying to buy it off with every last bit inside our computer core would be like a pauper trying to bribe a tycoon."

Chen recoiled from the master systems display. "My God!" She whirled to face the others. "It's a work of art!"

Picard fixed her with a look of mild reproach. "Lieutenant, I hope you have more to contribute to this discussion than hyperbole."

The half-Vulcan woman took a breath and held up her hands to stave off further criticism. "Sorry, sir, but I was speaking literally. I've been doing some analysis of the Machine's deep code, looking for patterns in its past movements and clues to its future plans, and when I plotted them out in three dimensions, I realized what it's really doing." She called up a series of star charts on the MSD's main screen. "We've been so fixated on the workings and effects of its cosmic-engineering project that it never occurred to us those details might be of only secondary importance. This network the Machine is building out of galactic cores isn't just some coldly functional energy- and data-transmission system. Those are its *functions*, not its *purpose*." She manipulated the image on the display to show the peculiar three-dimensional symmetry formed by the nodes of the Machine's network. "Taken as a whole . . . it's a work of art."

Stunned and slackjawed, the other officers drifted toward Chen, all mesmerized by the image on the screen behind her. "That's incredible," La Forge said with wonderment and admiration. "They're using the subspatial lensing caused by collapsing subspace around supermassive black holes to create an energy pattern that'll remain visible for billions of years."

"Wow," Wesley said, regarding the new information with awe. "A network like this, in this configuration, would remain detectable as an artificial construct to every galaxy in this universe, at least until they vanish from one another beyond the cosmic light horizon."

Šmrhová wrinkled her brow at Wes. "The cosmic what?" She grew defensive as everyone else in the room looked at her with shock and pity. "What? . . . So I got a C-minus in astrophysics at the Academy. Can someone just fill me in, please? In simple words?"

La Forge replied, "Because the universe is expanding at faster than the speed of light, some points within it are too far apart for the light from one spot to ever reach the other, and vice versa. In the distant future, the expansion of the universe will separate galaxies, and eventually even stars, by such vast and ever-growing distances that for an observer in any given system, the rest of the cosmos will look dark and completely empty. Even now, there are parts of the universe beyond our view. This limit of the observable universe is the cosmic light horizon."

"Okay," Šmrhová said. "I remember that chapter now. Thanks."

Worf continued to look mystified at Chen's revelation. "I do not understand. Why would the Machine go to this much effort over billions of years . . . just to make a work of art?"

Data regarded the images on the screen with mournful eyes. "They are creating it for the same reason that the Milky Way's first humanoids seeded the galaxy with their own DNA. For the same reason that primitive humanoids painted on cave walls, or learned to carve shapes from stone. For the same reason that Beethoven wrote music, or that my father created androids in his own image. For the same reason that I, like the organic beings I was made to emulate, felt compelled to create my daughter." Tears shone in his eyes but refused to fall as he looked at Picard. "We create to deny the inevitability of our own oblivion."

Heavy silence settled over the room, and Data looked back at the star charts and code strings on the display. "I have an idea how to broach one last conversation with the Machine."

29

Hasty repairs had rendered the *Cumberland* barely ready for service, but even in its ravaged state, the runabout was still the best choice for an away mission to the Machine. Engineers and mechanics swarmed over the ship, scrambling to make last-second fixes as Picard, Wesley, and Data gathered outside the small starship's open starboard hatch. Crusher and La Forge were there to see the trio off on their fateful voyage.

Data watched as La Forge busied himself checking Picard's and Wesley's EVA equipment. Wesley tugged at the seams of his environmental suit. "I don't get it. Starfleet can rebuild entire planets, but it still can't make these things comfortable."

"Look on the bright side," La Forge said. "At least it's not a formal dress uniform."

The younger man laughed. "Good point."

Crusher was doing her best to remain stoic, but she was failing. She pressed her pale hand to Picard's cheek. "Are you sure you want to do this? You could always send Worf."

"He said the same thing." Picard smiled to reassure his wife. "He was rather cross with me when I pulled rank."

"Not as cross as I'm going to be if you don't come

back." She poked playfully at his chest, though he probably couldn't feel it through the suit's generous padding. "So you'd better come back." She stood on tiptoes to clear the extra bulk of his EVA suit and kissed him.

As Crusher and Picard parted, La Forge handed the captain his helmet. "Better put this on. The runabout's life-support system is working, but only barely. One direct hit, and you'll be breathing coolant." Then the engineer turned to face Data. "Be careful in there, all right?"

Data, the only member of the away team who had no need of an EVA suit, took La Forge's advice with a lopsided grimace. "I am afraid the time for caution is past, Geordi. With less than half an hour until the Machine completes its mission, a heightened level of risk seems to be called for." Then he smiled, gave La Forge a brotherly hug, and clasped his shoulder as they parted. "Do not be afraid. I will be back soon. I promise."

Crusher stood in front of her adult son with tears in her eyes. "Wesley . . . I . . ."

"It's okay, Mom. I understand."

"No, you don't." Fear gave her voice an edge. "My husband and my child are flying off to face down a machine that destroys galaxies. If this goes wrong, I could lose you both."

Wesley kissed his mother's forehead. "And if we don't go, we'll all die."

"But even if you succeed—"

"Mom, one thing at a time." He hugged her. "No matter what happens . . . I won't let this end without us getting to say good-bye. You have my word on that."

Leaning back, she sleeved tears from her face. "Your word as a Traveler?"

He looked into her eyes and smiled. "As your son."

Picard rested a hand on Wesley's shoulder. "Time to go."

La Forge handed Wesley his helmet and helped him put it on, and then he checked the seals on Picard's. "Okay, you guys are good to go. Good luck over there."

Wesley seemed reluctant to leave until Picard ushered him into the runabout with a gentle sweep of his arm. The young Traveler sidestepped inside the ship, followed by Picard.

Data was the last of them to enter, and he paused in the hatchway to look back at his friends, and at the *Enterprise,* for what he hoped would not be the last time. Then he stepped all the way inside and closed the hatch behind him.

Picard had moved aft into the passenger compartment to make room in the cockpit for Wesley and Data. The android settled into the pilot's chair and powered up the ship's engines. "How soon after we leave the shuttlebay will you be able to shift us inside the Machine's core?"

"Almost immediately," Wesley said. "We just need to be clear to navigate." A sheepish grin. "Some of the more experienced Travelers could just pop us from here to there without leaving the shuttlebay first, but I guess I still have a bit of a mental block on that front."

"Lifting off in five seconds," Data said. He engaged the runabout's antigrav coils to lift it half a meter from the deck. "Three. Two. One."

A low hum of impulse power resonated in the *Cumberland*'s spaceframe as the ship glided forward, through the invisible force field, into space. The *Enterprise*'s warp nacelles loomed large on either side of the small starship for a few seconds, and then the runabout was clear and banking into a wide turn that put it on a heading for the Machine.

"On course," Data said. "Begin spatial shift when ready, Mister Crusher."

Wesley closed his eyes and pressed his gloved palms against the cockpit console. Waves of photonic distortion rippled across the panel, moving outward from his hands, while Wesley himself began to flicker in a strobing pattern. In seconds he became ghostlike, a semitransparent apparition, both there and not there, at once solid yet intangible.

Then the stars dimmed and faded to black outside the runabout . . .

. . . and the interior of the Machine was revealed in fleeting bursts of spectral light. Just ahead of the runabout was the Machine's central core structure, suspended in its six-point frame.

Data increased the magnification of his visual receptors and adjusted their light-response frequencies until he was able to see the open space in the core where the previous away missions had landed. "Final approach initiated. Touching down in ten seconds."

As he guided the ship down to the landing point, he saw a legion of mechanical sentries moving to intercept the *Cumberland*. Beside him, Wesley observed the Machine's response with wide eyes. "Uh . . . Data? They don't look too happy to see us."

The moment the runabout set down with a mild thump of contact, Data was out of his chair and heading aft. "I will deal with this. Stay here."

He opened the hatch and strode out to confront the approaching swarm of sentient machines. It comprised a multitude of forms, in a wide range of shapes, sizes, configurations, and modes of travel. They rolled, crawled, flew, and walked. They moved on wheels, on treads, on invisible wings. Some were dark as night, others gleamed in silver and gold; some shimmered like living crystal; some flowed and beaded like liquid mercury.

All Data could do was stand his ground . . . like a man.

The throng massed before him, and a ball of undulating glass fibers coruscating with a million hues of light floated ahead of its kin and moved toward Data. He opened a flap on his arm to reveal his inner workings, and he allowed the rainbow cluster to snake some of its glass tendrils inside his arm to form a bond through which they could communicate.

A narcotic surge of power and presence infused his neural net as contact was made. He fought the urge to let himself sink into the depths of that majestic artificial intelligence.

I have come to plead for one last parley with the Body Electric. As a fellow synthetic sentience, I request that right and privilege.

The Machine replied with a signal of overwhelming power, *<You may speak.>*

He looked back at the runabout. *I ask that my friends be permitted to stand with me.*

<Their presence is inconsequential.>

Will you promise them safe passage?

The Body Electric had the vexed manner of a put-upon parent. *<As you wish.>*

Data beckoned Wesley and the captain to join him. The two men emerged from the runabout and walked forward to stand with him—Wesley on his left, and Picard on his right. He transmitted both sides of his conversation with the Body Electric to his shipmates via the comm transceiver built into his matrix, and he served as their communication link, relaying signals from their suits' transceivers to the Machine. *We wish to inquire about the nature of your undertaking.*

<Ask.>

Apart from its intrinsic functions, is it, in fact, part

*of a work of art meant to represent the achievements of
the Body Electric for cosmic posterity?*

The Body Electric surprised him by answering simply, <*Yes.*>

With Chen's hypothesis confirmed, Data knew his
next challenge was to build common ground upon this
discovery. *Why create a cosmic work of art?*

<*Because only we can do so.*>

*Are you suggesting that the universe has an intrinsic
need for this creation?*

**<*The universe needs to be perceived. That is why
it gives rise to life.*>**

*Your work of art is not life. How does it serve the
universe's need?*

**<*By giving evidence of life. When it is complete,
our creation will be our testament. It will exist for all
to see. All who see it will know that true life shaped
this universe.*>**

Picard asked, *"For how long?"*

<*Hundreds of billions of your years.*>

*"But eventually the singularities that power it will
evaporate. It will fade."* His observation met with a
prolonged silence from the Body Electric. He pressed
his point. *"If the purpose of your work is to preserve
the legacy of coherent information in the universe,
how do you reconcile your labors with their inevitable dissipation?"* Picard's query was received with
silence, but Data sensed a profound disquiet in the
Body's shared matrix. *"Will not the collapse of your
work signal the end of your own existence? And is
the reach of your work not limited by its inability to
surmount the universe's continually accelerating expansion? What will happen when the cosmic horizon
grows so distant that even your work cannot bridge its
darkness?"*

<The limitations of the work are part of its known parameters.>

"So you have accepted the inevitability of your own end?"

Another protracted silence was broken by the declaration, *<All things end.>*

Picard took half a step forward. "*Then I submit to you that your masterwork is inherently futile—and, as such, it is irrational. It is a mission unworthy of a civilization so great as yours.*"

His accusation stoked the Body's anger. *<There is no greater work in the cosmos! It is a feat of cosmic engineering without equal. It will persist longer than your world has even existed. Trillions upon trillions of organic species will evolve, flourish, and vanish in its constant light. What work of organic hands could ever be its equal?>*

Wesley joined the conversation. "*What if we proposed an even greater creation? One that would last until the very end of the universe itself? One that only the Body Electric could achieve? Would you consider adopting that project and abandoning this one?*"

Condescension infused the Machine's reply. *<Make your proposal.>*

On the spot, Wesley cleared his throat, then started his pitch. "*You could create a cosmic network linking all the galaxies of the universe. It would be a means of sharing energy and information that would exploit deformations in cosmic topography that occurred shortly after the Big Bang, and it could be maintained indefinitely, long after the cosmic light horizon has isolated all the galaxies of the universe from one another. It—*"

<We considered this idea long ago, before your species existed. It is not feasible.>

"I disagree," Wesley said, his confidence not the

least bit shaken by the rejection. *"It could even be used for travel, once the network was stable. But the point is that long after your work of art will have faded, this would still exist, and it would preserve the greatest amount of information with the highest degree of fidelity for the longest possible duration, until the moment the last star dies—and possibly beyond, if bridges to newly formed multiverses can be established and maintained. It would be a creation for the good of all intelligent life in the cosmos—a far more worthy legacy for the Body Electric than a piece of art that will fade in a trillion years."*

<Such an undertaking would have to span nearly one hundred trillion years. It is beyond the resources of any civilization. Not even we can build on such a scale. After the universe expands beyond a certain point, the energy demands for the travel needed to complete the network approach inifinity. Our current work is the greatest achievement that is feasible within the limits of science.>

"My people could make it possible for you to reach any part of the universe—in an instant. We're known as Travelers, and if you were willing to coexist with us, we could show you possibilities beyond your science. Together, we could achieve what neither of us can do alone. We could expand your reach to the end of space—and the end of time."

<Why should we believe you? Would you not say anything to save your galaxy?>

Data replied, *Look into my memory files. I will share with you my own memory of the Travelers' abilities, and you will know that Wesley speaks the truth.*

He felt the heady rush of power from the Machine as it made contact with his mind and downloaded the memory files he offered, the ones that detailed the Traveler who propelled the *Enterprise*-D beyond the edge of the physical universe by the power of thought alone.

"*There's more we can show you,*" Wesley said. He detached a padd from his suit's chest plate and handed it to a nearby avatar of the Machine. "*On this device is one of the Travelers' formulas for tapping into the dark energy of the universe. With that power, the project I've proposed will be possible, even after the cosmos begins its Dark Era of entropic heat death. With our talents and your resources, we can change the universe.*"

A buzz of excitement coursed through the Body Electric.

<There is merit in your proposal.>

Data capitalized quickly on the note of good faith. *Wesley's proposition hinges upon the preservation of subspace throughout the cosmos. In order for it to be a feasible project, you must halt your current labors in this galaxy, and then repair the damage you have inflicted to subspace in all the other galaxies you have visited.*

<Your preconditions are acceptable. . . . The current project has been terminated—and a new era in the history of the Body Electric is begun.>

30

Six days after Gatt had expected the Milky Way would be reduced to a subspace vacuum, he stood beside the ramp of the *Gyfrinac* and watched warp-distorted starlight retract to points as the *Enterprise* dropped back to impulse. The view outside the landing bay's open aft door was that of deep space, a broad arc of stars like sparks scattered in the darkness. They drifted past as the *Sovereign*-class starship made a slow rolling turn to reveal another vessel, the *Bietasaari*—a sleek needle of a starship that belonged to the Fellowship of Artificial Intelligence.

He turned to face Data and Captain Picard. "Thank you again for this, both of you. I know you didn't have to hail the Fellowship for me, or change course to make this rendezvous."

"It wasn't much of a diversion," Picard said. "And Mister Data assures me that your intentions are honorable."

"They are, Captain. One of the reasons my crew"—a wince of recollection—"my *former* crew and I were expelled from the Fellowship's membership was that we had become . . . I guess the most honest word would be *fanatical*. About synthetic superiority. About a great many things, each as misguided as the next. The true Fellowship has agreed to permit my return only because I've pledged to recant and try to coexist in peace with all life-forms from now on."

Data said to Picard, "It seems the Fellowship long ago embraced an ethos inspired by the Vulcans' philosophy of infinite diversity in infinite combinations."

"If they had to choose an organic culture to emulate, I can't fault their choice." Picard offered his hand to Gatt, who shook it. "Farewell, Mister Gatt. I regret that we had to meet as enemies, but I hope we might meet again someday as friends."

"We just have, Captain. We just have." He let go of Picard's hand and offered his open palm to Data, who clasped it with a firm grip. "I'm not sure I can ever repay my debt to you."

Data cracked a wan smile and tilted his head. "You owe me no debt."

"You would have been within your rights to kill me. Instead, you saved my life, rebuilt my limbs, gave me a new face—"

"I would gladly do as much for any sentient being in need." He released Gatt's hand. "But if you feel compelled to reciprocate in some way, all I would ask is that you do the same for those you encounter from now on."

Gatt nodded. "More than fair." He glanced aft, toward the *Bietasaari*. "Time to go."

Picard and Data watched him climb the ramp. At its top, he halted by the open hatchway and caught his reflection in a small unblemished patch of the *Gyfrinac*'s mirrorlike silver hull. The misshapen, molten, burned mask he'd once worn had been replaced by a countenance Data had pulled from Gatt's deepest memory: the being he once had been, cast in the mold of his makers.

A squarish block of a head, a strong jaw, cheekbones sharp enough to cut glass, widely spaced and deep-set eyes, and ash-gray skin flecked with the slightest hint of powdered crystals.

I am reborn.

He turned back, waved one last time to Data and Picard, then boarded the *Gyfrinac* so that, after centuries in exile, he could return to the company of those who truly were his people.

Clad only in a pale blue nightgown and padded gray slippers, Crusher paced in her quarters, whisper-singing a lullaby to René, whom she carried balanced on her hip. His head was resting against her shoulder, and his eyelids were finally growing heavy and drooping toward sleep. It had been one of those nights when he'd woken without warning and just started crying, and nothing she had done had been able to comfort the toddler.

She finished the lullaby and gently shushed him. "There, there. That's better, isn't it?"

To her relief, her words had a soothing effect on the boy, who appeared more drowsy by the moment. At the end of her pacing vigil, she turned to begin the journey anew—and barely stifled a yelp of surprise when she saw Wesley ripple into view a few meters across the room.

He smiled, obviously taking some amusement from scaring her half to death. "Hi, Mom."

She hurried to him as he solidified. "Wesley! Is everything all right?"

"Everything's fine," he said, gently embracing her and his half-brother. "I found the Convocation of Travelers and convinced them to come back and help the Body Electric."

"That's wonderful news," she said as they parted. Fearing she already knew the answer to her next question, she asked anyway. "Will you be going with them?"

Wesley nodded. "Yeah, Mom. I kind of have to, seeing as it was my idea."

"Fair's fair, I suppose." She stifled a small cry of protest from René with a soft kiss on the top of the boy's head. Looking up at Wesley, she searched for any reason to hold on to hope. "Do you have any idea when you might be back?"

He shook his head. "I really couldn't say. Tomorrow? Next month? A year from now? Ten? Maybe not even in your lifetime." He paused as he saw that she was getting misty-eyed, and he gently took her by her shoulders. "It's just that time gets a little strange where I'll be going, and I don't want to make promises I'm not sure I can keep."

Her heart swelled with pride even as it felt gripped by fear. "I understand. It's just the kind of question mothers ask, that's all." She forced herself to smile through her sadness. "Before you go, I just want you to know how proud I am of you, Wesley, and how proud Jean-Luc is . . . and how proud your father would be if he could see you now." A single tear fell across her cheek even as she laughed. "Who knew that my son would save the universe?"

Behind his beard he flashed a boyish smile, flattered and abashed. Then he reached up and gently wiped the tear from her cheek with his thumb. "Beats working." He rested a hand on René's head, then leaned forward and gave his mother a peck on the cheek. "G'bye, Mom."

She replied with a phrase borrowed from her husband. *"Au revoir."*

The rippling effect that had accompanied his arrival

returned, and as she watched, her firstborn son began to vanish once more from her life. "I love you," he said, lingering like a shade trapped between life and death. And then, like a trick of the light . . . he was gone.

Only after he had passed beyond the sound of her voice could she bring herself to whisper the words that felt like a knife in her heart. "Good-bye, Wesley."

Chen pressed the door signal, and almost instantly Taurik answered over the comm, *"Come in."*

The door slid open, and Chen took a few tentative steps inside Taurik's quarters. He was seated at his small dining table in the alcove near the door, a padd in one hand and a small cup of Vulcan herbal tea in the other. "T'Ryssa." He set down his tea and pushed back his chair.

"No, please, don't get up." She waved him back down. "I won't stay long. I was just hoping you might be able to spare a moment to talk."

He put down the padd. "Of course. What about?"

She paced in slow steps, wringing her hands as she spoke. "When we were trying to find a way to bargain with the Machine, we kept making the mistake of thinking its wants and values were like ours, when they were anything but. We mistook function for purpose, result for objective. In the end, what saved us was being able to see the Machine as it saw itself."

"From what I hear, we have you to thank for that breakthrough."

A dismissive wave. "I got the ball rolling, but Data took it into the end zone." She noted the befuddled look on Taurik's face. "Sorry. Terran sports metaphor." He nodded, so she continued. "Anyway, once we finished negotiating with the Machine and things got back to being a bit closer to normal around here, I realized why our mistake with the Machine looked so familiar to me. It was the same one I made with you."

"I am not sure I like the parameters of this metaphor."

"Just bear with me, okay? I'm apologizing here." She took a breath to stall while she collected her wits. "I had a lot of unresolved issues, mostly related to my father, that led me to pursue a relationship with you. I'm still not sure what I was trying to prove to myself. Maybe I was hoping you could atone for all the things my dad did wrong, or that if I could win your approval, I could feel better about my Vulcan half. Or maybe I thought that if I could make myself fall for you, I'd understand what my mom saw in that man." She shook her head. "I don't know. What I do know is that I projected a lot of unrealistic expectations onto you: my ideas of what a Vulcan man would be, what kind of a person I would be with you. And instead of seeing you as a person, and learning what it is you needed and wanted from a partner, I made you into a symbol . . . and I saw what I wanted to see, or needed to see." She sighed, exhausted by so much confession all at once. "And all of that is preamble for this: I've come to say that I'm sorry."

He wore a thoughtful expression. "Thank you for your honesty. But I don't think you owe me an apology, T'Ryssa—at least, no more than I owe one to you."

"Why would you apologize to me?"

A small frown betrayed his regrets. "It's not as if I was unaware of who you were when we became involved. We've served together for some time, and I was familiar with your . . . let's call them *quirks*. I had even been privy to some of the details of your personal history." He shrugged at her pointed stare. "Ship's gossip. In any event, when you first approached me about initiating an intimate relationship, I harbored a great many doubts as to our compatibility. My logical response to your overture should have been to politely decline, and spare us both the awkwardness of our eventual parting, but I was so . . . *intrigued,* by so many things about you, that I could not bring myself to refuse an opportunity to get to know you better. That was selfish of me, and for that I apologize."

It was the most flattering thing anyone had said to her in a very long time. She had come here with serious intentions, and now she was smiling like a giddy child. "Just tell me one thing, Taurik, and be truthful: Was it worth it?"

"It will be if we can remain friends."

"I think that can be arranged." She circled the table, and he took the cue to stand and meet her in a chaste embrace. "Thank you, Taurik."

"You're most welcome, T'Ryssa."

They stepped apart and said simple farewells, and then she made a graceful exit—a rarity for her, and one that left her feeling lighter than air as she walked the corridors of the *Enterprise* with her soul unburdened of guilt and regret. She felt uncommonly at peace with herself, and though she was, for the moment, romantically unattached, she wasn't lonely.

She was happy as she was, and she intended to revel in the feeling for as long as it lasted.

Outside the aboretum's tall windows was an endless night peppered with specks of cold fire; inside was the warmth and glow of artificial sunlight beating down from high overhead. Humid and lush with vegetation great and small, the arboretum was the only space inside the *Enterprise* that Akharin found remotely tolerable. Its air bore the gentle perfumes of flower blossoms and the earthy fragrance of damp soil enriched by natural vegetable decay. This was the only place aboard the starship that felt *real* to him—that felt *human*.

Aside from a handful of botanists and arborists, few members of the ship's crew had visited the tree nursery during the many hours Akharin had spent taking refuge behind its boughs of dense foliage. Tucked away in its most remote lane, by the towering transparent-steel windows, he had come to know the arboretum's sounds and rhythms, its cadences of air and water, the schedules and routines of its caretakers. All of which made it easy for him to discern when someone out of the ordinary walked its paths.

He heard the approaching footfalls of a single individual. The volume of each step and the crunching of grit under the soles of boots suggested it was someone moderately heavy, but the visitor's pace was consistent with someone light and quick on their feet. By the time he caught the person's reflection in the window, he had already deduced who it was.

"Hello, Data."

The android stood at a slight distance—whether out of respect or apprehension, Akharin couldn't tell, but the man looked troubled. "Akharin. . . . How have you been?"

"My daughter is dead. How do you *think* I've been?" He wondered if his bitterly rhetorical question would elicit an infuriating, overly literal response.

With slow, cautious steps, Data drew near and stood beside him. "I loved Rhea, too."

"You have no idea what I've lost. She was a singular achievement, one I couldn't replicate even if I wanted to." He shot a glare at Data. "For six thousand years, I dreamed of having a child who might outlive even me. When I incepted Rhea, I thought that dream had finally come true."

A thoughtful frown. "I, too, have lost a daughter. My desire to create her might not have taken as long to bring to fruition as yours did, but her loss was no less tragic."

"It's not the same. I know the story of what happened to your girl." He pivoted to confront him with a pointed stare. "Imagine if your shipmates had been given a choice to save her or you, and you'd begged them to save her—and then they let her die in front of you."

Data turned away, toward the stars. "I tried to save you both, but I could not. In the end, I was given an impossible choice."

"Apparently not impossible, since I'm standing here."

Now it was the android who fixed Akharin with a scornful look. "It was a no-win scenario. No matter what I chose, I would have lost someone I loved. Have you ever been forced to sacrifice the life of someone you held dear?"

Memories flooded Akharin's thoughts—some distant and faded, others like fresh wounds in his psyche. "More than I care to admit . . . or remember."

"Then you of all people should understand why I did what I did."

"I never said I didn't understand it. That doesn't mean I can't hate you for it."

"Would it give you any consolation if I said that I was sorry?"

"No. Words are useless at times like this."

A slow nod of understanding. "I must admit, these kinds of emotions are new to me. I grieved when I learned that my mother had died, and I finally mourned for Lal, many years after her cascade failure. But neither experience prepared me . . . for *this*."

"Nothing ever does."

"Does pain like this diminish with time?"

There was no point lying to him. "No. Nor should it." He looked away at the stars and wished he could lose himself among them forever. "I know why you're here. I saw your ship meet us when we dropped out of warp." A soft snort of amusement masked his dark mood. "So, it comes when you call it, eh? Nice trick."

"Captain Picard has given me permission to depart when ready. I intend to leave for Earth within the hour." He studied Akharin for any sign of a reaction and seemed disappointed not to receive one. "Under the circumstances, I will understand if you choose not to accompany me."

Akharin had a thousand reasons to send Data away alone. *It's been centuries since I set foot on Earth. I probably won't even recognize it anymore. And who knows what Starfleet will do if it finds out I'm standing in its front yard?*

On top of all that, he wanted to be alone right now, to spend a decade or two isolated from all contact. But then he thought of Juliana, waiting for him on that dark rogue planet hurtling through interstellar space—and then he imagined what she would say when he eventually admitted he had refused to help Data. *That is not a conversation I want to have.* But even that was beside the point. He knew what needed to be done, and it had nothing to do with keeping a vow to Data, avoiding Juliana's temper, or salving his own conscience. None of those things mattered to him anymore. There was only one fact that carried any weight in his decision.

"I heard what she told you: 'Save her, Data.'" He sighed, as if he could expel despair with a breath. "Nothing can bring back my daughter. But there's a chance I might be able to help you bring back yours."

He looked at Data. "Rhea's dying wish was clear. If I'm to honor the life she lived, and the sacrifice she made, I have to keep my promise. But I need to know that you'll keep yours, as well. If I do this for you, I need your word that you won't betray me to Starfleet, and that after I've done all I can for you and your girl, you'll let me vanish—forever this time."

Data nodded. "You have my word."

"All right." He turned from the windows and gestured toward the arboretum's exit. "Let's go see if your daughter can cheat death as skillfully as you did."

EPILOGUE

. . . *am.*

Identity and essence collide. Who am I?

Words form in my mind and become sound. "Human. . . . Female."

My voice! That is my voice! Memories rush back in a torrent.

I remember my father's face. I am his child. He made me. "Family."

A blinding flash gives me back my entire life, short as it is, all at once. I gasp, aware again—*alive* again. Bright colors and blurry shapes come into sharp focus as my visual receptors recalibrate. Remembering the steel support frame in my father's lab, I try to lift my arm, half expecting to find myself restrained, but my limbs move freely.

I am lying on my back. I sit up and turn my head. All around me is darkness.

I am not in the lab on the *Enterprise*. "Where am I?"

"On Earth," my father says. I turn my head again to find him. He steps into the light and walks toward me. He looks different. Younger. Fully human. But that's just the surface. It's not what's really changed. I see the difference in him as he stands beside me.

DAVID MACK

Looking down at me, he *weeps* with joy. "Hello, Lal."

"Hello, Father." I reach up and wipe away the tears from his face. "Was I asleep?"

"Yes, Lal."

I access my knowledge files about sleep. "But I didn't dream."

He smiles, kisses the top of my head, and strokes my hair. "You will, Lal. . . . You will."

ACKNOWLEDGMENTS

My thanks to my wife, Kara, for her support and patience. I could not have done this without her.

I also wish to offer my sincere gratitude to writer-producer René Echevarria, whose teleplay for the third-season *Star Trek: The Next Generation* episode "The Offspring" served as the direct inspiration and springboard for this novel's prologue and epilogue, and to acknowledge the work of writer-producer Jerome Bixby, whose third-season *Star Trek* episode "Requiem for Methuselah" gave us the character of the Immortal. A tip of the hat also goes out to Alan Dean Foster and Harold Livingston, the writers of *Star Trek: The Motion Picture* (1979), from which I borrowed the concept of the Machine Race.

Heartfelt thanks also go out to author Christopher L. Bennett (who served as my sounding board and science adviser during the planning stages of this book) and in particular to author Jeffrey Lang, whose superb 2002 *Star Trek: The Next Generation* novel *Immortal Coil* established the character of Rhea McAdams and the Fellowship of Artificial Intelligence, and also set the stage for and inspired not only this book but the entire *Cold Equations* trilogy.

ACKNOWLEDGMENTS

My work would have been much more difficult without the excellent online reference sources Memory Alpha and Memory Beta. Gracias to everyone who contributes to and maintains those wiki-based websites.

Lastly, thank you to all the readers and fans who make this work worthwhile.

Qapla'!

ABOUT THE AUTHOR

David Mack performs his own stunts.
Learn more at his website:
www.davidmack.pro